The W H

Barbara Lawther

GROOMSPORT
PUBLISHING

Published in 2016 by Groomsport Publishing

ISBN Paperback: 978-0-9956696-0-4
Ebook: 978-0-9956696-1-1

A CIP catalogue copy of this book can be
found in the British Library.

IndieAuthors
World

Dedication

For Kieran Maloney

Acknowledgements

The writing of this book and the publishing process has taken me way out of my comfort zone in a way that nothing else ever has. The final publication would never have happened without a large dose of butt kicking, encouragement, love and wine.

For those of you subjected to the procrastination I will thank you tomorrow!

Giving this book, as a first draft to a few people, was the most vulnerable thing I have ever done. My expectations and secret hope was that you would tell me it was total bull. When you didn't, it meant an even bigger and scarier experience of actually publishing. This process has shown me that the greatest critic was my own voice. Once I had emailed the first draft, I should have realised that there was no going back. I had jumped off the cliff.

So thanks to the first responders:

Adrienne Kennedy, Oz; Karen Espley, UK; Kneisa Ralph, Oz; Alison Powell, Northern Ireland; Fiona Maciver, UK; Aly Richards, UK; Kate Griffin, Ireland; Rosie Lawther, Northern Ireland; Glenda Mailloux, Canada. And Koko.

And of course to Jenny Davis, my fabulous sister and Joan, my mum.

To my favourite boys: Niall, David, Fergus, Ruairi, Scott and Owen. And of course Roy and Peter.

My favourite girls: Lara, Mira and Astrid. Julie and Rosie Lawther.

To the other 'encouragers': Audrey McLaren, Paula Quiller, Susan Hooper, Ann Delargy, Clo Chohan

For the most patient and encouraging editor, Christine McPherson, Scotland.

For Kim and Sinclair at Indieauthorsworld, a huge thank you for making me laugh and giving me action points to get this book published. I definitely couldn't/wouldn't have done it without you.

Vulnerability is not weakness.

And that myth is profoundly dangerous.

Dr Brene Brennan

Prologue

He lay in bed, the pillow tightly wrapped round his head, but it made no difference. He could still hear the raised voices of his parents, then she would scream. The noise haunted him; it pierced right through his heart. He could hardly breathe.

It had got worse since his baby sister, Rachel, had gone to sleep one night and never woken up. That had been the worst morning of his life, as he'd watched from his bedroom window as the tiny body was carried away in her yellow nightgown. He heard a voice whispering to him that he could have saved her, but when he turned around no-one was there.

The screaming and the whispering always seemed to happen when there was a big thunderstorm, the clap of thunder drowning out her screams just for a moment. He hated the morning after. He would see the bruising, but by this stage they were pretending nothing had happened.

It did his head in. He hated them. He wished they were dead.

A few months later, he got his wish. The screaming had stopped. When he found their bodies lying in the kitchen the next morning, he walked to the neighbouring farm to ask for help. He was eight years old.

He wished he could have saved his baby sister, then maybe things would have been different.

Chapter One
Summer 1989

The caravan was magical. It could sleep eight people – though not all adult-size. The double bedroom was for Mum and Dad, the bunk room for me – Megan – while my brothers, Will and Johnny, would sleep at the top of the caravan on the seats at the big window.

I thought we had the best view. We could see right up the village main street, and even the chimneys at the power station near Carrickfergus, across the Belfast Lough, on a clear day. Out towards the end of the headland stood the Watch House. Every night I dreamed of living in that house. It sat remote from the other houses on The Point, or as my dad called it: The Posh! The row of large houses overlooked the village green towards the port and across to the Copeland Islands – the small isles that held the lighthouse where the Belfast Lough met the Irish Sea. These little islands always made me think of the book by Enid Blyton, *The Island of Adventure*, and I promised myself if I was to ever run away that is where I would go.

The Watch House glistened in the sunshine as a beacon. When the weather was bad, as it often was in this part of the country, it stood strong against the crashing waves of the sea. On those windy days, you could hear the tinkle of the boat bells from the little harbour port. I would imagine myself sitting at the window with the fire in the hearth to keep us cosy, looking out to the sea beyond, safe.

I loved Groomsport; it was the place we called home for the month of July. I loved it because I could run free much more than I ever could at our house in Belfast. Here, in this little sleepy village that came alive every summer, our parents worried less about The Troubles., and were relieved to get us out of the city during the marching season, away from the tensions that flared up there every year.

Groomsport was built around the port harbour. Small in comparison to many other such ports, its position at the head of the land at the end of Belfast Lough – before boats turned right for England or left for Scotland – had made it the ideal location for the Customs men in the 18th century. The harbour held small boats, safely moored from the tides and currents that crashed on the rocks just outside. Throughout the summer weekends the place would be mobbed with groups of guys and their girls looking over motorbikes, souped-up cars, and speedboats.

On those days, I wasn't allowed on my own round at the harbour, because too much trouble usually erupted. I never let on, but I would ride my bike to the path that led from the car park onto the first beach (it wasn't that big a beach, it could only hold about eight windbreakers comfortably or it would be overcrowded). The path wasn't strictly speaking the harbour, but I don't suppose I would have won that argument with my mum or dad.

One time, I caught my brother, Will, there when he had just turned 16. He was with his friends, Terry and Dave, and Dave's dog. When he saw me watching him, he came over and told me to go home. I stood my ground and said Mum and Dad wouldn't be pleased to see him there either, so he bought me a Whippy ice cream poke with a chocolate flake and strawberry sauce.

It turned out to be well worth the money for him. Just 15 minutes later, I spotted my parents walking along the main beach towards the harbour, so I rode back and warned him before he got caught.

Groomsport seemed to be the village that had two of everything.

There were two churches – the Church of Ireland and the Presbyterian Church. There were two pubs – the drinking man's pub, and the middle class bar that also served meals. There were two shops, if you didn't include the post office which also sold crab lines, buckets and spades, and blow-up beach toys – the Spar grocery shop and Mrs Adams' store. Mrs Adams scared me. She wore black, must have been about a hundred years old, and didn't like children.

There had been two chip shops, but this summer only one had reopened. It was beside the car park on the quay. Day trippers would buy their fish and chips and sit in their cars to eat the greasy suppers. My favourite was the pasty supper, with tomato ketchup and mushy peas and so much salt and vinegar your lips would sting. That was a real treat! There were some picnic benches, if you didn't mind the seagulls swooping in to nab anything that they could get. On a Sunday morning the area would be littered with the remnants of late night suppers that had been savaged by the gulls.

Two old cottages sat on the edge of the Harbour, known as Cockle Row. They were whitewashed and had been thatched, their thick walls keeping the bitter wind out. They were at right angles to the sea to keep the chilling North winds from biting.

They were smaller inside than our caravan, and I'd been amazed when my dad first told me that fishermen had lived in these cottages back in the 1840s, when a fleet of over 20 boats would sail from the harbour into the Irish Sea. The only time I had been on the Liverpool ferry going from Belfast, I had been seasick, so I didn't envy the poor men who would have sailed these boats. My mum said she felt sorry for the women and families they left behind, waiting and wondering if they would come home safely.

Inside the cottage was a big fireplace, which you could easily stand in; it would have held the metal pots and boiling kettles. The heat from the hearth would have kept the family warm, whilst the smoke would fill their lungs with ash. Outside the cottages was a concrete paddling pool that many a child – and probably an adult, too – had splashed through.

The only anomaly was the single pharmacy, known as the Drugstore. This was my favourite place, because it also had a small cafe at the back that was a take on an American diner and served ice cream floats. Heaven in a glass. The bubbles in the lemonade meeting the scoop of ice cream as it plopped into the glass created a taste so delicious that you always asked for another. I never did get a second one. Whoever I was with would just laugh and tell me I would be sick if I had two.

The Presbyterian church hall stood on the other side of the path that led to the park and two tennis courts. Beyond this, small rocky gorse bushes led onto the village green. The path beside the green and the sea led to 'The Posh' and on towards the Watch House.

The village green was where it all happened for us kids. During the summer there was always something going on – sports days, rounders, footie, cricket, and the ice cream van.

The path curving away from the Watch House was private property, and led out to Ballymacormick Point – an outcrop of sandy bays and a salt marsh, which belonged to the National Trust. The walk along the coast was a favourite with dog walkers, families, and lovers. To one side, the farmers' fields were sealed off with wire and wood fences. On the other side was the sea.

When the tide was out, the rock pool and seaweed were places you could play, but the smell of the decaying seaweed turned my stomach. When the tide was in, the path would be wet where the waves crashed onto it. And there were many places ideal for playing hide and seek, or for a wee quiet smooch!

From Groomsport, the path connected through to Ballyholme beach. The gorse bushes were intertwined with blackberry brambles, and we couldn't wait for the end of August when the dark purple plump berries would be ripe for picking. Mum would make a mean apple and blackberry crumble – a real treat.

***

In the summer of 1989, I turned 11. During the week it was just my mum, Johnny, and me staying at the caravan, as my dad worked in Belfast and our Will had his first summer job. Dad and Will would drive down in the old blue Ford Escort on a Friday night after work. I would stand at the window of the caravan at 5.45pm, straining to see the gate and the first glimpse of our car. On my shout, Mum would leave the two-ring stove, look in the mirror, smooth her hair and put on her lipstick, ready to greet Dad as he turned the car onto the piece of grass in front of the caravan. Will would jump out first, hug Mum, then smack me and Johnny on the head (his sign of affection), distracting us so that Dad could give Mum a kiss and a hug.

Before we even sat down, Will would have changed into his shorts and t-shirt, leaving his trousers and shirt lying. In those days, I would rush to pick them up before he was shouted at by either Mum or Dad, so that nothing could spoil us all being together again.

We'd eat our meat and two veg, Dad commenting it was the best meal he'd had all week. Mum would smile appreciatively, knowing he was lying, as he would have eaten at his mum's, her mum's, and his sister's that week, and in truth they were all far better cooks than our mum.

Will would be out the door as soon as he had finished his meal, off to see his mates. 'Be back by 11!' Mum would call after him. 'No drinking!' Dad would shout. We never knew if he heard them or not.

Johnny and I would do the dishes, while Mum and Dad would go off for a walk. Dad would slip us a coin each and Johnny would go off to meet up with his mates; I would go and see my summer friend, Hilary. She and I would ride our bikes round to the village park where, about an hour later, Mum and Dad would meet us. They always laughed as if it was a surprise to bump into us there, and Dad would buy us both an ice lolly from the van parked up beside the tennis courts. He would ask where my money was and I would smile my sweet smile and tell him it was in my money box in the caravan. When we heard the church clock chime eight o'clock, we knew it was time to cycle home.

The best time was during the 12th and 13th July – when tensions ran high in many towns and cities across Northern Ireland. The Protestants would take part in marches to celebrate the Battle of the Boyne of 1690, when King William of

Orange beat the Catholic King James II; the Catholics would protest against the marching.

As people all across the country held their breath, awaiting trouble, our family all got together in Groomsport. Nan and Granda (Mum's parents), Uncle Jack and Aunt Elsie (Mum's brother and his wife), and our cousins, Max and Eddie, all joined us. As there were only eight actual beds in the caravan, Dad would pitch a tent on the grass for the boys to sleep in.

I had always wanted to sleep in the tent. I cried, I pleaded, I offered to do all the chores, but the boys just laughed at me. I hated being a girl, especially the only girl. 'The Princess', Granda would call me, blowing me a kiss.

The Saturday night when we were all together was the most special. Dad would drive round to the chippy and buy us all proper fish and chips, wrapped in paper. There would be mushy peas, too, and it certainly wasn't the night you wanted to be sleeping in the tent when four boys would compete to see who could produce the best fart ripples. You could hear the laughter and shouts of 'Stinker!' for hours.

We would sit in front of our wee black and white portable tv, which was connected to the car battery, and watch an old movie, the picture getting smaller and smaller as the battery ran out. To this day I've never found a movie more scary than those Saturday nights in the caravan. It wasn't helped by Dad and Uncle Jack playing some joke on us to scare the living daylights out of us. One of them would sneak out and either start scratching or knocking on the windows and underneath the van.

The first time I was ever allowed to watch with the boys, I needed to go to the toilet in the middle of the film, which was *The Hand*. Now the toilet block was about 100 metres from the caravan (this was before posh caravans with toilets and showers), so my brothers – much to their disgust – had to escort me there. On the way back, Dad jumped out from behind the caravan, scaring me so much that I froze to the spot and screamed my lungs out. Mum came rushing out of the caravan with the frying pan to hit him, while my brothers just ran off and left me. We laugh about it now, but at the time I had to sleep with my mum for about a week – much to my dad's disgust, as he had to sleep in my bunk!

At some point on the Saturday night, Granda would announce that he needed to go for a walk to check on the boats to make sure they had been moored properly. He had been a merchant seaman for most of his life, so I had innocently assumed he still took his love of boats very seriously. This gesture of care was met by derision by Nan, followed by a bang of the caravan door shutting as he left. My dad and uncle were then dispatched after him to make sure he didn't do anything stupid. It was some time before I learned that he was actually off to the pub in the village for some of the 'black stuff', and it would take both Dad and my uncle to help him home.

Many a Sunday morning I would wake to find Granda fast asleep in the Ford Escort, his snores waking most of the neighbouring caravans. He was a big man, and always seemed to know when the bacon, eggs, and fried tattie bread were ready. On those mornings, he smelt of stale ale and cigarettes and there would be a stony silence between him and Nan.

He would slip my brother Will some money to buy him a paper and some chewing gum on his way home from church. Mum had stopped him asking Will to buy his cigarettes after she caught Will and his mates smoking behind the caravan.

I disliked going to church during the holidays. I didn't understand why God didn't take his holidays at the same time as us. Surely that would have been fair, but the pews of the parish church were bursting with holidaymakers. After church we would head home for the Sunday roast. Mum always put the meat in the gas oven just before we left for church, and prayed that the sermon wouldn't be too long or the meat would be overdone.

On the first Sunday of the month, we always had over-cooked meat, because it was Communion. On that particular Sunday, we were compensated by having home-made chocolate mocha pudding and custard.

After Sunday tea, Granda would line us up and pass out the pocket money. As the youngest, I always got the least. I felt hard done by and asked when I would get the same as the boys, but Granda would laugh, pat my head, and say, 'When you're as old as they are.' Everyone would laugh at my screwed-up face but in truth, I did better than them, as every week Dad would bring me my favourite comic, and Nan or my aunt would bring me a new ribbon or one of their knitted creations. After all, I was the princess!

My Sindy dolls had the best wardrobe in the world with Mum, Nan, Aunt Elsie and me stitching and knitting new costumes for them. Dad even made some wooden furniture for my make-believe house, but Mum drew the line at my brothers' Action Men playing with my Sindy.

***

It was 1989; the summer I turned 11. In late July, Mum took me up to Belfast by train from Bangor to buy my new school uniform. It was a big day. I had passed the eleven plus exam, so would be going to the same grammar school as my two brothers. We arranged to meet Dad in town during his lunch hour, so that he could take the uniform back home.

The three of us went to a proper sit-in restaurant for our lunch – The Skandia, behind the city hall. I was even allowed a knickerbocker glory for dessert; that magical concoction of ice cream, jelly, fruit, sauce, cream and sprinkles, topped off the best day ever.

On the train ride back, we sat in a carriage by ourselves and Mum told me about the girly things that would start happening to my body. I'd grow hair on bits of me, my boobs would grow and, most gross of all, I would start to bleed from down below. I wanted to know if the boys had that, too. 'No,' said my Mum, smiling and squeezing my hand, 'they go through different changes.'

It seemed like a lot to take in, but I couldn't ask her any more questions as an old couple got into our carriage. Later that night, though, as she was tucking me into my caravan bed, she gave me a little book to read that would explain everything we had talked about. She also suggested I hide it in case my brothers teased me, as brothers do. I hugged her goodnight.

It was the summer when the sun shone and scorched our bodies. No sunscreen then.

It was the summer Will cut his foot on a rusty tin can that had been lying on the beach, and had to go to the Ulster Hospital for it to be stitched, and to have an injection from the biggest needle he had ever seen. He denies to this day that he actually fainted when the nurse first showed him the needle. He did come away with her phone number, though; that was Will.

Every year the same caravaners would return, and friendships would be renewed. After breakfast, our chores complete, we would head off to the beach, or to cycle into the village to the green, or go crab fishing. There was so much to do, so many adventures to have. We had to tell our mums where we were going, though, and if we were caught somewhere we shouldn't be, then emptying the slop bucket was a favourite reminder that Mum's word was law!

It was the summer when I started to enjoy going off by myself. I loved to climb the rocks below the caravan park, or to go to the field between the two caravan parks and hide out in the gorse bushes. There was one place I could see out and watch the world go by, and where the world couldn't see me. It was a cave in the rocks below the caravan park; a child could climb into it when the tide was out, but you couldn't see it if you didn't know it was there. If you left it too late to climb out, though, you would be caught there by the tide coming in. Jonny warned me that would mean you would drown, or be battered against the rocks if you did manage to climb out.

It was our secret place, which adults couldn't see. The first time I had climbed in was when I was only eight years old. I hadn't wanted to then, but Johnny had dared me a coke float that I couldn't, and I would have done anything for one of those and to prove him wrong. I won the bet that day.

One other time I was in the cave, I slipped as I climbed out, and my foot got stuck between the rocks as I turned. As the tide was coming in and my fear was rising, I started to scream and was luckily heard by Will's gang down on the beach below. They had to pull hard to get me out, and I caught my leg and ankle badly. Will helped me home and Mum liberally applied antiseptic to my cuts, nodding at Will's story that he had seen me slip on the rocks. I knew she didn't believe him when I couldn't quite meet her eye.

That night she sat with me, applying cold flannels to my face when my skin burned up and the cuts on my leg throbbed every time I turned round. I was sick for two days, not wanting to leave my bunk, preferring to be left alone lying in darkness. 'Sunstroke,' Mum had said.

But while the cave may have nearly claimed me on that occasion, it would prove to be the place that saved me this summer.

Aunt Elsie and Uncle Jack had gone to England for their holiday that year, so we stayed on through August. The weather was glorious and we were as brown as berries. I had shot up a couple of inches and my favourite yellow dress no longer fitted me; it was now halfway up my thighs. 'Chicken legs,' Dad had teased. 'Roast chicken legs.' I just laughed. The dress had been my Sunday best the year before, but now I was allowed to wear it anytime.

I had been playing on the beach with Hilary, my summer friend who had a caravan at the bottom end of the field near the park. Hilary was blond to my dark, and I was either at her caravan or she at mine. We were allowed to do things together, like ride our bikes into the village or to the park, but not on our own. Our mums thought it safer for us to be together, while our dads just laughed and said, 'Double the trouble!'

After tea, we were always allowed an hour to play before 'going in time'. I don't quite remember what caused our fight that evening – the first one we had ever had – but Hilary stormed off from the beach. I decided I wasn't going after her. If I went home early, my mum would want to know what we had fallen out about and would march me down to Hilary's caravan to apologise. So I stayed on building my sand castle.

I wasn't aware that I was being watched until a shadow covered my castle. I remember he was tall – older than my dad, but not as old as Granda. He was friendly, helping me to finish the last part of the moat. As we worked, he asked me my name. I liked to play pretend, as I didn't really like my name; I'd been named after my great-grandma. So I told him my name was Rachel. It was my favourite name.

'That's a nice name,' he said.

'Thank you,' I replied politely.

He asked where my friend was that night. When I told him she had gone home, he said it was sad that I was alone, but he would keep me safe. I know I was only eleven, but I sensed something wasn't right.

He laughed, and it scared me. I wanted to run, but I knew from playing games on the beach with my dad and my brothers that he would catch me very quickly. I looked around me. There was no-one else left on the beach.

'Elizabeth' – Hilary's pretend name – 'will be coming back soon,' I said quickly.

'Will she really?' he replied, staring at me.

'Yes,' I said, determined, and bent down to pick up a handful of sand. 'I should go now as my mum will be waiting for me and she'll be cross if I'm late.'

'That's a shame,' he said, looking at me sideways. 'We were having such fun!'

'Bye,' I said, starting to walk towards the steps to the caravan park.

'Wait!' he called. 'Wouldn't you like an ice cream?' He pointed to the van parked at the opposite end of the beach.

I stared at him and shook my head, before turning to run towards the steps. He lurched after me and grabbed my ponytail as it blew behind me. I hated that ponytail. My brothers always used it to catch me when I was running away from them, too.

I might have looked slight, but years of wrestling with my dad and brothers had taught me a few moves. As he pulled me back into his arms, I wriggled hard but his grasp tightened. He slapped my face. That's when I threw the sand in his eyes and bit hard on his scarred hand. 'Dirty tricks,' my dad always called them; he once slapped my leg when I did it to my brother.

The only other dirty trick I knew was to kick the man hard in the bit between his legs. My foot caught him as his hands went to his eyes where the sand had hit him. Then I ran as fast as I could across the sand.

'Focus! Focus!' I heard my dad scream in my head. He had taught me that one night before sports day, when he told me to keep looking straight ahead.

I took one look behind me and saw the man lurching towards me. I knew I couldn't make it up the steps into the caravan park before he'd catch me, so I darted left towards the rocks. It would take longer to go up the path, but the tide was out and if I could get into the cave I would be safe.

I climbed frantically and made it into the cave, then lay still, my heart racing so fast in my chest I was sure he would hear it. He was standing just above the entrance, but he wouldn't have been able to see it.

I could hear him muttering, 'I'll get you, you little bitch!' I held my breath, then heard him say, 'I just wanted to save you. Save you.' He repeated the phrase several times.

I don't know how long I lay there, but my feet started to get wet as the tide was coming in. I had a choice – to die in the cave, or to chance my luck against the angry man. It seemed a lifetime before I heard a voice in the distance. It was Johnny.

'Meg! Meg! Meg!'

I crawled out of the cave and Johnny grabbed me. 'Mum's going to kill you!'

I laughed hoarsely. That was one other way I could die that night.

'She went down to Hilary's and found you weren't there, and she'd gone in ages ago. Mum's thrown a blue fit!' fumed Johnny, dragging me along.

I pulled away from him and looked back along the beach. The man was standing there. He saw me, too. He raised his hand and waved. Johnny looked to see what I was looking at, but the man dipped down behind the rock.

'Who's that?' he asked, puzzled.

'The bogeyman!' I said, turning and running for home.

When Jonny caught up with me and asked me what had happened, I told him the man had just scared me, shrugging my shoulders. I wouldn't look at him.

Mum came running down the path to meet us, her face a mixture of fury and fear.

'Sorry, Mum,' I mumbled, not able to look at her.

She shouted at me, grabbed my arm, and pulled me back to the caravan. It was only then that I realised I was bleeding and my dress was torn.

She lifted my chin so I had to look her in the eye. 'What happened?'

'I slipped on the rocks when I was coming home, and I think I bumped my head,' I said, tears running down my face.

She looked at Johnny, who just shrugged.

'Those damn rocks. I've told you before you shouldn't be climbing them, haven't I?'

'Yes, Mum,' I whispered.

When we got back to the caravan, she sent Johnny to find the first aid kit, while she pulled off my dress to see the cuts and bruises. She gasped.

'I hate being a girl,' I whispered.

'What?' she said, holding my chin up to look me in the eye again.

'I wish I was a boy!' I winced as she hugged me.

Her face softened; she thought I was referring to my changing body. 'I know, love, I felt the same way when I was your age!'

She washed my cuts and put cream on them, which stung. She gave me some cream on my fingertip to rub into the bruise that was starting to show on my face, then she made Johnny and me hot chocolate and gave us each two biscuits. That was a treat.

When I climbed into her double bed rather than my own bunk, she just looked at me closely, then nodded. As she kissed me goodnight, I held onto her for ages.

I lay in the dark, with the light shining through the gap in the door from the lantern at the far end of the caravan. I could hear voices talking quietly. Mum was quizzing Johnny about what had happened. He said he didn't really know, just that he'd found me in the hiding place we always went to, and that I had been really scared. He said he thought he had seen someone on the beach, but couldn't be sure. He told Mum he'd asked me, and that I'd said I had been chased by the bogeyman.

Later, I felt her get into bed beside me and pull me close. 'It's okay, my love, you're safe. I won't let anyone hurt you,' she whispered.

***

The next day I awoke feeling sore. I wasn't allowed out of the caravan, and even Johnny wasn't allowed to go off. He was made to play Monopoly with me. I didn't want to go out anyway. Mum went down the field to speak to Hilary's mum, and after lunch Hilary came and we played with our Sindy dolls.

One afternoon, a few days later, I was playing at the back of the caravan and Mum was weeding the little flower patch at the front, when a car drew up. There was a man driving, and a girl sitting in the back seat.

He rolled down his car window and told Mum he was looking for the caravan of his daughter's friend. The girl was called Rachel and had long, dark hair. I couldn't see him from where I was hiding, but I could hear his voice. I froze, then I started to shake. My teeth were chattering. I crouched lower, behind the large box container at the back of the caravan that stored our bikes and Dad's tools.

I heard my mum say that she only had boys and she didn't know any girls called Rachel, then the man thanked her and drove slowly away. I was sure he had seen me; at least, the girl in the back seat had.

When the car turned the corner, Mum called me. 'Meg, Meg, where are you? It's okay, love, I'm here!'

I crawled out from behind the box and ran into her arms.

'Meg, was that the bogeyman?' she asked.

I nodded, tears streaming down my face. 'It's okay! It's okay!' she soothed, holding me close.

When Johnny came back, Mum sent him down to Hilary's caravan with a note for her mum, Joan. It wasn't long before she and Hilary arrived.

Hilary was sent into the caravan with me, and Mum closed the door. She and Joan stood a distance away from the caravan, so that we wouldn't hear what they were saying, but I could see they were both frightened. Joan put her hand over her mouth as if in shock, then took out a cigarette and lit it.

Mum came back into the caravan, grabbed her handbag, and left. Joan sat outside smoking until Mum came back about fifteen minutes later.

That evening Dad arrived, even though it was only Thursday.

He gave me a big hug and I tried not to wince. He stroked my hair. 'Meg, love, did some man try and hurt you?'

'I was on the beach, Dad,' I whispered. 'Hilary had gone home and I wanted to finish my castle,' I gulped. 'I didn't see him, and he came up behind me and asked me my name. I said I was called Rachel. He offered to buy me an ice cream, and when I said no, he grabbed my arm and I tried to run away but he caught my ponytail.'

'Okay, and then what?' he asked gently, as Mum sobbed quietly in the background.

'I threw sand in his eyes, and bit his hand, then I kicked him... where I shouldn't kick a boy, and then I ran. I got up to the rocks and he was chasing me, so I hid. And then Johnny came and found me.'

Dad hugged me close, and Mum came and wrapped her arms around us both.

***

Joan looked after me that evening while Mum and Dad went out. I didn't know then, but they went looking for the car of the man who had spoken to Mum. A massive thunderstorm had started. I always loved thunder and lightning.

We packed up that weekend and headed back home to Belfast. School was due to start in ten days. It was the summer I got my long ponytail cut off. As the hairdresser started to cut, Mum shed a tear and asked to take a big handful of hair home with her. But I liked my new bob; not quite a girl, but not a boy either.

The events of that summer faded in my memory with the excitement of starting a new school, but Mum and Dad didn't. A couple of weeks later, a girl of fifteen was reported missing near Groomsport. She had run away several times before, but had always gone home. This time her body was found washed up several days later.

I had overheard it on the news, and didn't understand when Mum had said to Dad that at least the girl hadn't been 'hurt'. The police were calling it a tragic accident.

Mum and Dad didn't tell me, but they went to the police station to report what had happened to me earlier in the summer, but were reassured that the girl's death had definitely been an accident. She had been seen drinking earlier in the day and had wandered off after a fight with her friends, they said. She had long, dark hair. Her name was Rachel.

**

A couple of months later – December, 1989 – Nan collapsed in the street and was rushed to the Royal Victoria Hospital. She'd had a heart attack. Nan died four days later, having regained consciousness briefly to see her husband, son, and daughter at her bedside. Granda seemed to wilt overnight. Mum was devastated.

Christmas came and went. I knew Santa didn't exist and I, too, was very sad about Nan, but I have to admit I was disappointed in my presents. Mum had been in a fog for weeks. She'd go into a room and just stand there, completely forgetting why she had gone in. She would rub away the tears running down her face, and look so lost that one of us would take her hand and show her to a chair then just sit with her.

We never went back to the caravan at Groomsport.

Nan had left Mum a bit of money, and me her shell jewellery box. Instead, we went on our first foreign holiday to Spain the next summer – the events of the previous one well and truly forgotten.

A year after Nan died, Granda was diagnosed with lung cancer. It wasn't a surprise to him, as he had smoked forty cigarettes a day since he was a boy. He had worked in Gallagher's tobacco factory in York Street for nearly 20 years, once the largest tobacco factory in the world.

When Johnny and me went to say goodbye to him, he was gaunt, his skin a mix of grey and translucent and bruising. As I turned to go, he called me back and slipped a twenty pound note into my hand, and one into Johnny's, too.

'There you go. You're as big as the boys now, Princess!' he said, stroking my cheek.

I gave him a big hug, not knowing it would be my last. Dad smiled later that night when I showed him the money and told him what Granda had said.

He was buried beside Nan in Carnmoney Cemetery. I went to the funeral, but wasn't allowed to go and see the coffin being lowered into the ground. I was relieved.

With the money Granda had left in his will, we moved home later that year, out to Templepatrick. It was a longer bus ride into school each day, but I didn't mind. I enjoyed living out in the country.

Will bought a car with the money Granda had left him, but Johnny and I weren't allowed our money until we turned eighteen. I decided that I would travel the world with my inheritance, and even bought a map to plan my adventures.

Dad laughed and said it was safer than having pictures of pop stars on my walls. Little did he know that my dreaming would take me away from Belfast and home for almost twenty years.

Chapter Two
The Meeting – May 2009

Megan Scott stood in the departure lounge at Gatwick Airport, waiting to board her flight to Belfast. It was the beginning of May. She was a million miles away in her head, and didn't notice the man standing beside her until he offered to lift her carry-on case into the overhead compartment. She was going to say she could manage until she noticed his twinkling blue eyes and dimpled chin, and found herself saying yes instead. He lifted the bag with ease and swung it into the overhead. *He must be over six feet tall,* she thought; his t-shirt showed he worked out.

He had noticed her when he checked in. Her long, brown hair flowing down her back, the way she smiled at the check-in staff. He had used his charm to get the seat beside her, flashing his own smile and batting his blue eyes. He had, of course, first checked her ring finger to see it was clear. He didn't want a messy situation.

As they sat down, he offered her his hand. 'Kieran. Kieran Maloney.'

'Megan. Megan Scott,' she replied, shaking his hand and returning the smile.

'Going home?' he asked.

People who left Northern Ireland, or the Republic of Ireland, to study or work abroad – even just to England or

Scotland – always talked about 'going home' when they were returning. It was usually said with longing, even though the vast majority who left had created a life beyond anything possible in their home town.

'Kind of,' she answered, sighing. 'My mum's just been diagnosed with breast cancer, and I'm going home to stay with her for a while!'

'I'm sorry to hear that, I really am!' He frowned. 'My mum had it about five years ago, but she is still doing very well now.'

'That's really good to know.'

'Your mum'll be glad to have you home. Me, Dad, and my brothers were useless. It's the only time she wished she'd had a daughter, though my sisters-in-law are a godsend.'

'Yes, my two sisters-in-law are great, too. What about you, are you married?' She tried to sound casual.

'Nope, never married,' he said, showing her his ring hand. 'You?'

'The same,' she replied, flashing her left hand.

'Where's home for you now?' His brain was racing – single, beautiful, family-orientated, clever... This could be a very good flight.

'That is the million dollar question,' she laughed. 'I have a mortgage on a flat in London, but I spend most of my life travelling for my job. What about you?'

'I moved back six months ago. I spent three years in Australia, three in Dubai, two in South Africa.'

'What do you do?' she asked.

'I'm a carpenter by trade, though I now do project management of big building developments. With the recent boom in investment, it's a busy time.' She nodded. 'Though I do like to keep my hand in.' He showed her his scarred hands.

Megan smiled. 'Maybe it's better you do the management, with all those scars!'

He laughed with her. 'It's easy done – a momentary distraction and a tool can easily slip.'

'And why did you come back home after all those glamorous locations?' She was genuinely interested; it was a question she often asked herself.

'Are you saying Belfast isn't glamorous?' He tried – and failed – to look shocked.

'It certainly has changed over the last few years since peace has come about,' she replied.

He shrugged. 'Peace! My dad has a building firm and I always swore I'd never go and work in it, but he wants to retire. I'm getting on, and so I thought: why not? I'll come back and give it a go! And when my ma was sick, it kind of put things in perspective being so far away.'

She nodded, understanding that point only too well. There was an invisible string she had always fought but which gently tugged her back every so often.

'What about you, ever thought of coming home?' asked Kieran, trying not to sound too keen.

'No more than yes, if you know what I mean. I do think about it from time to time; now being one of them. Being in London, it's always easy to hop on a plane, and Mum and Dad do come and stay when I'm there. But Belfast still feels small town, and it's hard to stop the wanderlust in me.'

'Small town? Don't let the tourist board hear you say that! There is a lot to do now – good bars and restaurants, and it's easy to jump on a plane with the two airports. Not so provincial any more, really.'

'I'm back for a couple of weeks for now, so I'll see how it goes,' she said. She smiled as she imagined how delighted her parents would be if she met a nice boy from the Province and settled down close to home.

'What about work?' he asked.

'Work? I'm an accountant, and my company have kindly given me a temporary assignment here so that I can be with Mum,' Megan explained.

'That's brilliant.'

'Yes, I've worked for them since university and travelled the world with them, so I have a good relationship with them.'

During the flight, they chatted easily about business, family, places they had travelled. Kieran spoke of his three brothers – one in the police force, one a solicitor, and the other an engineer – all living in and around Belfast, all married with kids. He was the youngest.

'Four sons? Your poor mother!' Megan laughed.

'Aye, when she saw I was a boy, she said "no more", and sent me dad for the snip!'

'My mum was lucky. I was her third, after two boys. She got her girl, though I think she considered I was more a tomboy when I was growing up.'

'Well, you don't look like a tomboy now!' he smiled warmly, and Megan blushed. He seemed a nice guy, and had been the perfect distraction to stop her worrying about her mum for a little while.

As the plane neared the landing gate, they exchanged mobile numbers. She had baggage to collect, but Kieran only had hand luggage. He had been at a stag weekend with some friends in Spain, flying back via Gatwick, so hadn't needed much.

***

Megan's brother, Johnny, was waiting to pick her up and drive her to their parents' home. As she got in his car, her phone beeped with a new text.

Dinner this weekend?

She smiled and text a reply.

Yes, but let me check how things are at home. M

Sure. If there is anything I can do, please let me know. K

Thanks, I will. M

***

Jane Scott was delighted to have her daughter home. Whilst she didn't want to be a burden, there were just some things you preferred to have your daughter for. Her sons and her daughters-in-law had been great and practical; her husband, Jack, useless. He followed her around like a puppy and wouldn't let her lift a finger.

Jack, too, was delighted to have his 'princess' home. He was scared. Terrified, if he was being honest. He and Jane had been together since she was seventeen and he eighteen; nearly forty-five years. He couldn't think what he would do if something... No, he shouldn't think. He had to be strong.

It was purely by chance that Jane had gone for a mammogram and mentioned that her breast and left arm were aching slightly. She had hated the mammogram – the most undignified experience of having to squeeze your breasts against a metal plate – but at least the nurse had been a middle-aged woman and not some wee lass whose boobs were still pert.

The call to come back had scared her. She had always routinely checked her breasts, and even now she couldn't find any lumps or bumps. Perhaps they were just being extra cautious. The hardest part had been telling Jack. He had tried to be strong, but she knew him too well. They had agreed not to say anything to the kids until anything was confirmed. No point in worrying them unnecessarily.

The results from the biopsy weren't good. Nor were they bad; she had to remember that. 'Caught very early, prognosis very good,' that's what the lovely specialist had said. Jack had gripped her hand. All he had heard was that his wife had breast cancer. It had been down to Jane to phone her daughters-in-law and her daughter to break the news; Jack couldn't speak.

Megan had known as soon as she heard her mum's voice that something was wrong. They spoke every couple of days as a rule, but her mum never called her before 6pm, knowing she would be at work. Jane explained that she was due in hospital in two days' time and that her operation would take place the day after.

Immediately, Megan gone to her boss, and booked time off to go home. She and Ed had worked together for years, and it was he who had offered her the opportunity to work out of the Belfast office, if she needed to stay close to home for a while.

She'd been able to get a flight that evening, so had left the office, quickly packed a case with all sorts, and got the train to Gatwick.

***

Jane came through the operation well. The surgeon was very positive about the results. He had gently explained that she would be a bit vague from the anaesthetic, and may even be sick from the side-effects. All being well, if the wound healed and she had no fever, she could go home in five days. He recommended radiotherapy, but would wait until the tumour results had been completed before assessing the period and strength of treatment. He assured her it would be at least two weeks before any radiotherapy would start.

To distract her mother from thoughts of the operation, Megan had told her mother about the lovely man she had met on the plane. She knew her mother still wished for her daughter to get married and settle down, preferably closer to home.

With the operation over and her recovery underway, the family were taking it in turns to visit Jane, so as not to tire her out. Her grandchildren were desperate to see her, and had sent in hand-made cards – even 17-year-old Fergus!

Megan agreed to meet Kieran in a café on the Lisburn road after the evening hospital visit on Saturday night. He looked good in black jeans and open-necked shirt, and his blue eyes twinkled.

'My mum lit a candle for your mum today at the chapel,' he said, taking her hand and giving it a gentle squeeze.

'That was good of her. Tell her thanks,' said Megan. Lighting a candle was important for many people who wanted to help prayers to get to the right people. Although it wasn't part of Megan's family's own beliefs, it still meant a lot to her.

'Aye, she wanted to know why I'd had a dreamy look on my face all week. I never could hide anything from her.' Kieran laughed.

When their meals came, Kieran was glad to see that Megan liked her food. He couldn't stand a girl who didn't have a healthy appetite. When she pinched a handful of chips from his plate, he gently slapped her hand away and told her to stop.

Megan pretended to be upset. 'An ex-boyfriend once stabbed me with his fork,' she said, 'when I tried to take a chip of his plate.'

'You're joking!'

'No, deadly serious!'

'What happened?'

'That's why he's an ex!' she laughed.

Kieran lifted his plate and pushed more chips towards her.

'What are you doing?' Megan asked.

'Just making sure I'm not an 'ex'!' he replied with a smile. 'Any other hints?'

'Hmm.' She dipped a fat chip into tomato ketchup and then placed it into her mouth as she considered her answer. 'Do you like garlic?'

'Love it,' he said.

'Good, that's another relationship killer. I do, too! What about you? Relationship killers?' she asked.

'Girls who don't like their food and pretend they need to go on a diet!' Kieran raised his eyebrows, making it obvious she had passed that test. 'And smoking. There are probably other things, but those are the key ones.'

As they ate, they chatted as if they had known each other for years. Although they had been brought up on what was often called 'different sides of the divide', religion wasn't an issue for either of them. Having both travelled and lived in many different cultures and countries, they knew there was good and bad in all religions. They had learnt tolerance and respect from their parents, and through their own experiences.

Conversation turned to summer holidays they'd enjoyed as kids, and it turned out they had both stayed in the caravan parks in Groomsport – Megan's family in the 'posh' park overlooking the village; Kieran's in the 'workers' site' further from the village, towards Orlock Point. Both families had obviously had the same idea of getting away from Belfast during the traditional marching season to avoid the political tensions that came with it.

They reminisced about coke floats, ice cream from the Cabin in Donaghadee, blackberry picking, dulce (Megan loved it surprisingly, whilst Kieran hated it), and day trips to the Copeland Islands. They had both read the Enid Blyton books and harboured the same plan that it was the place they would run away to. Kieran admitted he had even decided to run away one day and his mam had packed his backpack for him. She put some jam sandwiches in it and waved him off. He had walked for what he thought was hours, sat down and ate his sandwiches, and was back at the caravan just thirty minutes after leaving! How his dad and brothers had laughed that night.

'Do you know the house that sits on the headland out past the harbour?' Kieran asked. Megan nodded. 'It's called the Watch House,' he went on, 'and was built in the early 1800s to act as a customs house, handling the ships that sailed between the US, the Caribbean, and the flourishing trades in Belfast.'

'Yes.' Megan nodded, as she finished her dessert. 'It's at the end of The Point, or as my dad calls it 'The Posh'. I always wanted to be able to sit in the window seat upstairs, drinking coke floats, and watching the waves crash onto the rocks below.'

'Well, that's the house I want. I decided when I was younger that when I owned it, I would have made it. It's on my to-do list to buy!' Kieran announced seriously.

'Mine, too!' replied Megan, laughing at the coincidence. 'Do you not want to build your own house?'

'That's the funny thing about builders, they spend all their time sorting other people's houses out but don't do their own! I like doing up old properties, but not new ones,' he explained. 'I have a loft flat in the old foundry on Ormeau Road. I bought it as a shell and it has taken me two years, but I think it is finally done. I'll need a new project soon.'

'I don't think the Watch House has been on the market for years, so you might have a wait,' said Megan.

'Ah, that's where you're wrong!' Kieran tapped his finger against the side of his nose knowingly. 'I've had a tip-off that it's coming on the market soon.'

'Wow!' said Megan. 'It must be a sign.'

'Possibly, but I'm sure a lot of people will be interested in it.'

'I'd be scared to go and see it in case it spoilt my dream,' Megan admitted.

'Well, I'd love to go and see it, but I'm scared I can't afford it and it will be another thirty years before I can buy it!' Kieran laughed. After a few minutes, he leaned forwards towards Megan. 'Let's do it. Let's go and see it if it comes on the market.'

'Seriously?' Megan looked at him as if he was mad.

'Yes, why not? We would always wonder.'

Megan was amused. Was this guy suggesting they go house-hunting together? They had barely met, but his words sparked a little shiver through her body. Was it the house, or was it the guy?

At that moment, Kieran made a bet with himself. If he got the house, he would get the girl; or was it the other way round? If he got the girl, he'd get the house. Either way, he'd be happy with the result.

'I'll call the estate agents and let them know we're interested and want to arrange an appointment when it comes on the market,' he said as he paid the bill, waving away Megan's suggestion to split it. 'You pay next time,' he suggested.

'You think there'll be a next time?' she asked innocently.

'Oh yes, no doubt. After all, we have a house to see.' He sounded more confident than he felt.

When he drove her back to her parents' house and stopped outside, Megan started to giggle.

'What's funny?' he asked.

'This is like being a teenager again, and getting dropped off at my parents. My dad will probably be sitting up waiting, pretending to watch some movie.'

'Aye, my ma would never go to bed until we were in,' replied Kieran.

He bent over and gave her a gentle kiss. 'Not bad,' he said, pretending to think about the kiss. 'More practice needed, though.'

Megan pushed him away gently with a smile. 'That's your ration for tonight,' she said, getting out of the car. 'Only one kiss on the first date.'

'I'm looking forward to the hundredth date then,' he said, smiling.

Her dad was, indeed, still sitting up watching the football, and they chatted for a while before Megan headed off to her room.

As she was getting into bed, her phone beeped with a message. There was a picture of a pair of lips! Despite everything, she had a good feeling.

Chapter Three
More than friends

When Megan visited the hospital the next day, she was delighted to find her mum feeling a good bit better. As expected, she was bombarded with twenty questions about the previous evening's dinner date.

'Yes, Mum, it was very good. Yes, I am seeing him again next weekend. No, he has never been married. Yes, he wants kids.' Megan couldn't help but laugh, but was nevertheless relieved when her brother, Will, his wife, Lesley, and their children, Emma and Simon, arrived.

Thankfully, her mum didn't mention Kieran in front of her brother. Megan still remembered the grilling her brothers had always given any of her poor boyfriends when she had brought them home. Her dad had encouraged them! Any boy wanting to date his daughter had to pass the brother test first. And given that both her brothers had been rugby players, there was no messing with them.

***

On the Monday morning, Megan started work in the Belfast office. She already knew several of the people who worked there, and had visited the office a couple of times. The manager she would be working for had collaborated with her on previous projects.

Within an hour she was settled in, reviewing the budgets, and the day seemed to fly by. After work, she walked up to the hospital to visit her mum. Jane was doing well and the doctors agreed she could soon go home.

When she was discharged on Wednesday, Jane was delighted to get back home and have her own things around her. She'd been warned not to do too much, and her husband had taken the doctors at their word, making her snacks and cups of tea, and constantly checking she was okay.

By the time Friday night came, Jane was glad to see her husband head out to a local football match so that she could get a break from his fussing. Megan and Jane decided to have a quiet evening together, watching an old episode of *Pride and Prejudice* – one of their favourite TV series.

'So, Meg, is Kieran your Mr Darcy?' Jane asked with a little smirk.

'Mum, honestly, what are you like!' Megan replied, shaking her head. Throughout the week Kieran had sent Megan texts to check how her mum was doing, and she was looking forward to meeting up with him again the following day.

She told her mum about how, over dinner, they had discovered they had both spent summer holidays in caravans in Groomsport, and casually mentioned that they planned to visit the old Watch House when it came on the market. Megan wished she'd had a camera handy, as she watched Jane's jaw drop in shock.

'Honestly, Mum, it's just nosiness. We're both curious to see the house.'

'So will you be selling your flat in London?'

'Mum, will you not be building your hopes up? And don't be saying anything to Dad or the others! Give us some space. As Nan would say, what's for me won't go past me!'

'True enough, love!' replied her mum, with a smile.

Megan could see her mum was already planning her mother-of-the-bride outfit, but she didn't mind if it gave her something positive to look forward to.

***

Saturday morning was dry and bright, if a little cloudy, as Kieran and Megan drove up to the North Antrim coast and stopped off for a walk to the Giant's Causeway. The place was packed with foreign tourists, all snapping photos of the giant stones.

Neither of them had been there for years; it had been an annual pilgrimage for most schools. The bigger thrill for schoolkids had always been the visit to Barry's amusement park in Portrush, and a ride on the Big Dipper.

Kieran confessed that the first time he had gone on it – just six years old and thinking he was a big boy – he'd actually wet himself, and had never heard the end of it from his brothers. Megan revealed that on her first visit to the amusement park, she had put some of the pink candy floss in her hair, thinking it would be cool to have pink hair. Instead, it had just turned into a sticky mess.

'Mum spent ages trying to pick it out,' she laughed, remembering the incident, 'and in the end I had to wait until I got home to have it showered out.'

They bought fish and chips and mushy peas and sat on the seafront, laughing as the annoying seagulls dipped and swooped trying to swipe any food they could get. Then they drove on into Portstewart, and surprisingly managed to find a parking space.

The sun was just setting, and the shadows were starting to appear on the convent wall that overlooked the sea. It was a scary building – a grey, castle-like structure at the end on the rocks; 'a place to send naughty children' had been the threat of their parents.

Kieran bought them each a poke – an ice cream in a cone, with strawberry sauce and a chocolate flake – and they walked along the strand beach to sit and watch the final rays go down. It was getting chilly, but it had been a lovely day. Kieran put his arm around Megan and pulled her close as they walked back to the car, both feeling as though they had known each other for years.

***

During the week, Megan had arranged to meet her old schoolfriend, Alison Kennedy, in a new restaurant bar which had opened on Linenhall Street. Alison's husband, Ade, said he would join them about nine o'clock, giving them a couple of hours to gossip beforehand. He also wanted to check out Megan's new fella, so she invited Kieran to pop along for a drink then, too.

As the couples chatted, Ade told Kieran how Megan had made him jump through hoops before giving him the seal of approval to marry her friend. He recounted how the feisty 5ft 4in Megan had warned him – a lofty 6ft 3 – that she'd kick his ass if he hurt Alison. As they all laughed at his story, Ade added, 'And I don't doubt she would, an' all!'

The two men shared a love of motorbikes, and agreed to give their racers a go some Sunday together. Alison and Megan just rolled their eyes.

As the four left the bar, promising to meet up again soon, Alison gave Megan a hug, and whispered, 'Seal of approval!'

Then, turning to kiss Kieran on the cheek, Alison said in a stage whisper, 'And I'll castrate you with my bare hands if you hurt my friend.'

Kieran cringed, and the two men laughed.

'I don't know what you're laughing at. She will!' said Megan, as they walked back to his car.

It was late, so Kieran dropped her off at her parents' house, but didn't go in.

'Three kisses tonight,' he said, rubbing his hands with glee.

***

Over the next few weeks, Megan and Kieran met up at the weekends and headed out on day trip. As they both loved walking, they took a hike over the newly-opened Black Mountain path, marvelling at the breathtaking view over Belfast city. On another occasion they took Kieran's motor-bike for a trip down to Newcastle on the Irish Sea coast, where the Mourne Mountains swept down to the sea. And they enjoyed an outing with Alison and Ade, with a walk and then lunch. The area had recently undergone a revamp, and the two couples bought fish and chips and sat on the wall looking out at the sea.

Kieran and Megan had occasionally discussed being introduced to each other's families, but agreed there was no rush; they were keen to get to know each other first.

It was a Friday near the end of June, and Megan was at work when Kieran texted her to say that the Watch House was finally on the market. He had arranged an appointment to see the house at 11am the following day. Megan felt rather bemused by the idea, but nervous, too.

Friday night was her night at home with her mum. She would have a quick drink with her colleagues and then collect a Chinese takeaway or something similar on the way home, arriving just as her dad was heading off to watch the summer league football.

That night, Jane was just chomping on a spare rib when Megan told her she would be going to see the house in Groomsport the next morning with Kieran.

Jane stopped chewing and sat quietly for a minute. Pleased to see her daughter happy, she had been trying her hardest not to be too nosey about Megan's budding relationship. She tried to sound casual, but couldn't hide the excitement in her voice. 'So, is it serious?'

Megan sighed. 'I do like him, Mum, he is the nicest bloke I've met in years. But I want to take my time and be sure. It's also, I know I'm feeling emotional at the moment because of you being sick. If I decide to come back to Belfast to live, it has to be for the right reasons.'

Her mum nodded. 'Yes, it does. You know how much it would mean to your dad and me if you came back, but we have always wanted to encourage you to find your own path. We are proud of you. If a wee bit of romance is taking your mind off your worries, then that is a good thing. Enjoy it!'

Chapter Four
The Viewing

The next morning at breakfast, Jane couldn't hide her excitement. Delighted to see her more like her old self, her husband thought she was thrilled at his plan to take her out to the garden centre for a break and a coffee... until he caught her and Megan exchanging a look. He hadn't seen *that* look in years.

Whenever Megan was up to something, or planning some new outfit, or bringing home a new boyfriend, she would tell her mum and then regret it when Jane couldn't hide her excitement.

'What is it, you two?' he asked warily. 'You look as if you're up to mischief!'

They both laughed.

'Go on and tell him,' encouraged Jane, but Megan just made a face at her.

'Is it this new fella?' he asked.

Megan said nothing. Jane laughed again.

'Do I need to be getting your brothers to check him out?'

Megan couldn't hide her amusement at that. 'I'd be more scared of Simon and David, or Emma and Jenny, than I would my brothers these days.'

'Tell him what you are doing today, love!' her mum said excitedly.

Megan rolled her eyes then told her dad about their trip to Groomsport.

'Just a nosey, you say?'

'Yes, Dad!'

'It's been years since we've been down that way,' he replied.

'Yes,' Jane agreed. 'Not since they built the houses on the old caravan park.'

'Well, we will just see what you think then,' her dad added.

Megan got up from the kitchen table and cleared away the breakfast dishes. As she left the room to head upstairs and clean her teeth, she could have sworn she heard her dad whistle *The Wedding March*. She shook her head in resigned amusement and went off to get ready.

***

Kieran arrived just before 10am, looking 'presentable' – or so her mother later told her friends. He had brought a carrier bag of magazines for her mum, so Megan invited him in to meet her parents.

'My mum sent you these,' he explained to Jane, as he handed over the bag. 'She found it easier to read short stories rather than a book during her treatment.'

Megan had already told her mum that Kieran's mother had been treated for breast cancer five years before.

'She says if you need a chat anytime with someone who has been there and done that, she would be only be too happy,' he added.

'That's really lovely of her.' Jane smiled at him warmly and took the magazines. 'And, yes, I would like to do that sometime. Thank her very much.'

Tick! thought Megan to herself. Kieran had just passed the first test.

***

As they drove down the M2, Megan took in the stunning view of Belfast Lough, the sun sparkling on the water, the big yellow cranes – Samson and Goliath – shining brightly in the shipyard. Forty minutes later, they pulled off the Donaghadee Road into Groomsport village, and parked the car just beside the war memorial. From the road they could just see the new housing estate which had replaced the caravans. They walked across the village green to the house, enjoying the view of the harbour and the tingle of the boats, to find the estate agent waiting for them.

'Perfect weather to see the house at its best,' she commented, as she shook their hands.

'I think it's even better when there is a big storm,' Megan replied, the excitement bubbling up inside her. She squeezed Kieran's hand and he grinned back at her, his own excitement showing in his eyes.

'Oh, so you know the area?' the agent asked.

'Yes, we both used to have holidays in the old caravan park, and both of us dreamed of owning this house,' Kieran explained.

'Some things have changed, but not a lot,' said the woman, warming to the friendly young couple. 'The house could do with a bit of a clear out and updating inside, but it is a beautiful house in an amazing location.'

Inside, they could see that the interior badly needed redecoration. The current owner – an elderly gentleman – had lived there almost 40 years, most of the time on his own. The building was solid and structurally in good repair and, although every room would need redecorating, the house itself was better than either of them had dreamt.

After she had shown them around the house, the estate agent went outside to take a telephone call, leaving them to wander around on their own. Megan was sitting on the window seat looking out to the view she had dreamed of so many times during her childhood, when she turned to see Kieran looking at her.

'Well, Missus,' he asked with a grin, 'shall I buy it?'

***

Across the harbour, a man stood on the pier, looking through a pair of binoculars. It had been a long time since he had set foot in the village, but he had felt the urge to return when he saw the house advertised for sale on the internet. He was furious. That house belonged to him. He should be the master there.

Something caught his eye. There were three people coming out of the front door of the house. He raised his binoculars so he could get a better look. He could not believe what he was seeing. She had come back to him.

'Rachel!' he said to himself. 'You've come home!'

He watched the trio leave the house, walk back along the coastal path towards the harbour, then cut up the side of the tennis courts. And that's when he lost sight of them. He assumed they had got into a car, so he made his way quickly back along the pier to catch sight of their vehicle, swearing as he realised he had lost them.

***

When they said goodbye to the estate agent, Kieran and Megan decided not to go straight back to the car but doubled back through the park, down past Cockle Row, and along the path towards the main beach where a couple of people were walking their dogs.

They walked to the water's edge and Kieran started to throw flat stones into the water, trying to make them bounce. Megan picked up a couple of stones and laughed as her first stone bounced five times across the water.

'Wow!' shouted Kieran. 'Lucky throw!'

Her second throw bounced five times, and her third six.

'Lucky?' she shouted back, laughing.

They walked on along the beach, and Megan stopped to watch two young girls building a sand castle. One was blonde, the other dark; they reminded her of Hilary and herself. She took a deep breath and wrapped her arms around herself.

'What is it?' asked Kieran, putting his arm around her. 'You look as if you've seen a ghost!'

'Not quite,' she said. 'Just a very old memory I had forgotten about.'

'A pretty horrible one, by the look on your face,' he said, concerned.

She pointed towards the rocks and they walked over together. She could just see the cave hole, though it was now overgrown with grass. She wondered how many kids had hidden in it since the last time she was there.

She pointed to the cave. 'Can you see the hole in the rocks there?' she asked.

Kieran shielded his eyes to get a better view. 'Just about,' he replied.

'That cave probably saved my life!' she said, a sudden sob breaking in her throat.

As he pulled her closer, she could feel his heartbeat. It felt safe to be in his arms.

'What happened?' he asked gently.

She pointed towards the two girls playing. 'That was me and my friend, Hilary.' She stopped for a moment. 'Let's go to the coffee shop in the village and I'll tell you the story.'

They walked back along the beach to the old drugstore, which was now a cafe, and ordered coffee and sandwiches. When the coffee arrived, Megan recounted the incident of that summer in 1989 when she was eleven years old.

Kieran listened in silence as she told him about the evening on the beach and the man who had frightened her. She hadn't realised just how much it still affected her.

'I've never told anyone the whole story,' she said.

'You must have been terrified!' said Kieran.

'Yes, but the worst bit was that a few weeks later another girl went missing. She died!'

'Oh my God, I remember that. Sean – my brother who's a policeman – it was his first case when he started, and he was involved in the search for the girl. They found her body. But they said it was a terrible accident.'

'I know. I didn't know at the time, but my parents went to tell the police what had happened to me because they were worried in case it was something similar. But the police said they were sure it was a tragic accident, as the girl had been drinking alcohol even though she was only fifteen. My parents never discussed it with me, but I overheard them talking about it.'

Kieran took her hand as she carried on talking.

'The thing is,' said Meg. 'I told the man my name was Rachel, not Megan.'

'Why?'

'I didn't like my name then. I wanted to be called Rachel. But the girl who died, she was called Rachel.'

'That could be a coincidence?' Kieran smiled, giving her hand a gentle squeeze.

'Yes, of course it could... only I was wearing a yellow dress that night I was on the beach, and so...' Megan gulped '...so was that girl.'

Kieran's jaw tensed. He wasn't sure how to respond.

'Sorry.' Megan shrugged her shoulders.

'You've nothing to be sorry for,' he told her, leaning over to kiss the top of her head. 'I'm just very thankful you managed to get away.'

'I never really thought about it over the years, but every now and then when I hear of a girl going missing, I do realise I was very lucky.'

Kieran was lost for words.

'Sorry to spring this on you,' said Megan, looking miserable.

'No, it's okay. I'm glad you told me.' Kieran put his arm round her and hugged her close, dropping a gentle kiss on her forehead this time.

'Let's order some cake and change the subject!' Megan was keen to recapture the cheerful atmosphere they had enjoyed earlier that morning.

They ordered a slice of Bakewell tart, a slice of chocolate cake, and two more coffees.

'Let me guess,' said Kieran, desperate to see her smile again. 'You'll want to try a bit of my cake?'

'Absolutely, and if you're cake is nicer than mine, you'll offer to swap,' she laughed.

'So what did you think of the house?' she asked, taking a mouthful of chocolate cake.

'I loved it far more than I wanted to.' Kieran nodded, helping himself to the Bakewell tart. 'I know inside needs a total revamp, but you'll never get a better location anywhere in Ulster, I don't think.'

'Yes, it's really magical. I love it,' she agreed. Then, with a coy smile, she asked, 'So, are you going to buy it?'

'Well, it's too big for one person...' he said. 'It would really be an ideal family home. Want to come live with me and be my love? Or do we have to get married first?'

Megan coughed, almost choking on her cake. 'You're not serious?'

'Totally,' he replied, helping himself to the last of the chocolate cake.

'Oy, that was mine!' Megan pretended to stab him with her fork.

'Oh dear, have I ruined my chances now?' Kieran pretended to be upset, but he still had a twinkle in his eye. 'Look, Meg, we've both been round the world and had other relationships. I know it's early days but this just feels different from anything I've had before, and at the same time so very right,' he said, taking her hand.

Megan held her breath. Surely he wasn't going to go down on bended knee in the coffee shop?

'And besides,' he added, 'I could get both the house and the girl, so what more could I possibly want? Well, apart from the Ferrari, and a new motorbike, and maybe a wee boat to park outside.'

Before she could answer, they were interrupted.

'Excuse me, I don't mean to be rude, but are you Megan Scott, by any chance?'

'Yes. Yes, I am.' Megan looked closely at the blond lady; her face seemed a little familiar.

'My name's Hilary, Hilary Bennett. I'm not sure if you remember me, but we used to have a caravan in the park here in the 1980s,' she explained, putting out her hand.

'Yes. Hilary. Oh my gosh, I can't believe you would recognise me after all these years.'

'Well, you haven't changed much. Still got that lovely brown ponytail and that cheeky laugh. It was the laugh that made me turn round.' She smiled at them both. 'I live in one of the new houses over on the old caravan park, and I own this place now. Do you remember when it was the drugstore and we used to come here and have coke floats?' she asked.

'Yes I do. It's lovely to see you after all this time. By the way, this is Kieran,' said Meg.

Just then they heard a voice in the background. 'Mum, come on.'

'Sorry,' said Hilary, with an apologetic smile. 'That's my daughter, Rachel. She's going to a party.'

Kieran and Megan smiled at the young girl.

'I have to go, I'm sorry. Daughters, honestly!' Hilary scribbled something on a piece of paper and handed it to Megan. 'Here's my number. Please give me a ring and maybe we can meet up for a drink or a coffee sometime. I'd love to hear about your travels.'

'How did you know I travelled?' asked Megan, surprised.

'Oh, our mums still meet up in Belfast every couple of months for lunch, and your mum is always going on about where you are now. I'm very envious. Especially when my two kids are doing my head in.' Hilary laughed. 'How's your mum doing?' she asked.

'She's well, thanks. Taking it easy for now.'

'Give her my regards, won't you? And I hope I'll see you soon.'

As Hilary left the cafe with her daughter, Meg turned back to Kieran. 'Wow, that was a surprise, wasn't it?'

Kieran sighed. 'As I was saying...'

Meg laughed nervously. 'I think... if only to live in that house... it would be a... maybe.'

Kieran leaned over to kiss her briefly, then whispered, 'Well, I'll just have to buy it then!'

They went back to the car and drove along the coast to Donaghadee, where Kieran pointed out the Copeland Islands. 'We used to take a wee motor boat and a dinghy, and row over there then camp for the night,' he said.

'Who, you and your brothers?'

'My dad, brothers, uncle, cousins, friends. Never any girls, mind you. They would have just spoiled it for us.' Kieran flashed her a cheeky grin. 'We'd catch fish and Dad would gut them and fry them. God, they tasted so good. We'd have sausages as well, just in case we didn't catch enough fish. Dad would always tell us the story of Jesus and the loaves and fishes. My Uncle Connor always said it should have been the story about water into wine!'

They stopped in Donaghadee and bought an ice-cream each and a bag of dulce. When Megan took a handful of the dried seaweed, Kieran screwed up his face.

'How can you eat that stuff?' He looked disgusted.

'Love it. I love oysters, too; any seafood, in fact' she replied, chewing the dulce with extra gusto.

'If you love oysters, we should go to St George's market and pick them up there. It's fab on a Saturday.'

'Yes, we should. I remember going down to Strangford and getting the oysters there fresh off the boat. They were delicious.' Megan smiled at the memory.

'Well, maybe that can be another date,' he said. 'I might even cook for you!'

They walked along the pier to the lighthouse, stopping to admire the view back across the bay. They reminisced about climbing the moat as kids, pretending that it was their castle and they were saving it from invaders.

On the drive back to Belfast, Megan asked Kieran if she should perhaps tell his brother her story about the man on the beach.

Taking his eyes briefly from the road, he patted her hand. 'It wouldn't do any harm,' he said. 'Sean and Angie are away with the family for a week, with the school holidays, but I'll mention it to him when he gets back.'

***

A week later, Sean was at home watching football on TV when his brother rang. He had been enjoying having the house to himself; the kids were out with their friends, and his wife had gone into town.

'Do you mind if I bring a friend over to talk to you?' Kieran asked.

Sean laughed in response. 'Sure, come on over. Is this the imaginary girlfriend that we haven't met yet? Ma keeps on about it.'

Meg liked Sean immediately. He was an older version of Kieran and a bit more portly, but still had the same big smile and twinkling blue eyes.

'You're unique, you know,' he told her, as he got them both a drink from the fridge.

'How?' asked Meg.

'First girl he's brought home in twenty years. We all thought he was gay but too scared to tell our mam!'

Kieran punched his brother on the arm, but Sean was enjoying his younger brother's obvious discomfort. 'Aye, Mum'll be so relieved she'll start the knitting.'

'Knitting?' asked Megan, looking from one brother to the other. Kieran groaned.

'Aye, baby clothes.' Sean grinned.

Megan laughed. Kieran's brothers were just like hers. She knew she would be on the receiving end of some similar banter when she eventually introduced him to her family.

'Sean, we need to tell you something–' Kieran began.

'You're not pregnant already, are you?'

'NO!' They shouted in unison.

'Thank God, or Ma would have you down at the priest faster than you can say Hail Mary!'

Realising from their expressions that they had something serious to discuss, he gestured for them to sit down at the table. 'Okay,' he said. 'I'm listening!'

Meg began to tell her story about the incident almost twenty years before. She couldn't tell from Sean's face what he was thinking, but he gently prompted her on a couple of occasions when she stopped.

Listening, Kieran was thankful for his brother's sensitivity. Being a Catholic in what was perceived to be a hostile police force had been difficult for Sean and his family at times over the years. Despite the pressures – and being shot on one occasion – Sean had always been determined to carry on with his job.

When Megan finished talking, Sean reached across and squeezed her hand. 'I'm sure that was very difficult recalling that,' he said, his voice sounding a little choked.

Megan nodded.

'That case haunted me,' he told her. 'I had just come out of police training college and was on the team searching for the girl. I was there the day they found her body. Awful. Such a stupid waste.'

'Was that the only one?' asked Kieran.

'Yes, in that a body was found. There have been other runaway girls over the years, but they've usually been found because they had to go away for a few days on the Liverpool ferry.'

Megan and Kieran nodded with understanding. Abortion was illegal in both Northern and the Republic of Ireland, so girls and women who got 'into trouble' would take the ferry across to England where they would be able to get 'the problem' sorted. It was a heart-breaking and lonely journey for those who undertook it. It was rarely discussed, but it was known that if a young girl went away for a few days, that was usually the reason. The shame for the girl and her family meant it stayed a closed secret.

'My mum and dad went to the police station after the girl's body was found,' Megan told Sean. 'They were scared it was something more sinister.'

Sean heaved a sigh. 'At the time, all the indicators were that it was a tragic accident. The girl had been seen buying alcohol a couple of hours before. She had a row with her friends and was walking home alone. She was seen by a couple out walking their dog. There was a terrible storm that night and it seems with the alcohol and the weather, she was swept away.' Sean shook his head sadly.

'She'd not been raped or anything like that. She had bruises, but that was consistent with her falling on the rocks,' he recalled. 'Her fingernails had broken, but the coroner concluded that had happened when she was trying to grab onto the rocks in an attempt to save herself.'

'That's awful!' said Megan.

'I remember it, because... because I was new, and I was sent in to see the autopsy. I lasted no more than five minutes before I threw up my stomach contents.' Sean squirmed at the memory. 'Tough love, our commander called it in those days.'

'Tough love?' asked Kieran.

'Aye, he wanted to ensure that we would be prepared to see horrific things – you know, body parts, bomb victims, etc. He wanted to ensure we wouldn't spoil any crime scene by throwing up at it, or losing our nerve.'

'That's bloody awful,' said Kieran, his mouth twisting in disgust.

'Aye, maybe so, but do you remember that police sergeant who took a group of teenage boys into a morgue to show them the results of drink driving?' They both shook their heads. 'He was severely reprimanded, but those lads never ever drank and drove again. In fact, all of them said it was the best wake-up call they ever had.'

'I suppose that is one way to get the point across,' Kieran agreed.

'I'm thinking of doing it for our Sam and Sian and their mates, but I think their mother and grandmother may have my skin for it!' Sean grinned briefly, before his expression became serious again. 'The girl's mother said it wasn't an accident. She had been drunk herself at the time, and was known to have a drink problem. She was distraught. Sometimes it is hard for the relatives to accept it was just an accident, but...' He looked out the window as he gathered his thoughts.

'She said the clothes her daughter was wearing when she was found weren't hers. It was assumed that she had borrowed it from one of her friends, or that the mother was so wasted she couldn't actually remember what her daughter wore.'

There was silence for a few moments before Megan found her voice.

'What was the girl wearing?' she asked quietly.

'A yellow sundress. Nothing out of the ordinary about it,' Sean replied.

Megan looked at Kieran, then back at Sean. 'I was wearing a yellow dress that evening,' she whispered, her voice cracking with emotion.

'Shit!' said Sean. 'That's too much like a coincidence, and I don't believe in coincidences.'

Kieran's mobile rang. 'It's the estate agent,' he told Megan as he checked the screen. He got up and went into the kitchen for a few minutes, then came back smiling.

'What?' asked Sean, as he saw his brother nod towards Megan.

'Secret, big bro!' Kieran smirked.

'I'll take you in for interrogation, lad, and you won't last five minutes!' Sean warned, shaking his head.

'I think I need to introduce Meg to Mum first, or you know she'll have a fit if she thinks someone else knows something first.'

'That's true,' said Sean, then turned his attention back to Meg. 'Thanks for telling me your story. I know it can't have been easy.' He had a good feeling about this girl. His brother was clearly besotted with her; Sean really hoped she would last the course.

'I'll have a look back at the notes on the old case, just out of interest,' he added, 'but twenty years means there will probably be little to see now.'

'I understand that,' Megan replied, standing up to leave. 'It was good just getting it off my chest after all this time. Thanks.'

Chapter Five
Looking deeper

S ean couldn't sleep. When he finally rolled out of bed at
4am, Angie grunted at him.

'Going to the office, love,' he whispered, kissing her on
the cheek.

'Why?'

'Just something I want to check.'

He arrived at the central station barracks in Belfast
shortly after 5am, to the surprise of the guards; they weren't
aware of anything important going on.

Sean logged onto his computer, his methodical brain
whirring. He tried a few different searches in the hope that
his gut instinct was wrong. But he didn't believe in coincidences, and this just seemed too big a one for his liking.

At 9am he called in his two senior officers – Dougie Spencer and Catriona Murphy – both Detective Sergeants. They
had both been looking forward to a quiet weekend before
the usual July 12th chaos, when everything usually kicked
off.

Catriona Murphy was frustrated at having to go to work
on a Sunday. She had just bought her first flat, and had
planned to use the day to start decorating her bedroom.
She had spent the previous day clearing out the room, with

the result that its contents were now spread over the living room and other bedroom.

Dougie Spencer, on the other hand, was relieved. He had been due to go to his brother-in-law's for lunch that day, and the guy really got on his nerves – work was a great excuse to get out of it.

***

For four hours the three checked, rechecked, and trawled through masses of information. When they finished, Sean called the Chief Constable, Chris Davis. An hour later he, too, arrived at the station. If Sean's gut feeling was right and their analysis accurate, another girl/young woman was due to disappear sometime in the next six weeks.

They decided to set up an incident room away from any prying eyes, so that they could continue their investigations. No-one in the station, except those chosen to be on the team, should know what had been uncovered.

The Chief Constable then contacted the Home Secretary to advise her of the situation; he knew she didn't like to be caught unaware. They agreed that the matter should be kept under close guard and that he would brief her if anything significant came up. She said that she hoped that these incidents were coincidences, but the team had her full support.

Central Police Station, Belfast - Monday, July 6. 3pm

Officers from eight police forces across the UK and Ireland had quickly assembled for a vital, hush-hush briefing from Chief Inspector Sean Maloney and his team. And for the next two hours, they briefed their colleagues on what they had found.

Sean explained that over the previous twenty-five years, in a number of different locations, a total of twenty-eight teenage girls or young women had gone missing, or suffered accidental deaths, or committed suicide, or suspicious death. The number itself was not unusual, but what concerned him was that all the reports had been filed in and around the August bank holiday – the last weekend in August.

The computer records did not show all the relevant information, so it would be the officers' jobs to go back to their own forces and analyse the cases concerned. Some of the older files might not have been fully included on the computerisation of old records, so they might have to check through paper reports or microfiche records. Each officer was tasked with checking a number of vital details: what the girl had been wearing; if she had had a boyfriend at the time; and any reports of a man in the area acting suspiciously.

There were seven cases in Northern Ireland – by far the biggest number – spread over the twenty-five years and in different parts of the Province, so it would have been difficult for anyone to detect any kind of pattern. The cases were split between the Belfast squad, and they were asked to look for anything that might link them together.

Everyone was told to report back within seven days, although anything critical should be flagged up with him or his two deputies immediately. There was to be no discussion with anyone other than those directly briefed, and the press were not to be informed; a media blackout was ordered.

Sean highlighted the difficulties involving the cases of women recorded as missing persons. Once someone turned sixteen, they were considered to be an adult and likely to have left voluntarily, so limited resources had been put into searching for suspected runaways during the 1980s and 1990s, unless there was a history of abuse or mental illness. Many of the youngsters who ran away tended to head across the water to England or Scotland, or down south across the border to Dublin. To complicate the issue, the person notifying the police of a disappearance didn't always update them if the missing person returned home or was found.

Sean warned that this meant some of those going missing could have slipped under the radar. There were also a couple of gaps in incidents during the twenty-five year spell, which raised the possibility that this was genuinely just a coincidence.

'I'll be honest with you and admit that this whole investigation might be a stab in the dark,' he told the officers. 'But I can't ignore it if it means saving the life of even one girl or young woman.'

When the briefing was over, the officers who had travelled for the meeting headed back to their own forces, while the Belfast team wasted no time in getting to work.

Megan, who had told him she had pretended to be called Rachel, had been approached in 1989, just a few weeks before the body of Rachel Porter had been washed up near Millisle, a couple of miles along the coast from Groomsport. The Rachel Porter case was the one Sean had discussed with Kieran and Meagan as his induction into the gruesome side of police work.

But Sean was also keen to look closely at the accidental death of a girl in Groomsport – Rachel Fitzpatrick – who had drowned the year before Megan's encounter on the beach in the same village. It was believed she had fallen off the harbour wall during a storm and drowned.

The address on the computer record for Rachel Fitzpatrick was The Watch House, Groomsport – a house Sean vaguely remembered from holidays he had spent on a caravan site there as a youngster. He knew the chances of the Fitzpatrick family still living there were pretty slim.

Dougie Spencer, Sean's DS, recognised the name of the dead girl's father – Hugh Fitzpatrick. A professor of history, he had recently completed a popular Irish history series on TV. The first piece of luck they had was finding that he still lived at the Groomsport house.

After a few calls, Dougie tracked the professor down to Dublin, where he was attending a series of lectures, but would be back home by the end of the week. Keeping his reason for calling vague, Dougie arranged an appointment to meet the man on Saturday at noon.

As the week progressed, the team managed to eliminate several names when investigations showed that the women concerned had been found alive and well, or where the circumstances of their death had been unforeseen, like a car accident.

There were, however, other cases where the information did match. If this was a single killer, the team decided he must have travelled a lot and had quite probably served spells in prison, though not necessarily for crimes against women.

Each morning and evening that week the team met to review their findings, liaise with their colleagues in the other forces, and update the huge board in the incident room. Appointments were made with the families of the girls on the list, in an effort to discover if there was anything else which could be followed up. Dragging up old memories wouldn't be easy for anyone.

Chapter Six
A house with history

K ieran was surprised when the estate agent called to say the house owner wanted to meet prospective buyers himself before agreeing a sale.

'I know it's unusual,' she said, 'but he's a historian and considers the house to be of significant historical value, so he wants to be sure that whoever buys it will preserve and appreciate it.'

Nervous to be interviewed, Kieran arranged that he and Megan would go to Groomsport on Saturday. There was a slight haze over the sea and a nip in the air when they arrived, but the house still felt right. The door was opened as they approached it, by an elderly gentleman who looked familiar.

'Hugh Fitzpatrick, pleased to meet you,' the man said, extending his hand and inviting them in.

'I thought I recognized your name,' said Kieran. 'You made some TV programmes about the history of Ireland, didn't you?'

The man nodded. 'Yes, which is why there are so many books sitting around the place.'

The house was as beautiful as they both remembered, and Kieran and Megan exchanged smiles as they stood for a few moments at the window to admire the view.

'I'm sure you think it a bit strange that I wanted to meet you before agreeing to any sale,' Mr Fitzpatrick said, gesturing for them to sit down.

'A little,' admitted Kieran, 'but we understand that the house has an amazing history and that you want to ensure it is preserved for the future.' Megan smiled and nodded in encouragement.

'I've lived here for almost forty years,' the historian revealed, 'but I'm moving to the United States, where my late wife's family live. I've been offered a fellowship post at Harvard, near Boston, and I'm looking forward to better weather. The cold wet climate is playing havoc with my arthritis.'

Over coffee, Megan and Kieran shared their stories of their childhood holidays at the nearby caravans. He told them that he, too, had often gone over to the Copeland Islands with his young daughter and son to camp and fish.

Mr Fitzpatrick was keen to know what Kieran's plans were for the interior of the house, admitting that he had neglected it somewhat over the years. He seemed impressed when Kieran told him that as a carpenter by trade, he would want to hand-build the kitchen, as he enjoyed cooking.

Megan smiled and added that she would enjoy sitting in the glass room and watching the world go by while Kieran cooked. 'What can you tell us about the history of the house?' she asked.

'Groomsport was an important port in the 17th century, as Donaghadee was the main gateway between Ulster and Scotland. Even before Belfast had become the city it is now. The name was derived from the Irish meaning – port of the gloomy servant,' he explained. 'The building itself was a customs house in the early 1800s, when Sir James Hamilton had placed a customs officer here for the trade coming to and from Belfast.

'In 1781, free trade had been established directly between Belfast and the Caribbean, and this trade route would be more important to business than trading with Europe. Belfast, as you will know, grew into the city through ship building and maintenance, though Harland and Wolff – famous for building *The Titanic* – only opened in 1862.

'The city grew with chandlers making soap and candles, and even shoemakers, but it is most famous for the linen which was produced in homes in and around the city. These goods were part of the export, but more importantly the import of sugar and tobacco built Belfast. Factories grew up to process these goods before they were in turn shipped to mainland Britain and on into Europe. At one stage the old Gallaghers' factory on York Street was the largest tobacco factory in the world.'

Megan told him that her grandfather had worked there for many years and, as a chain smoker, had died of lung cancer.

'That's no surprise,' Mr Fitzpatrick continued, clearly warming to his subject. 'Many workers had free cigarettes included as part of their wage packet. What you might not know is that Ireland had been a source for the white slave trade that saw almost half a million Irish men, women, and children be forcibly sent to work in plantations in the Caribbean, US, and countries in the north of South America.'

Both Kieran and Megan were surprised and shocked; neither had ever heard this aspect of their country's history before.

'Yes, it is overshadowed by the African slave trade, but was no less brutal in its impact,' the older man went on. 'As brutal as the potato famine. It was abolished finally as part of the 1807 Slave Trade Act, but many of the slaves were not themselves freed until 1833.'

'What happened to them?'

'None of them ever made it back to Ireland,' said the professor, shaking his head. 'Many were forcibly interbred with the black African slaves as a way of making more money for their owners.'

'Seriously?' gasped Megan.

'Yes. In fact, my wife was a descendant of two such slaves. That is how we met, when I was researching the history.' He got up and lifted a framed photograph from the mantel shelf and handed it to them.

'I proposed to her on our third date, and we were married six weeks later!'

Kieran reached for Meg's hand. 'I can understand that,' he said, smiling.

Hugh Fitzpatrick nodded. 'Yes, she was a beautiful woman, too.'

Megan blushed, but the older man struggled to hide the sadness in his voice. 'We never had one fight in all the time we were together. She loved this house, especially when there was a storm. She would sit on the window seat at the landing and watch it.'

'Yes, that is what I imagine doing, too,' Megan said, keen to change the subject.

'Well, I do hope this house will bring you the happiness we had, but not the tragedy.' The professor didn't elaborate, but rubbed his hand wearily across his eyes.

Feeling uncomfortable, Kieran caught Megan's eye and gestured that it was time to leave. They thanked the man for his time and headed towards the front door.

'I really do believe you will bring good luck to this house,' Mr Fitzpatrick said, shaking their hands. 'Goodbye Kieran, goodbye Rachel.'

'My name is Megan.' She felt a prickle of unease.

'Yes, yes, I'm sorry, my dear. For a moment you reminded me of my daughter, Rachel.'

As Kieran and Megan walked back across the village, they were deep in discussion about what they had heard. Was there a connection? Did it affect how they felt about the house?

***

They were so engrossed in their discussions that they didn't see the man walking towards them. For the last hour he had been sitting on the bench overlooking the port, waiting for them to come out of the house.

He walked towards the Watch House. *Time to come home,* he thought. As he drew near the gate and was about to enter, he noticed two men getting out of a car parked nearby. *Policemen. He could spot pigs a mile off! What were they doing here?*

He continued walking along the path towards Ballymacormick Point, looking back to see the two men entering the house. His plan was scuppered. But he would be back.

Rachel had finally come home, and he would be waiting for her.

Chapter Seven
Friendship rekindled

After their 'interview' with Professor Fitzpatrick, Megan had arranged to pop into the coffee shop for lunch and a chat with Hilary while Kieran went into Bangor to pick up some things for his bike. He would collect her on his way back in about an hour or so.

Hilary was delighted to see her childhood friend, and they chatted easily together. Hilary and her dentist husband, Ben, had two children – Rachel, the 12-year-old Megan had met on their previous visit, and nine-year-old Paul.

'We moved from Belfast four years ago when the housing development first went up on the old caravan site, and we love it,' explained Hilary. 'The commute into the city isn't too bad for Ben, and the children have settled well into the schools.'

Hilary laughed. 'Rachel has just started at the grammar school in Bangor, and feels so grown up getting the bus every day by herself.'

Megan was interested to know more about the coffee shop, which seemed to have a steady trade.

'We bought it three years ago when the previous owner wanted to sell up. It has worked out well for me because it allows me to work part-time round school hours. Thankfully, it does a steady trade even in winter, although weekends can be pretty hectic.'

Megan talked about her travels and work, recounting how she had met Kieran recently on the flight back from London.

'Really?' Hilary couldn't hide her surprise. 'I thought you must have been with him for ages. You seem really comfortable together. In saying that, I met Ben at a party at university and we got married about a year later, much to everyone's surprise. We were practically living together anyway – though our mothers never knew – and it was a good excuse to split the rent. Actually, he was a kept man for a couple of years whilst he finished his degree. I don't let him forget that!' she said with a laugh.

Megan took a sip of her coffee. 'Do you ever regret it?' she asked quietly. 'I mean, marrying so young, or so quickly?'

Sensing something was troubling her childhood friend, Hilary chose her words carefully.

'I would have married him no matter what. It hasn't always been easy, of course, but we have worked at it together. I just knew... I just knew we were right for each other.' She leaned across and squeezed Megan's hand. 'Are you having doubts?'

Megan paused for a moment to think. 'It does feel a bit quick. I mean, I know I've never met a guy who I have gelled with so well. But – and it's a big but – do I want to move back here for good? I just don't know. I worry that I feel drawn back here because of mum's illness and wanting to be closer to the family.'

'From an outside point of view, I think you two – from what I've seen – do have something special,' Hilary replied.

'I do also think, and you know this yourself, that the person to help you with this is him. Talk to him.'

'Yes, I know. I will.'

The two friends smiled. It was good to have reconnected.

***

When Kieran arrived to pick Megan up, he ordered a coffee and another slice of the Bakewell tart, adding that he hoped to be able to get a full portion for himself this time.

'I hear you're thinking of buying the Watch House; or the White House, as we used to call it,' Hilary said.

'Yes, I loved that house when I was a boy, so I'm very interested in it,' Kieran replied between mouthfuls of cake.

'Same as this one then.' Hilary nodded towards Megan. 'She always loved it when we were youngsters.'

'We met the owner this morning, Megan probably told you. Fascinating gentleman,' Kieran went on. 'Wants to ensure no riff-raff buy the place.'

'That rules us out then!' Megan joked.

'He is an amazing man,' Hilary agreed, 'but he keeps himself very much to himself. A couple of years ago, it was the bicentenary of when Cockle Row was built, and the village decided to hold events over a couple of days. He organised everything to ensure it was authentic, and the village was packed for not just days, but weeks afterwards.' She laughed. 'It was great for business, I have to say!'

'Yes, he shared some of the history of the house with us, and it was fascinating. We really would be getting a piece of history,' Kieran agreed.

'You would, but he has also sadly had his tragedies.'

'In what way?' Megan was intrigued.

'Way back before we were born, his wife died in a car accident on the road to Belfast. She was American, still only in her twenties, but their baby daughter managed to crawl out of the wreckage and was found by a passerby.'

'That's terrible! How sad,' said Megan.

'Yes, but then his daughter drowned off the pier just before her 16th birthday. The man practically became a recluse after that.'

'My goodness!' Megan was shocked. 'That would send anyone demented!'

'Apparently it did. His second wife and son left him soon after.'

'How much tragedy can someone cope with?' asked Megan, remembering Professor Fitzpatrick's comment to them about tragedy.

'I'm surprised he continued to live there,' said Kieran.

'He did go away for a while and the house stood empty. As I said, when he was helping with organising the celebrations he was so kind and really got people involved. I learned such a lot about this place. There is so much history in this area.'

Before leaving, Megan and Kieran arranged to come back some evening to meet Hilary and her husband for dinner.

As they strolled back to where Kieran had parked the car, Megan stopped suddenly. 'Didn't Professor Fitzpatrick say his daughter's name was Rachel?' she asked, frowning.

'Yes, I think he did. What a strange coincidence,' replied Kieran, pulling her close to him.

Chapter Eight
A history lesson

Sean and Dougie arrived in Groomsport just after midday, and knocked on the door of the Watch House. When they introduced themselves to Hugh Fitzpatrick and showed him their ID cards, he ushered them into the sitting room and offered them tea or coffee.

Clearing away three used cups, he explained that he had been meeting a lovely young couple who hoped to buy the house. 'Lovely couple,' he said. 'Strangely, she reminded me a lot of my daughter.'

'You're planning to sell the house?' asked Sean.

'Yes, I'm moving to the US where I'm taking up a new research post at Harvard.'

'Congratulations, sir. I very much enjoyed your TV programme on the history of Ulster,' said Dougie.

After a brief discussion about the programme, Hugh asked the two officers how he could help them.

Sean explained that they were investigating a couple of events from some years before – one involving a young woman who had gone missing, and another who had been approached and chased by a man on the beach in the North Down area. In carrying out their research, they had come across his daughter's unfortunate death and, whilst they were sorry to bring up the tragic situation, they wanted to be sure to rule any possible connection out.

'I believe they are called cold cases in the US,' said Hugh Fitzpatrick.

'Yes, sir, that's right,' said Sean.

'Well, I'm not sure what more there is to tell you that you don't already know. My daughter, Rachel, was 16. She had gone out that night for whatever reason, without telling my wife. I assume there must have been a boyfriend, though her friends all said she didn't have one at the time.'

He gave a deep sigh and looked out of the window towards the harbour. 'For whatever reason, she was on the pier and there was a storm, one of the worst in years. It seems she was blown off the pier. People heard her scream and ran to help, but it was too late. She got swept away. Her body was recovered the next day.'

'I'm very sorry, sir.' Sean genuinely felt bad about making the man relive the tragic events again.

'Yes, it was a double agony, as her mother had died in a tragic road accident fourteen years before.'

'Her mother?'

Hugh Fitzpatrick nodded. 'She was driving our car one night and crashed, on the road to Belfast. My wife was killed in the accident but my daughter, who was only two, survived. My wife was American. The police said there was evidence that she had been driving on the wrong side of the dual carriageway and swerved to avoid an oncoming vehicle; the car hit a wall and burst into flames.' He looked at the officers squarely. 'And no, she hadn't been drinking. She didn't.'

He shook his head as if he wanted to shake off the memories. 'I was in Dublin at the time, at a historical society meeting. Ironically, I was at the same meeting fourteen years later when I got the dreadful call about my daughter.'

No-one spoke. How could such tragedy strike twice to the same family?

After a few minutes, Mr Fitzpatrick went on, 'I've hated that journey from Dublin ever since. I have never been able to forgive myself that I wasn't here. I never understood why my wife was out driving that night, as she wasn't a confident driver and hated storms. Nor why my daughter was out either, for that matter. I've beaten myself up for many years trying to understand that.'

Sean cleared his throat. 'I'm extremely sorry, sir, to be bringing all this up. But the following summer, the year after your daughter died, would you remember where you were?'

'I was in the US with my wife's family – or rather, I should say my first wife's family. After Rachel died, things came unglued with my second wife. She left me a few months after Rachel's death, and quite honestly I couldn't blame her. My grief was... overwhelming. I couldn't bear to be here, so I went to the US three months after Rachel's death. The house would have been empty, but for the housekeeper coming in.'

'I see. And your second wife's name, sir?' Dougie prompted.

'Arabella. The last time I heard she had remarried – a solicitor from Galway. Some chap named Fullerton, I think.'

Dougie made a few notes in his pocketbook. 'And where would you have been staying in the US at the time?'

'I would have been in Boston. I rented a house; in fact, I bought the house there ten years ago. I now split my time between here and the US, as a lot of the history research I do links Ulster with America and the Caribbean,' the older man explained. 'I couldn't face renting this house out, but nor could I face coming back to it. That would have been between 1989 and 1999, so I just asked my solicitors to deal with all bills, etc, in my absence. If you need to check that, I can give you their details.'

'Thank you, sir, that would certainly be useful.' Sean nodded. 'How long were you married to Arabella?'

'Ten years.' Mr Fitzpatrick smiled wistfully. 'We were very happy during that time. She was a wonderful mother to Rachel, for which I was always thankful.'

'So the house here would have been lying empty?'

'No, we had a housekeeper who looked after the house for us. She was a local lady, Hilda Adams.'

'So she had a key?' Dougie looked up from his notebook.

'Yes she had, though there was always a spare key hanging on a nail behind the wood shed.'

'Who would have known about the spare key?'

'Not many people – my wife, daughter, son Thomas, Hilda, and my cousin, Barry Fitzpatrick. Probably the sourface that was his wife, too, Leah. I think the key is probably still hanging there, in fact!'

'Do you have any details of where Hilda Adams and Barry Fitzpatrick might be now?' asked Sean.

'No, I don't. I actually lost touch with Barry... a fight at my daughter's funeral, of all places. He was drunk and obnoxious, and I took a swing at him. He was married to Hilda's daughter, Leah, and they lived along the coast in Millisle, but I haven't heard from them in years. Probably doing time, the pair of them. Arabella didn't have any time for them, either.'

'Why would that be?' Sean couldn't hide his interest.

'She felt Barry was a bit odd. He would turn up when I was away, apparently to check that everything was okay. She felt uncomfortable with him. She actually thought the house was haunted, but shew as only unsettled on the nights that I was away.'

'And Hilda Adams?'

'That was a shock. She had looked after me, the house, and even Rachel after her mum died, then suddenly out of the blue she wrote me a letter and told me that she couldn't work for me any more. No explanation. When I came back to live here, I discovered that she had left the village.'

'When did she stop working for you, sir?' Dougie was scribbling frantically.

'Just after the first anniversary of Rachel's death. The timing seemed weird, but I had other things on my mind. I expect she probably had too much on her hands trying to bring up her daughter, Leah's children. She was a useless mother, quite frankly. I heard both her children left home as soon as they could.'

'Do you know where they went?'

'Yes, actually... I have the daughter, Sarah's address. She wrote me a lovely letter when the history programme came out. She told me how much she had enjoyed coming to our house, how much she had loved Rachel, and that she had named her own daughter after her. Just a moment and I'll find her address.'

The professor went out of the room and returned a few minutes later with a piece of paper on which he had written an address and phone number. Sean thanked him.

'Her brother, Gordon, is a solicitor in London, I believe. They both turned out very well, in spite of their parents.' He sat back down. 'I'm sorry that I can't be of more help to you. As I've said, I wasn't here that summer.'

As they turned to go, Sean couldn't resist commenting that he hoped that the professor's prospective buyers followed through on their interest on the house.

Hugh Fitzpatrick smiled. 'Yes, I think they are very keen. I felt quite bad as I called her Rachel, she so reminded me of my daughter, but I think they liked the house.'

***

Back in the car, Sean directed Dougie to drive further into the village then pull over. 'I could do with a half to collect my thoughts. Let's go into this bar and grab some lunch.'

Once inside and their orders given, he turned to his sergeant. 'So what do you make of all that then?'

'I think we might be wanting to check on this Barry Fitzpatrick. I think Hugh Fitzpatrick seems to be out of the frame, but we should check his alibi anyway.' He paused. 'The name Rachel comes up a helluva lot, doesn't it? Maybe it's a family name. You know how the Americans name their sons Junior the third, or whatever,' Dougie suggested.

'Yes,' Sean agreed. 'My mother would have a field day, what with all the biblical names... Rachel, Leah, Sarah...' He sipped his drink. 'Call the office and get them to check the databases to see if any of the people he mentioned feature.'

'Do you want a wee wager that they do, boss?' Dougie had a reputation as the office bookie.

'Nah, I think it is a certainty at least one of them will,' said Sean. He handed Dougie the piece of paper Hugh Fitzpatrick had given him. 'And give this woman, Sarah, a call and see if she has anything to add. She must only have been about twelve or so when Rachel Fitzpatrick died, but it is surprising what a child observes. And see if you can track down Hugh's ex-wife, and also this Barry and Leah.'

They hadn't even finished their food when Dougie got a call to say checks had thrown up Barry Fitzpatrick's name as having a history of spending time at Her Majesty's Pleasure over the years. The list of convictions included petty crime, assault, grievous bodily harm, and more recently some drug and gun crime. He had been released from jail five months before, but hadn't kept any probation appointments in the last two months. As he had violated parole, there was an arrest warrant currently out for him.

His ex-wife Leah Fitzpatrick had a number of misdemeanours on her record – shoplifting mainly – but no jail time. The last address on her file was the one in Millisle which Hugh Fitzpatrick had given them. Millisle was a small village, but Rachel Porter's body had washed up near there. Another coincidence?

Chapter Nine
Meeting the family

Kieran finally gave in to his parents' hints and agreed he would bring Megan for lunch. His mother pulled out all the stops, making her son's favourite Sunday roast and a delicious melt-in-your-mouth pavlova for dessert.

A tiny woman, who was clearly the boss of the family, she took no nonsense from the strapping sons who towered over her.

'A nice Ulster girl, I can't believe it!' she said, shaking Megan's hand as she escorted her into the conservatory. 'Just what our Kieran needs.'

'Don't you mean a good Catholic girl, Mum?' her son asked.

'Kieran, my boy, I'm just very glad it's a girl you've brought home!'

Everyone laughed as Kieran just shook his head.

Over lunch, his dad teased Megan about what football team she supported, and his mother chatted away, asking question upon question. It was when she went to get out the photograph album that Kieran decided it was time to leave.

When they arrived back at Megan's parents' house, Kieran was ready to leave her at the doorstep, but her brothers' cars were there so it looked like it was to be his turn in the spotlight.

'Glad to see he has two arms, two legs and one nose,' said one brother, as they were introduced.

'Aye, he even has all his own teeth, or so it looks like!' said the other one.

Their wives, Rosie and Lesley laughed, remembering the teasing they had received the first time they had been brought to the family home.

'If you don't stand up for yourself, or you take offence easily, then you won't last two minutes in this family,' Rosie warned Kieran.

Megan's parents, Jane and Jack, were just delighted to have their family around them. They missed Megan very much, and secretly hoped this was the man that would finally bring her back home.

Chapter Ten
Widening the inquiry

Sarah Drummond, nee Fitzpatrick, did not feature on any database. When Dougie made a call to her, she admitted to being surprised that the police were looking at her cousin's death after all this time. She said she had not been in contact with either of her parents in years, confirming that she had left home when she was sixteen, desperate to get away from them before something happened.

When Dougie asked what she meant, she was hesitant in replying.

'I didn't want to turn into my mother, and the Fitzpatrick women seemed to be cursed,' she explained. 'I didn't mean anything in particular, just that there was a lot of tension at home after Rachel's death. Actually, there was a lot even before she died.'

Dougie felt it would be a good idea to pay Sarah a face-to-face visit, to find out what more she had to say. With Sean's approval, he arranged that they would go to England and interview her the following Tuesday. Her brother, Gordon, would only have been seven years old when Rachel died, so they felt it unnecessary to contact him for now.

Before their trip to England, Sean decided to pay Leah Fitzpatrick a visit, as it would also give him a chance to check out the location where Rachel Porter had died. He also arranged to meet with Rachel Porter's mother, Angela.

Leah Fitzpatrick (nee Adam)'s house, Millisle - Thursday, July 16. 10am

Catriona drove Sean from the station out down the Ards Peninsula across to Millisle. It was a route she was familiar with, having lived down on the coast near Portaferry. Her parents still lived there and she enjoyed going back occasionally for a rest, the pace of life was still significantly slower than in Belfast.

Millisle was a small village a couple of miles along the coast from Donaghadee, and about 32 miles from Belfast. It sat on the Irish Sea, but its rocky shoreline and seaweed beaches made it less popular.

The main street formed part of the coastal road down to Portaferry – a popular drive for day trippers – but during the winter months it had an eerie emptiness about it. Today, in early July, it was busy with families enjoying the traditional fortnight shut-down. The bars were always full at lunchtime, while the ice cream vans did a roaring trade from their positions just beside the small beach.

It was relatively easy to trace Leah Fitzpatrick. When she got divorced, she had moved to a house just around the corner from her marital home, but she had changed her name back to Leah Adams as her ex-husband's name was not welcome around the town. The owners of the old house had been able to point Sean and Catriona in the right direction. No doubt word would spread quickly that the police were back on the trail of the Fitzpatrick family.

Leah may have only been in her mid-fifties, but she could easily have passed for someone in their seventies. Years of smoking and eating fried food had taken their toll, along with the cheap booze. She spat venom when the officers asked about her ex; there was clearly no love lost there. She moaned that because of him she had lost her children, her looks, and her respect.

She claimed that she'd had no contact with Barry; the last she had heard, he was back in prison. But she became immediately suspicious when their questioning turned to events around the time Rachel Fitzpatrick had died.

Sean told her vaguely that they were looking into a girl's disappearance and drowning, and checking back over old similar cases, but he could see Leah's brain trying to work out the connection.

'We believe your daughter ran away when she was sixteen?' he said.

'Yes,' sniffed Leah, pulling out a scruffy hankie. 'Sarah Rachelle was my princess. I'd have done anything for that girl, but she went and got herself pregnant. I had to send her away. Barry would have killed her and the lad – and probably me, too, for letting it happen.'

'Rachelle or Rachel?' asked Catriona, checking the spelling.

'It was Barry's idea to call her Rachelle, it was after one of his ancestors from some history journal diary that his cousin Hugh had found. He really wanted to call her Rachel, but that name had been taken by his damn cousin for *his* daughter.'

'The daughter who died?' Sean suggested.

'Aye, God rest her soul. When our Sarah went missing, Barry went ballistic, shouting that something could have happened to her like happened to Rachel. Surprisingly, he was going to go to the police, so I had to tell him the truth.

Sarah wouldn't tell me where she had gone, because she knew Barry would beat it out of me.' She sniffed some more. 'I haven't seen her since the day she left.

'As it turned out, Barry beat me black and blue anyway. He would have killed me if some of our neighbours hadn't called the police. Barry was arrested. Gordon got taken into care and ended up going to live with his nan, my mother. I divorced Barry, and I've been on me own ever since.'

There was silence. She took another drag of her cigarette, her fingers stained brown from the tar. 'He left me with nothing. I was going to sell the fancy car he drove, but it turned out it wasn't even his, it belonged to that damn cousin of his. When I went to clear it out, I realised he must have had a bit on the side, because there were women's clothes stuffed in the boot.'

'What kind of car was it?'

'Dunno.'

'What kind of clothes? Do you know whose they were?'

'I had my suspicions, but the clothes wouldn't have fitted her. They looked more like our Sarah's size, but they definitely weren't hers.'

'Do you remember what they were?' Sean tried to sound casual.

She shook her head. 'It must have been a dress, or a long t-shirt. There was a broken silver charm bracelet down the side of the seat – a cheap thing. I threw it out.'

'Whatever happened to the car?' asked Catriona.

Leah shrugged her shoulders. 'It was taken back to Hugh's place, I think.'

'Do you remember what it looked like, or the make?'

'It had four doors, a kind of beige colour, but I couldn't tell you the make.'

It seemed to dawn on Leah that if Barry was out of prison he might come after her. 'Barry held a grudge. He never liked anyone to get something over him. He doesn't forgive or forget,' she explained.

'What was his relationship with his cousin like?' asked Sean.

'That's the strange thing, they had nothing in common – what with Hugh being all clever and high and mighty – but they were close. They'd grown up together and were more like brothers. Barry was proud of his cousin's success, but at the same time he resented it. He felt that Hugh had been given all the opportunities but he hadn't. And he was besotted by Hugh's wife, that Irish nigger!'

'What?' Sean couldn't hide his shock at her words.

'Oh aye, seems she was descended from slaves, or something – an African man and an Irish woman. It was before Barry and me got married.' She frowned. 'It was a right tragedy what happened to her. We got married not long after she died. Barry's arm was in a plaster thing, as he had been badly burnt in an accident at work. He was distraught when he heard about the accident. Kept saying he should have saved her. Then when the child Rachel died...' She started to weep as she lit her third cigarette, took a drag, and began to cough.

'It was just dreadful. He felt he had let Hugh down, not looking after them. He kept saying he should have saved them. It didn't make sense to me. I mean, surely it was Hugh's responsibility to look after his family.'

There was a short silence, whilst Leah blew her nose.

'Dear God, why did you have to bring all this up? It was such a terrible time.'

'I'm sorry,' Sean said, his voice softening a little. 'We have one more question. Do you know why Hugh and Barry fell out?'

'It was that bloody second wife of his, Lady Arabella. Stuck-up cow.'

'*Lady* Arabella?' Catriona asked.

Leah gave a harsh laugh. 'Not really; it was just the name I called her. She was so stuck-up; thought she was a cut above us all. She would snub us, not invite us to things when Hugh had important guests. The final straw was at young Rachel's funeral – everyone had had a few drinks, something was said, and Hugh punched Barry. We left and never went back.

'After that, Barry was always in a bad mood. I was thankful he worked away such a lot, as it gave me peace. He moved away for a couple of months the following summer, but came back when his money ran out. Things weren't good for us, and when our Sarah left it was probably the final straw. Now look at me... a bag of nerves and on my own. Miserable bloody life.'

'We understand your mother was their housekeeper?'

'Dead years, she was, and I didn't even know. No-one thought to tell me! I mean, I didn't deserve that.'

The officers had heard enough and got up to leave. Leah Fitzpatrick seemed to have aged before them.

Back in the car, Catriona turned to Sean. 'Well, boss, that woman has certainly done me a favour,' she said with a laugh.

'How come?'

'I reckon I've just quit smoking!'

Sean laughed. He called Dougie, who had been trying to track down Arabella Fullerton. He'd discovered that she was living in Galway, and had agreed to meet with them the following day. She had sounded nervous on the phone.

Angela Porter's house, Ballywalter Village - Thursday. 11.50am

Angela Porter lived just off the main street, in a modern terrace house with a small front garden. The years had not been kind to her – thanks to a combination of circumstances and a liking for vodka and a pack of cigarettes a day. She had hardened over the years, which wasn't surprising with the tragic loss of her only child.

Still bitter that her suspicions had not been listened to twenty years before, Angela was not over-welcoming when Sean and Catriona arrived. It still rankled that, as a single mother, fingers had been pointed at her over what had happened. She still felt guilty that she had been out drinking and hadn't noticed until the next day that her daughter was missing.

'I always said there was something suspicious about my Rachel's death, but no-one would believe me!' She drew deeply on her cigarette, eyeing the two officers sitting in her modest living room.

'At the time, you said your daughter didn't have a boyfriend, is that correct?' Catriona asked kindly, trying to put the woman at her ease.

'Yes, she was studying for her A levels, determined to get out of this hell-hole.'

'Does the name Barry Fitzpatrick ring a bell?'

'That bastard!' Angela's features changed from bitterness to fear. 'What has he got to do with anything?'

'How do you know him?' Sean asked.

Her face stony with anger, she didn't reply, but took another long drag from her cigarette.

'His wife thought he was having an affair with another woman. Was it you?' Sean persisted.

'It wasn't an affair!' She spat.

'What was it then?'

'Sex. Just sex.'

'Did he pay you?' asked Catriona. Angela threw her a filthy look, but didn't answer.

'Weren't you a bit old for him? We heard he liked his women younger – maybe your daughter's age?' provoked Sean.

Angela reacted to both the insult and the accusation. 'Absolutely bloody not!' she snapped.

'It must have been hard realising that he preferred your daughter to you,' Catriona suggested.

There was silence for a few minutes, then Angela began to cry. They waited for her to regain her composure.

'It wasn't like that. Rachel was a good girl,' she sobbed. 'She was studying hard and wanted to go to university. She had got good grades in her O levels, and I was so proud of her.

'I came home one night and he was here. He had no reason to be. She asked me to tell him to go. He laughed and said he was just keeping her safe, as there were a lot of bad people out there.'

She drew on the cigarette again before continuing. 'She went to her room and I told him if he ever laid a finger on her, he'd be sorry! She swore he had never touched her, and I believed her.'

'When was that?'

'The week before... before she died.'

'Would she have got into a car with him?' asked Sean.

'No, no way.' She paused. 'I don't think so.'

'Is there anything else that you remember about the week leading up to that night?' asked Catriona.

'I've gone over and over and over it in my head. Rachel wouldn't have stayed out that night, so I don't know why she did. I was at my friend's house.'

'Why wouldn't she go out?'

'Rachel had a dog, Skip. She loved that dog, but he was terrified of thunderstorms. She'd had him since he was a puppy. He died the month after her, he ran in front of a car. That nearly killed me all over again.'

'Did you ever see Barry after your daughter died?'

'Just the once. He came to her funeral, he was crying... tried to say he was sorry he couldn't have saved her. He was rambling and I didn't know what he was talking about. I never saw him again.'

Angela's initial hardness had given way to reveal the fragile woman that hid below the layers of grief. Her daughter had clearly been the one good thing about her life, and that had been tragically torn away.

Sean explained that they were looking at some other missing girls, more recent cases, and they were just trying to tie up any possible connections. He said he understood their visit was difficult for her, but asked if there was anything else Angela could remember.

'There were a couple of things that always bothered me, but no-one would listen,' Angela said, almost in a whisper. 'The dress she was wearing, I'd never seen in my life before. Rachel didn't like yellow. And the little charm bracelet I bought her for passing her O levels was missing. She never took it off. I would like to have had that...' Her voice cracked and she dabbed at her eyes with her handkerchief. 'I suppose it probably came off in the water.'

Sean thanked her for her time and told her if there was any new information at all, they would be back in touch. As they turned to leave, she put a hand on his arm.

'She was the one good thing in my life, and there is not a day goes by when I don't beat myself up and blame myself for her death. She would have been a remarkable woman had she lived.'

She closed the door behind them and, as they walked down the path, they could hear her sobbing.

***

As they drove back towards Belfast, both officers were quiet until eventually Sean spoke.

'It just all seems too coincidental – the name Rachel, the yellow dress, the lost jewellery. We have a connection to Barry Fitzpatrick. Could they both be tragic accidents?'

'Well,' replied Catriona, glancing briefly at him as she drove. 'If you didn't have Megan's story, then yes, they could just be two accidents a year apart. After all, it was summer, and yellow is a popular summer colour for girls to wear. But I do think Megan's story brings them together. Was Rachel Fitzpatrick's death the first one and the killer got a taste for it?'

Sean nodded and thought for a while. 'Let's see what the other cases have brought up.'

***

Back in the incident room, the team was continuing to collate feedback from other forces around the country. There was some good news where a few of the missing girls had eventually turned up safe and well. But a picture was building of a number of still missing or dead girls with the same profile – long dark hair, aged 14-18 years old, wearing yellow, and missing jewellery. Investigations showed there was roughly a year between the incidents, though some gaps of several years.

The team's initial reaction was that if there was a single perpetrator, he travelled for his job, and possibly had served time in prison as well. That would explain the different locations and the gaps in time.

Sean asked Dougie to track Barry Fitzpatrick's prison record times against the dates and times of victims, to see if there was any correlation.

'Do we have any idea of his whereabouts now?' Sean asked. 'I think I'd like to meet this guy.'

'No, boss. My initial checks on him show that he was released from Magaberry Prison in May,' Dougie explained, 'but he has failed to turn up for his probation meetings in the last four weeks. The address he provided on leaving jail turned out to be an empty house which squatters used; none of them had heard of him.

'It seems our friend Barry is a wanted man, for parole violations.'

Chapter Eleven
Across the sea

Guildford, England - Monday, July 20. 10.15am

S ean and Dougie took an early flight to Gatwick, hired a car, and met Sarah Drummond, nee Fitzpatrick, at her home in Godalming, just outside Guildford. She had the 'Irish' colouring – strawberry blond hair, freckles, and green eyes – and gave them a warm welcome with coffee and bacon sandwiches, as she assumed they'd be hungry after such an early start.

Once they were settled with their food, Sarah admitted to being surprised that the men had felt the need to come all that way to talk to her about something that had happened nearly 20 years before. She had been fourteen when her cousin Rachel had died, but remembered how life at home had become unbearable after the girl's death. Sarah recalled that her parents hardly spoke to each other without it turning into a slanging match, and that her mother began to smoke and drink heavily.

'My father became really strict with me, citing Rachel's death as a reason for his over-protection. He always picked me up from any party or disco; I could barely leave the house without him.'

'So how did you manage to get pregnant then?' asked Dougie bluntly.

Sarah laughed. 'Pregnant! There's two parts to that story. Firstly, my dad thought that if I was in my own house, I couldn't get up to trouble. He was often too drunk to know that my boyfriend often stayed over and slept in my room, and my mother couldn't have cared less.'

'And the second?'

'It was the greatest possible sin in my father's eyes, so it was the one sure way to get my mother to give me money to leave the country or he would kill me and my boyfriend. Or rather, if you were to believe my mother, he would kill her, too! She was always the victim.'

'So you lied to your mother?' asked Sean. 'You weren't actually pregnant?'

'That's right.' Sarah seemed bemused to be justifying her teenage decisions to a policeman. 'A couple of weeks later, I phoned and told her I had lost the baby, and by then I couldn't go home. But I was never actually pregnant.'

There was silence.

'I know it might sound callous, but it was the only way I could think of escaping,' she explained. 'The only bad thing was leaving my brother, Gordon, behind.'

'And when was the last time you saw your mother and your father?'

'My mother? Not since the day I got on that boat to Liverpool!'

'And your father?'

'Probably the night before I got on the boat. He was hardly ever at home by then, anyway. I picked the day that he would be away for a week so he that had no chance of tracing us. I heard he ended up in jail not long after that, and I heaved a huge sigh of relief, as did my boyfriend.'

'Boyfriend?'

'Yes, Jamie came with me. I should say my husband now.' Sarah smiled. 'We've been married for nearly fifteen years.'

'And you've never been back?'

'Well, yes, a couple of times, but I made sure Mum didn't know!'

'When was the last time you were there?'

She hesitated, and her smile faded. 'I've been going back more recently, to see my nan. Her husband died two years ago, and she is in a home now.'

'Your nan.' Dougie referred to his notes. 'That'll be Hilda Adams?'

'Yes, but she's Hilda Hunter now. She is living in the residential home in Ballyholme. Nan and her husband moved there about five years ago.'

'When was the last time you spoke to her?'

'Sunday morning, before she went to church. We usually speak on a Monday morning for a good chat after the weekend. She likes to hear what we have been up to, but she was going away for a few days with some of the other residents, down to the Mournes.'

The officers looked at each other, bemused.

'Your mother said she was dead,' said Sean.

'Well, she would. They haven't spoken in probably twenty years. Not since the year Rachel died. There was some terrible row.'

'Do you know what about?'

'It had something to do with Peter, but I'm not sure what exactly. Nan always remained tight-lipped about it.'

'Peter?' Dougie looked up from his notebook.

'Yes. Peter Adams. He was my half-brother. His mum was my aunt; my mother's younger sister, Rachel. Ironic really that my dad had a bastard child, as my mother called him, given his views on children outside wedlock. Peter was Rachel Fitzpatrick's boyfriend that summer, though they had split up before she died. He was going off to join the army.'

This was a lot of new information to take in. 'Would you know where Peter would be now?' Sean asked.

There was a brief silence.

'No. No, I don't.' There was hesitation in her voice.

Was she lying? Sean studied her face closely.

'When was the last time you did see him?'

'It's been nearly a year since he was last here.'

'What, at your house?'

'Yes, when he had time off from his job, he would either come here or go and stay with Gordon, or my nan.'

'This would be your brother, Gordon?'

'Yes. And before you ask, he's dead to my mother as well.' Sarah gave a hollow laugh.

'Why would that be?'

'The second cardinal sin... he's gay! Gordon lives up in London; he left home when he was 16, too, and came to live with Jamie and me for a while. We helped support him through college and university. Peter often stayed with Gordon and his partner, Mike, but neither of us have heard from him since last August's bank holiday Monday.'

'Why would that be?'

'I don't know. We were having a barbecue here. It was hot. Peter doesn't hold his drink too well, so he is always careful about how much he has. He seemed a bit agitated, but he was due to be posted back to Afghanistan. His best mate had been killed the last time they were there.'

'Afghanistan?'

'Yes, he's in the army. He joined the year Rachel died.' She stopped and gazed out the window for quite some time.

'Please, go on, Sarah,' Sean prompted gently.

'He'd received a letter from our father. Dad would write to him care of the BFPO address. Peter usually just tore the letters up, but something made him read it. We went inside because there was a thunderstorm, and the news came on the TV. I don't know what was on it but Peter went berserk. He just kept saying, "He's done it again. He's done it again", then he started to cry. No, not just cry, but sob, heart-wrenching sobs. We tried to calm him down, but he just ran off. His last words were that he would have to sort it.' Sarah started to cry quietly.

Sean and Dougie exchanged glances but sat quietly, waiting until she calmed down.

'I tried to get in touch,' she went on eventually, 'but he never returned my calls or Gordon's. He was due to be posted out a week later and I've watched the news every day for the last year, dreading that he will be killed out there.' She turned back towards Sean. 'The army won't tell us anything, because we are not officially next of kin. Is there anything you can do to help us contact him?'

'I'm not sure, but we'll certainly see what we can do,' Sean replied, realizing how worried she was. 'Sarah,' he went on, 'you've been very helpful, and we are extremely sorry for the upset that this might have caused. I do have one final question, if that's okay?'

'Yes, of course.'

'Have you any idea where your father might be now?'

'Hell, I would hope. God forgive me, but that man made so many people's lives a misery. I never had confidence when I was a teenager, not with curly ginger hair. And he would regularly tell me I was lucky that I wasn't as beautiful as Rachel. I never quite knew what he meant. I mean, she *was* beautiful, with her lovely colouring and her long brown hair, but she was also dead.'

'Sarah, I'm sorry to ask, but what do you mean by her colouring?'

'Oh, that must sound racist. I don't mean it to be. Dad would call her cappuccino, and every time he had one, he would laugh and say, 'I'm enjoying my cappuccino!' It was a bit off, really.'

'Why?'

'Rachel's mum was descended from an African slave man, so she was partly... I don't know the politically correct word, but partly black. Mum would call her "the nigger child", but Rachel was always so kind. I believe it was something to do with history, when black African slaves and white Irish slaves were inter-bred. Rachel's great-great-grandparents, I think it was, had been slaves.'

'I heard that mentioned on the TV programme which Hugh Fitzpatrick made,' remarked Dougie.

'I know, it's shocking. Actually, Hugh is my father's cousin. When he was away, we often stayed at his house, the Watch House. Do you know it?' Both men nodded. 'Dad would lord it up as if he owned the place. Apparently, Hugh had a diary of some sort from the late 1700s that he had found in the house, and the name of the guy who wrote it was Barry Fitzgerald. My father always thought he must be a descendant of him, reincarnated.'

The two detectives simply nodded, but the information was clearly processing around their brains.

'I think,' she added, 'you can see that our parents weren't the best of people. If it hadn't have been for our nan, goodness knows where we would be.'

'And your Aunt Rachel, Peter's mother. Do you have any contact with her?'

'Yes, we email each other. She lives in Australia now, with her husband and kids. I met her seventeen years or so ago. When Nan married Alex, she managed to persuade Rachel to come home for the wedding. My aunt only agreed to come back because Dad was doing one of his stretches in prison, and Mum wasn't invited.' Her smile reappeared, as she remembered what had clearly been a happy event. 'It was a really lovely day. Surprising that they had fifteen years of marriage; fifteen good years, at their time of life. Nan deserved it, though, after all those years of putting up with my parents.'

'Might Peter have gone to Australia to visit his mother?'

'No, absolutely not.' Sarah shook her head. 'I don't think he has ever actually met her, as it was Nan who brought him up. He could never face my aunt; hearing the truth of how he was conceived nearly broke him.'

'What do you mean, how he was conceived?' Dougie asked.

Sarah sighed, and shifted uncomfortably. 'You probably should speak to my nan, as I only know a little about it. But apparently my father raped my aunt when she was just sixteen years old... and Peter was the result.'

'Raped her?' Sean struggled to hide his surprise.

'Yes. He denied it, of course. I can't honestly believe that my mother would have married him after that. I'm sorry I don't know the details and, as you can guess, it isn't something that was talked about.'

'You said that Peter knew Rachel Fitzpatrick – the girl who died – and that they had dated?' Dougie was checking through his notes as he spoke.

'Yes, they were besotted with each other. The summer of 1988, they were inseparable. They tried to pretend they were just friends, but you could see the way they looked at each other...' Sarah smiled wistfully.

'So what happened?' asked Sean gently.

'She had got her 'O' levels, and done really well. She was going back to school and, sadly, they broke up. She said she needed to concentrate on her studies, and unfortunately Peter was a major distraction. He was heartbroken, and that is why he left Groomsport. He went off to join the army.'

'Do you know when that would be?'

'It was the week before she died. So tragic. And he has never married. I don't think he ever met anyone he felt for in the same way. He always gets me to arrange for flowers to be put on her grave every year if he is away. I didn't know what to do this year, so I arranged for a posy to be put there anyway; it seemed the right thing to do.'

'When would that be?'

'Last week actually. He prefers to mark her birthday, rather than the date she died.'

'Did he join the army straight away after he left?'

'Hmm,' she considered. 'It certainly wasn't long after. He had some almighty row with Dad, and next thing he had left. It was only through Nan that we were able to keep in contact. She persuaded him to come to our house when she was visiting, and we've kept in touch ever since. Well... until last year!'

Sean and Dougie thanked Sarah again and asked her to call them if Peter got in contact with her or her brother.

They assured her they would be in touch if they found out anything through their own enquiries or with the army.

This was turning into a family of twists and turns.

Chapter Twelve
Raking up the past

Dougie and Catriona were dispatched to Galway to meet with Hugh Fitzpatrick's ex-wife, now Arabella Fullerton. On crossing the border they were met by colleagues from the Gardai, the Irish police force.

Although the appointment had been arranged with Arabella herself, they were met on arrival by her husband, Colum. A rather pompous man, he was a local solicitor and obviously used to being a big fish in a small town.

When he led them into a grand sitting room, Dougie's first thought was that Arabella could easily have been a lady; he could immediately see how she had earned the nickname from Leah Fitzpatrick. Elegant and poised, her silver hair was swept up into a bun at the base of her neck. She wore a pale blue linen dress, and could easily have passed for a woman in her mid-forties.

They had barely sat down on the Chesterfield sofa, when Colum Fullerton demanded to know why police officers were disturbing his wife. Catriona decided to take the lead, aware that Dougie's hackles were rising.

'Thank you, sir, we do appreciate your time, and we understand that this is an unusual situation, Mrs Fullerton.'

'Arabella, please.' The woman smiled calmly at them.

'Yes, ma'am.' Dougie directed his attention solely on the woman. 'We're sorry, but we need to ask you some questions about your step-daughter Rachel's death.'

Arabella's hand flew to her mouth, shock registering in her eyes.

'Oh my God, that was more than 20 years ago. Why now?'

'It's a complicated story, ma'am, and we would appreciate if you could share with us your recollection of the events.'

'Is my wife in anyway under investigation?' interrupted her husband.

'No, sir, not at all,' Dougie assured him.

'Rachel was a beautiful, beautiful girl,' said Arabella, her eyes watering. 'She... She was swept off the pier in Groomsport one night in a storm!'

'Yes, we are aware of that. We've spoken to her father,' said Catriona.

'Hugh?' Arabella looked surprised.

'Yes, he said he was away at a historical event in Dublin when it happened. Is that correct?'

'Yes, yes it is. I could never forgive myself for what happened. I blame myself... There isn't a day goes by that I don't wish I could have done something... I wish it had been me, not that beautiful child!' Gentle sobs broke from her, and she put her face in her hands. 'I couldn't forgive myself, so how could I expect Hugh to forgive me?' she said, almost pleading.

'Bloody man, always going off for his own ego,' spat Colum Fullerton.

'Colum, please.' Arabella glanced across at him, frowning.

'Well honestly, he expected you to bring up that child of his–'

'Mr Fullerton,' Catriona interrupted gently.

Arabella Fullerton reached over to touch her husband's arm. 'Colum, please. I know this upsets you, but please go back to your study. I will deal with this. Please.' She patted her husband's hand and smiled encouragingly, her eyes still watery.

'But really...' he spluttered.

'No, my dear. I have to deal with this.' Her tone was cooler now.

Fullerton reluctantly got up and left the room, glaring at the officers as he passed them.

'I'm sorry, ma'am, we appreciate this must be difficult.' Dougie relaxed a little; it was easier to talk to Arabella now that her husband had gone.

She nodded briefly at his comment, then walked over to the bookcase and pulled out a photograph album. She handed it to Catriona then sat back down.

'I married Hugh when Rachel was seven. Her own mum had died five years before, in a dreadful car accident. I knew I wasn't the love of Hugh's life – Rachel's mum was – but I loved him, and I adored her. She was a special child. Always laughing, so loving and very bright. I loved living in the Watch House. I'd walk the children to school every day, no matter the weather.'

'Children?'

'Yes, my son Thomas was two years younger than Rachel,' Arabella explained. 'My first husband died of cancer when Thomas was only two, and we went through a difficult time. Then I met Hugh, in Dublin. We bonded over our grief and the fact that our kids adored each other so much. They got on fabulously well.

'Rachel was like a mother hen. On the nights there was a storm, Thomas would be terrified, but rather than come in beside me, he would go to Rachel's room. She loved storms.' Arabella smiled briefly at the memory.

'It nearly killed Thomas when she died. He... he...' She looked towards the window, collecting her thoughts. 'Thomas had a breakdown, and tried to kill himself. He ended up in hospital for quite a long time.'

Catriona cleared her throat gently. 'I'm sorry, ma'am. Where is Thomas now?'

'He lives in the US, in Boston.' She got up again and picked up a silver frame of two men laughing together.

'Thomas is in blue, and this is his partner, Colin, at their civil partnership ceremony. It was Colin who helped Thomas to recover. They've been together for about ten years. They are very happy now, it's wonderful.' Hers was a genuinely happy smile this time.

'Ma'am, did Rachel have a boyfriend?' asked Catriona.

Arabella shook her head. 'I would like to say emphatically no, but she was sixteen and very lovely. I can't be sure if she did or not. She had a group of close-knit friends, but others would come and go. You know how kids are at that age.'

They nodded.

'Her father had always said no boys before she got her first!' Arabella laughed.

'Her first?' Dougie was puzzled.

'Yes, it was a joke between them. Rachel wanted to study history, like her father. She wanted to go to Trinity, and the first was the class of degree he expected her to get. They would spend hours together talking about and researching history. She loved it. They were very close.'

Arabella stopped to think for a moment, memories flooding back. 'She had just passed her 'O' levels and started back at school. She was studying English, History and French.'

'How did Thomas feel about it?'

'My son wasn't as bright as Rachel, but he would spend hours with them sitting in listening. Funnily enough, Thomas thought Rachel had a boyfriend. He was convinced she had left the house that night to go and meet him. We only knew she was missing when he went to her room, because a bad storm had started and he was still afraid of storms.'

'How did Hugh and Thomas get on?'

'Hugh was very good with Thomas. He was a very caring man.' She stopped, her face changing as a flicker of annoyance passed over it. They waited for her to say something more, but she didn't.

'Did Hugh adopt Thomas?' asked Dougie.

Arabella bent her head, shaking it.

'No, no he didn't. Hugh may have been a brilliant man when it came to history, but he was rubbish at all other paperwork or organisation. After Rachel died, it came to light that Hugh had never filed the adoption papers for either child. I was devastated, as it meant that I couldn't be acknowledged as Rachel's mum. This hurt me so much. I had been her mother for ten years, and because of a stupid piece of paper...' Her voice broke.

'It caused a massive row between us. Our one and only row. Things were said. Hurtful things that couldn't be taken back. I left, and took Thomas with me. I didn't really mean to stay away. I thought he would come after us... I hoped he would come after us... but he didn't!'

'He didn't?' prompted Catriona.

'No, he was too wrapped up in his own grief. There was no going back for us. Thomas was in a bad way, so I needed to focus on him. We were separated for ten years before we actually divorced,' she added, wringing her hands together.

'Have you seen or spoken to him since?' asked Dougie.

'Not directly! About ten years ago, he wrote me a letter asking me to divorce him on the grounds of unreasonable behaviour. I assumed he had met someone else. In the letter he thanked me for being a wonderful mother to Rachel and Thomas, and wife to him. He said he was sorry how things had turned out.' She was silent for a moment. 'I just wish he hadn't waited ten years,' she whispered.

'I'm very sorry that this is bringing up such difficult memories for you,' said Catriona softly. 'Is it okay for me to ask a couple more questions?'

'Yes, yes of course,' replied Arabella.

'Barry Fitzpatrick, Hugh's cousin. Can you tell us what you know about him?'

Arabella visibly stiffened. 'I never really felt comfortable with him.' The disgust was evident in her tone of voice.

'Why was that?' probed Catriona.

'He gave me the creeps, quite honestly.' She shuddered at the memory. 'He'd appear out of nowhere. I would turn round and he would just be standing there looking at me or Rachel. When Hugh was away, he took it upon himself to act as a self-imposed guardian. He would come to the house and tell us he was there to keep us safe!'

The officers looked quickly at each other, before Catriona spoke. 'And what did Hugh say about that?'

'I tried to speak to Hugh about it, but he said Barry was harmless and that he felt relieved someone was looking out for us when he was away.'

'Were they close?'

'Well, that was the strange thing. They had nothing in common, really. Have you met Barry?'

'No. No, we haven't. We've met his ex-wife, Leah.'

Arabella made a noise of disgust and shook her head. 'Well, let's say they deserved each other. I've never in my life met a more obviously nasty creature than her. God forgive me, but that woman should have been drowned at birth.' There was a pause before she carried on.

'Hugh hated confrontation of any kind, and it always felt like Barry had some kind of hold over him. I tried to speak to him about it, but he just said to leave it that Barry had had a tough life. I'm not quite sure in what way, as he always seemed to land on his feet, but it seems he had once saved Hugh from drowning. They had been on the Copeland Islands, and when Hugh fell in the sea Barry had saved him. He liked being the hero... rushing to save people! Quite often, I felt he just enjoyed the drama. I wouldn't be surprised if he had pushed Hugh into the sea just to save him.'

Neither officer commented, but the thought had crossed their minds, too.

'Your husband, sorry, ex-husband, said you thought the Watch House was haunted. Was that right?' Dougie asked.

She gave a brief laugh. 'I don't know why I'm laughing, as it wasn't funny at the time. It wasn't so much haunted, but as if there was a presence there.'

'A presence?'

'Yes. Hugh told me I was just scared of ghosts, or that it was the wind. There was one night I plucked up the courage to go downstairs. It felt very cold, as if a door had been left open, but I checked and all the doors and windows were closed or bolted, so no-one could get in. And, of course, there was no-one there. But there was a smell.'

'A smell?'

'Yes, like stale cigarettes. But neither Hugh nor I smoked. There was also a smell of fish.' She gave another little laugh. 'I mean, I know we lived by the sea, but still... It was as if some old fisherman had been in the room.'

'Was there anything else?'

'I know it was an old house, but...' she paused, '...it felt as if someone was watching me.'

'Was there any particular time?'

'Always when Hugh was away, and usually when there was a storm. One night I looked out and I... I saw a small dinghy being tossed about by the waves. I thought to myself that it was in trouble, but whoever was sailing it clearly knew the rocks round that way, as they are very dangerous. The boat looked as if it had come... come from our house, but that didn't make sense. I just assumed that it had been blown off course.'

'Was it okay?'

'Yes, yes it was. The two people on board were clearly experienced. Probably local fishermen.'

Dougie made a note to check if there was a landing area at the house.

'Can I ask about Leah Fitzpatrick?'

'You can,' Arabella replied almost haughtily, then grinned, 'and I'll try not to swear! I couldn't stand the woman. I may sound like a snob, but she was as common as muck. As soon as she came to the house for some family get-together, she would grab the nearest bottle. I took to locking anything valuable away when she was there, as I had a couple of pieces of jewellery go missing. I can't, of course, prove that she took them, but...'

'Do you mind if I ask what jewellery?' Catriona prepared to make a note.

'I had a jade charm necklace go missing. It had a ying and yang charm, which Hugh had brought me from China. It wasn't expensive, but it meant a lot.'

'Anything else?'

'Sadly, yes. More importantly, Rachel's mum's engagement ring – Hugh's first wife. Hugh went ballistic when he realised it was gone. It was the only time I saw him really angry. It was always kept in a drawer in his office, along with other jewellery which Rachel was to be given when she turned eighteen.' She sighed.

'And you have no idea where it went?'

'I have a good idea, but I can't prove anything!' she snapped. 'I'm sorry. I genuinely think it was Leah, as she was always snooping round.'

'When was the last time you saw either Barry or Leah?'

'To speak to? It would have been the day of Rachel's funeral. He turned up drunk and kept crying that he could have saved her, he could have saved her. That really upset Hugh. They had words – I don't know what was said – and Hugh punched him. Knocked him to the ground. It was a delight to see, if it wasn't for the fact that it was a funeral, and that whatever was said had clearly upset Hugh.'

'You have no idea what was said?' asked Catriona.

'No, I don't. Hugh had been a boxer as a teenager and... it took Barry a while before he got up. Leah went for Hugh and...' Arabella enjoyed a genuine giggle. 'I had the pleasure of smacking her one, too. They were thrown out by some friends, and that was the last we saw of them. Though, sadly, it did cause problems for our housekeeper.'

'Your housekeeper?'

'Yes, Hilda. Hilda Adams. She was Leah's mother. After what happened, she must have thought she wouldn't be welcome, but you have never met two more different people. Hilda was kindness itself. She had been with Hugh all the time he lived in the house. I think he inherited her when he bought the place. She practically raised Rachel after her mum died, until Hugh and I got married.'

'Do you know where she is?'

'I don't, sorry. She lived in one of the council houses in the village. In fact, she could see our place from hers. Rachel used to flash a torch at her at bedtime to say goodnight. It was very sweet.'

'Did she resent you taking over as mum to Rachel?'

'Oh no. No, I never felt that. She had enough on her hands with Leah's two children – I think she practically brought them up herself. I often gave her some of Rachel and Thomas's old clothes to help her out. I was always sorry that we lost touch, but...' She shrugged.

'Did you know a Peter Adams?' asked Catriona.

Arabella thought for a moment, then shook her head. 'No, I'm sorry. The name doesn't ring a bell. Who is he?'

'Hilda's other grandson – the son of Leah's sister. He was adopted and brought up in England, but we think he was staying with Hilda the summer before Rachel died.'

'Oh yes, the name does ring a bell, but I don't think I ever met him. Rachel and Thomas had lots of friends coming and going. There was a summer youth club and they would all go and play games on the village green, or in one of the church halls. I'm afraid I don't remember him.' Her answer seemed genuine. 'Maybe one of Rachel's old friends would know, though I don't keep in touch with any of them now.'

'That's okay.' Catriona smiled at the older woman. 'I think we have taken up enough of your time. We can't thank you enough and, as we said, we're very sorry for bringing up what must have been a very difficult time for you.'

'I understand.' Arabella stood up to show them out. 'Have you seen Hugh?' she added tentatively.

'Yes,' Dougie replied. 'He is in the process of selling the house at the moment.'

Arabella looked thoughtful. 'He loved that house, despite the tragedies. It must be a wrench for him.'

As they prepared to leave, Catriona asked if they could borrow the photo album and return it as soon as possible.

'Yes, but please look after it,' Arabella replied. 'There are photos of Rachel that were taken shortly before she died but I didn't discover them until about a year later, when I got the film developed. It was before digital cameras, you see. In fact, Hugh may never have seen the photos either. I should have sent him some.' Arabella couldn't hide her sadness.

***

When they reached the car, Dougie took the driver's seat and started the engine. 'She still holds a torch for him,' he commented, as he manoeuvred out onto the main road.

'For who?' Catriona looked puzzled.

'For Hugh. Who else?'

'Hmm.' She nodded in agreement. 'What a sad tale.'

As Dougie drove, Catriona flicked slowly through the photo album. Arabella was right, Rachel had been a stunningly pretty young girl. The photos oozed happiness.

As she turned the pages, one photo caught her eye. There was a group of friends. On the back, someone had written: *Crawfordsburn Park, August, 1988. Rachel and Thomas and friends.* It was probably one of the last photos taken of Rachel alive.

Another photograph showed Hugh and another man – *Barry Fitzpatrick, maybe?* –leaning against a beige-coloured car.

She called the incident room to ask one of the PCs to follow up any information on the car, but the photo did not show the number plate or the make of vehicle, so it would not be a relatively straightforward search.

'While you're checking,' she told the young officer, 'I'd appreciate if you could have a look at the driving licences for both Hugh Fitzpatrick and Barry Fitzpatrick, and see if either of them has had any penalty points awarded.'

Chapter Thirteen
Another visit

Leah Fitzpatrick's house, Millisle -
Thursday, July 23. 11am

The following day, Sean and Catriona paid another visit to Leah Fitzpatrick. When she opened the door, she made no attempt to hide her annoyance at seeing the DCI again.

'What do you want now?' She dragged on her cigarette and blew smoke towards them.

Sean coughed. 'We can do our chat here in the street, if you like?' He looked around and nodded towards one of the neighbours.

Grumbling, Leah stepped aside and gestured them into the living room where daytime TV was blaring.

'Your sister, Rachel–' Sean began.

'I've no bloody sister!' Leah interrupted, her face furious.

'Yes you do! She happens to be the mother of your ex-husband's son,' Catriona replied with an innocent smile.

'That holy bitch! Always at church, and never told anyone she was carrying on. Never told anyone who the father of her baby was. She scurried off to Liverpool quick enough, mind, as she couldn't face the shame. Whore!'

'When did you find out about the baby and who the father was?' Sean ignored her vile comments.

'It was pretty obvious when she disappeared suddenly and my ma was crying. She always was my mother's favourite. It broke my dad's heart, but they forgave her. If it had been me, they would have kicked me out without a goodbye.'

'So do you know what happened to the child?'

'He was fostered, then adopted by my father's nephew in England. The brat came looking for his mother when he turned eighteen. He was the spit of his father, anyone could see that. Ginger hair and freckles. All hell broke loose, I'm telling you. The cow said it was rape, but Barry thought it was hilarious that he had a son.'

'He hadn't known about Rachel being pregnant?' Catriona asked.

'No. He went away on a wee holiday at Her Majesty's Pleasure, and when he came back she had gone. Good riddance!'

'And is that when he took up with you? Second choice?' Catriona tried the innocent smile again.

Leah didn't quite get the comment, or chose to ignore it. 'We started courting and, let me tell you, I was *certainly* not pregnant when we got married. No shotgun wedding for me.' She sounded pleased with herself.

'Do you have any contact with your sister now?' Sean asked.

'Don't care one bit. Could be in hell, for all I care.'

'By the way, Mrs Fitzpatrick, we went to see Arabella, Hugh's ex-wife.' Catriona stared intently at the older woman, watching her reaction.

'What did that stuck-up cow have to say for herself?'

'She mentioned some jewellery that had gone missing when she lived at The Point.' Leah's hand automatically went to her throat. 'She mentioned a Chinese ying and yang charm necklace – just like the one you are wearing. Unique, in fact, because Hugh had brought it from China.'

'She's a damn liar! This one's a copy,' snarled Leah.

'There were other things.' Catriona looked quickly at her notebook before continuing. 'A very expensive ring that had belonged to Rachel's mother. Again, very unique.'

Leah Fitzpatrick pulled the necklace from her throat and threw it at Catriona.

'Take the fecking thing and ram it down her throat. A good luck charm? It brings nothing but evil. I don't know what I did to deserve this!'

Neither officer spoke. Catriona bent down and picked up the necklace. It would become important at some point, she was sure.

***

Dougie had managed to contact Barry Fitzpatrick's probation officer, who confirmed he had not had contact with the former prisoner for more than a month. The officer explained that he had been on holiday himself and, with the Twelfth annual holiday, the time had passed by, but he was due to follow up with Fitzpatrick the following day.

Dougie asked the probation officer to let him know if he made contact with Barry, as the investigation team would like to talk to him, too. Once they'd finished talking, Dougie tried the mobile phone number which the probation office had for Barry, but there was no reply and the mailbox was full.

He put in a request to have the phone records obtained. It might give an indication of location and who Barry had been in contact while the phone was in use.

Chapter Fourteen
Prison pal

West Belfast - Friday, July 24. 7.45am

Sean decided to pay a visit to a former cellmate of Barry Fitzpatrick. Billy Brown had been in and out of jail since his first stint as a juvenile thirty years before. What had started as low level crime had, as is often the case, built up to guns and drugs. His most recent stint inside had been for three years, but he'd been released four months ago for good behaviour. It was probably just a matter of time before he was back in again.

Aware that the police weren't popular in Billy's neighbourhood, Sean and Dougie headed for the back door to avoid attention. Billy's long suffering missus, Cheryl, answered the door in a grubby fleece dressing gown.

'What are you trying to pin on him now?' she asked, lighting a cigarette as she stood back to wave the two into the kitchen. Billy was sitting at a Formica-topped table, eating a good old Ulster fry-up.

'It's not him this time.' Sean smiled at Cheryl. 'It's a mate of his.' He took a seat opposite Billy at the kitchen table. 'Hiya, Billy, long time no see!'

'Officer, my old mucker, how are you doing?'

'Straight to the point. Barry Fitzpatrick.' Sean looked directly at Billy, watching the other man's reaction.

'Not sure I know anyone of that name. And if I did, he'd be no mate of mine.' Billy sliced his sausage and put it into his mouth.

'You shared a cell with him.'

'Ah, that Barry. Know nothing.'

Sean got up and walked over to the fridge where a photograph of a young schoolgirl with long brown hair was pinned with a magnet.

'Cheryl, got a moment?'

Cheryl came back into the room and snatched the photo off Sean. 'What are you doing with that photo?'

'Your granddaughter?'

'You've no right to be threatening us,' she fumed, pointing her finger at Sean's face.

'Oh, I'm not, love. I'm just trying to protect your nearest and dearest. And I don't mean Billy.'

'You what? That'll be the day,' she scoffed.

'What was Barry in for again?' Sean turned back to Billy.

'He found his wife was cheating on him so he beat her up, and the lad he suspected.'

'Really?'

'Yes, and you can't blame a man for that, can you?'

'Luckily, I disagree with you, Billy, on that point.' Sean sat down at the table. 'He didn't mention young girls, by any chance? I mean, when the two of you were locked up for... how many hours a day?'

'No he did not!'

'Young girls around fifteen or sixteen, with long dark hair?' Sean spoke slowly, ensuring every word was heard by Cheryl.

'You what! I wouldn't have any perv anywhere near me. I swear I'd kill him myself.'

'Just wondering what age your granddaughter was?' asked Sean.

'Billy, you tell him what he wants to know or, so help me God, if anything were to happen to our Jodie, I'll frigging kill you meself,' stormed Cheryl, stepping forward to poke her husband in the chest with a bony finger.

'So, Billy, when was the last time you saw Barry?' asked Dougie.

'Last month.' Billy looked uncomfortable at the thought of being a grass, but obviously fiercely protective of his granddaughter.

'And where would this be, and why?' demanded Sean.

'A month ago, at the Lagan View Arms. He needed some new ID – a driver's licence and passport.'

'Did you get him one?'

'I... I passed him to a man who I used to know.' Billy tried not to meet his wife's eyes. They all knew he would be in for a hard time after Sean and Dougie left.

'Anything else?'

'He was wanting the name of a taxi firm in Bangor who would hire him. He needed a job.'

'Which one?'

Billy was silent until his wife poked him hard again. He flinched. 'I passed him to another old mate – Joe Abbot. He would use him.'

'For what?' asked Sean.

'That I didn't want to know about. If you ask too many questions, they get suspicious. And anyway, I don't do drugs. I do have some principles.' Billy sat up a little straighter in his chair.

Sean smiled at the man's indignant tone. 'Well, Billy, if there is anything else that might have slipped your mind, then please give us a call. There's a lot more going on with Barry Fitzpatrick than you know, and you wouldn't be wanting to be associated with him.'

As Sean stood up to leave, Cheryl stepped in front of him, barring his way.

'What about protection for us? For my granddaughter?' she demanded.

'Well, Cheryl, your husband knows enough people, doesn't he?' Sean nodded towards Billy.

Cheryl wilted. 'I don't give a shit about him, but I do about my daughter and granddaughter.'

'Aye, I understand that,' Sean explained patiently, 'but we need to make sure that he doesn't get any tip-offs.'

Cheryl was quick to spot an opportunity. 'What's it worth?'

Sean laughed at her cheek. 'Let's see. Your nephew is up in court next week, isn't he?'

'Aye, but his brief is confident,' she replied.

'Reckon he will get 10-15 easily. Might have a word and it could go as much as 18-20! But you make sure that no-one gets wind of our visit today, and it might come down a bit.'

'He won't be hearing it from us, rest assured. Isn't that right, Billy?' Cheryl glared at her husband.

'Good. Now, you might be wanting to head off to that place of yours in Spain for a couple of weeks,' Sean suggested.

'Spain! What are you talking about?' Billy's face was the picture of innocence.

'Ha!' laughed Sean. 'Billy, don't be trying to play the innocent, we know you have a place in Spain. We also know that the social security people don't know about it.'

'We'll do that, and thanks for the heads-up,' said Cheryl, and she led the detectives to the door. They left the way they had come in, knowing that they would have been seen.

When they got back to the office, Sean asked Dougie to check out any investigations going on regarding Joe Abbot, the man Billy had mentioned. They would need to pay him a visit, but were wary of treading on any other enquiries that might be going on.

Chapter Fifteen
A meeting of mums... and dads

Jane Scott was recovering well. She still got tired easily, but the nausea which she had initially felt was becoming bearable. The Macmillan nurses had been excellent in taking their time to explain to her the impact the treatment would have on her body.

One of Jane's biggest fears had been about her hair falling out, and she had confided as much to Megan.

'If it helps. I'll happily shave my head to keep you company,' her daughter had offered.

'There's no need for that, love,' said Jane gratefully. 'But I appreciate the offer.'

Megan had suggested that it might help if her mother met Sean's mum, Bernie, who had been through the same operation and was happy to chat.

Jane, who was keen to meet Kieran's parents, had readily agreed and invited Bernie to come for the afternoon and allow the two dads to go to the football.

Within minutes of meeting, Jane felt that she had known Bernie for years. Once the men had headed off to the match, the women made themselves comfortable with a pot of tea and shared their hopes that Kieran and Megan would stay together.

'I know how you feel about wanting Megan to move back home,' Bernie said. 'I missed Kieran terribly when he lived away. It's grand to have the whole brood around. It wouldn't be right to stop them heading off around the world, but there's nothing better than seeing them settle again back here.'

Jane was keen to ask Bernie about some her treatment and some of the side-effects of the chemotherapy. 'I'll be honest, Bernie, I've been worried about Jack's reaction. My boobs have always been something he's enjoyed,' she said blushing.

Her new friend laughed. 'That's understandable. We're in our sixties and no-one talks about the impact this has on your sex life. You don't want to be asking initially because you are so focused on the word cancer, but as time goes on you want to be getting back to normal and sex is still part of your life,' she said. 'When you feel tired during the treatment, you still want to be cuddled. At the beginning, Seamus had been reluctant to come near me in case he hurt me.

'To be honest, I was really sad when they had to remove my breasts. After all, it was part of what my husband loved about my body and had fed my four sons. Initially, I wasn't keen to have reconstruction surgery. I thought it was maybe a bit vain, but I wanted to feel that I was still a woman so I went ahead. I would never have considered having a boob job, but I have to say I am very pleased at how they've given me breasts I would have been proud of in my twenties!' She leaned forward to add in a stage whisper, 'Seamus is very happy about that, too!'

'If our kids could hear us, they would be mortified!' laughed Jane. It felt good to be with someone who had been through a similar experience and was so positive.

Bernie helped herself to more cake. 'This is another good thing,' she said, taking a bite of Victoria sandwich. 'I appreciate the simple things like good cake much more now. Life's too short not to eat cake. If you feel you want something, then don't deprive yourself any more. Just enjoy it!'

***

Across town, the two husbands were also getting on like a house on fire, and were enjoying a half bitter shandy and pasty in the pub at half time. Bernie had told Seamus that it was important for him to talk to Jack about how he had supported her when she was going through the cancer treatment. Her husband was mortified, but promised he would.

Over their drinks, he asked Jack how he was coping. The other man simply shrugged.

'You know, part of the problem when Bernie was sick, is that men don't talk about how it feels. I mean we don't talk about our feelings, do we?' said Seamus. Jack shook his head. 'I was terrified, Jack, I won't lie. I found myself having to go out to the garden shed and cry because I was so frightened. I've known Bernie since she was ten, and the thought of what she was having to go through was just awful. I cursed God every day, but I never prayed as much in all my life. It wasn't easy. I mean you are expected to be the strong one, but I just felt I was falling apart, too.' Seamus wiped away a tear that had rolled down his cheek.

'We had probably our first ever row when she was sick. I was ashamed of myself, I have to say. She got fed up with me treating her with kid gloves because it just reminded her that she was sick. She wanted to be treated normally. What brought the row on was that...' his voice faltered a little with embarrassment, 'I couldn't touch her. I was scared of hurting her, but we had always had a... a kiss and a cuddle, but I couldn't. I mean, I thought she wouldn't want to be touched. But she thought that I didn't... didn't fancy her any more, and she got very upset.'

He cleared his throat a little then took a quick sip of his shandy. 'She said she still needed to be loved and to be made to feel attractive. I think that was the hardest part of the whole treatment, I mean, you think that the person won't want to make love any more, and no-one tells you if it is okay or not. If I'm honest, we're closer together now than we ever were.' Seamus stopped talking and looked at Jack, whose head was bowed to hide the tears.

Seamus reached over and gently patted the other man's shoulder. 'Believe me, Jack, you will get through it. It brought our family closer together.'

Jack nodded. 'Thanks. And thanks for telling me about that stuff, Seamus. I had no idea and it hadn't crossed my mind, but it is very important.'

Seamus smiled. 'Women are good at sharing stuff like that, but we men aren't. Bernie told me to tell you, as she said it was the most important thing that would help Jane in her recovery.'

'Thanks. I do appreciate it.'

Chapter Sixteen
Who is Peter Adams?

I t was almost the end of July. DS Niall Levin had searched the records and found Peter Adams' birth certificate relatively easily. But while there was no criminal record for anyone of that name, the detective could not access records from the man's time in the army. Levin knew that wasn't unusual; there was an official process to go through.

Within twenty-four hours, the team had been notified to speak to a Colonel Robert Smith, but he was currently based in Germany, so it took another two days before a Skype call could be set up.

DCI Sean Maloney led the call, with Catriona and Dougie sitting in. Sean and the colonel had built a mutual respect when they'd worked together through some tough years in Northern Ireland's history.

'Thanks for taking my call,' Sean opened.

'Good to see you, Sean. It's been a long time. Hope the family is all well?'

'Yes, Robbie, thanks.'

'I take it this isn't a social call. How can I help?' asked Colonel Smith.

'Do you know a Peter Adams or Peter Fitzpatrick?'

'Unfortunately, yes.'

'It seems his record is sealed,' said Sean.

'Yes. Can I ask what this is in connection with?' Colonel Smith looked none too happy to be opening up an old and difficult wound.

'We're investigating the disappearance or deaths of a number of teenage girls over a number of years. Peter and his father, Barry Fitzpatrick, are potential suspects.'

'Over what period?'

'Twenty-five years,' Sean replied.

'Hell, you're joking!'

'I wish we were.' Sean sighed. 'We're at the early stages of the investigation, and Peter's name is connected to one of the girls. He was also in the area when a second girl went missing.'

The colonel looked puzzled. 'There's been nothing reported in the news.'

'No, it's still under tight review at the moment, so anything you have on him would be very useful.'

It was Colonel Smith's turn to sigh. 'Peter Adams, as he was when he worked for us, was both hero and villain. He was part of a special forward plan team that under-took special operations in Iraq and Afghanistan. He was Mentioned in Despatches for work he undertook there. For that and other activities, his record is sealed.'

'Is he still in the army?' asked Sean.

'No.'

'Robbie, I need you to be a bit more open than that. Please.' Sean tried not to sound desperate.

'He resigned his commission last September, before he faced a court martial. As I said, the man was both hero and villain.'

'So his services to his country made him a hero?'

'To some people, yes; to others, a target for revenge.'

'Go on.'

'Peter was a great foot soldier, never a leader. He was known for finishing the job. He was good at following orders and he did that to the letter.'

'And the villain part?'

Colonel Smith paused before replying. 'Peter had an issue with women. He was awkward around them, and couldn't hold his drink. A difficult combination. He ended up in one too many fist fights over them. He said he was protecting them from scumbags who were coming on to them, but unfortunately it caused more than one incident.'

Sean took in the information for a few minutes before posing his next question. 'Were the situations ever to do with women rejecting him?'

'I can't say for sure; they always happened off-camp. Coming back from assignments of months with only men around you, and having to get back into social situations with women, isn't the easiest thing. Some men adapt no problem, others don't.'

'But surely that alone must be grounds for dismissal?' Sean asked.

'Difficult times... He was exceptional in his role, and at a time when we were under a lot of pressure, we couldn't lose a man that good. So we overlooked some of the situations. He was, though, on warning.'

'So what happened?'

Smith shook his head. He seemed reluctant to go into detail. 'Out of the blue, Peter attacked an officer's wife. That couldn't be overlooked, as it was an unprovoked attack on-camp. The woman didn't press charges.'

Sean and his officers looked at each other, stunned. Dougie swore quietly.

'Where is he now?' asked Sean.

'He resigned his commission. He could do that and, with the years of service he had and the holidays owed to him, he left almost immediately.'

'And the woman?'

'She's fine, but the trust of the squad had been compromised by his actions. There was no reprieve for him. No-one would want to serve with him after something like that.'

There was silence for a few minutes. Then Sean spoke quietly, almost apologetically. 'Robbie... was the woman your wife, Rachel, by any chance?'

The colonel cleared his throat. 'Yes,' he replied quietly. 'Yes, it was.'

'I'm very sorry to hear that. Is she okay? Can you tell us a bit more about what happened?'

The other man shifted uneasily in his chair, clearly uncomfortable at the conversation. Eventually, he replied.

'It was last September. Rachel was in the garden of our home. Peter and another officer were there to collect a number of things for me, as they were due to be deployed a couple of days later. I had already been gone for about two months and wasn't due back for another four, so Rachel was sending out some little gifts from the family.' He stopped and thought for a moment, as though choosing his words carefully.

'She was talking to our neighbour in the garden when suddenly Peter jumped on her, pushing her to the ground. It took my neighbour and the other soldier to get him off her. She was badly shaken up and suffered some grazes. I was only made aware of the situation a couple of days later when

Peter was not deployed. By that stage, he had been given the opportunity to resign. I'm sure you will understand, I would probably have killed him had he been deployed. It would have been difficult – for him, the regiment, and for me.'

'Thanks, Robbie. I apologise for having to ask about it. Do you know if anyone knows where he is? His half-sister has said she has had no contact from him in about a year. There was apparently some kind of episode at a family event, probably around the time of the incident with your wife.'

'Sorry, I've no idea. You would need to get the information from HQ. I'm sure you know the channels you need to go through.'

'Thank you. I do. One more thing from me... Would it be possible to speak to Rachel to hear her version of events?'

The Colonel looked as though he was about to refuse, then hesitated. 'I'll ask her, Robbie. But, to be honest, she hasn't really spoken about it – not even to me!'

'Colonel,' said Dougie. 'We have dates that we would appreciate cross-checking with Peter's location at the time, to either rule him out or to warrant further investigation. Would it be possible to send these over to you?'

The Colonel nodded. 'I will only be able to tell you if he was "out" – meaning out of the location – but not where exactly he would be. If it turns out that he was near the location, then we will need to have a further discussion. Is that sufficient?'

'For now, yes thanks,' Sean replied.

'Okay, and I will get back to you regarding Rachel. And, Sean, I would appreciate any early heads up on this before it goes public. The press could have a field day, not to mention other parties.'

'Understood, Robbie. We will be in touch. And thanks again.'

When the Skype call disconnected, the three police officers sat quietly collecting their thoughts. Were they looking for one killer? Or did they have two suspects working together?

'I'll fax those dates over immediately,' said Dougie. 'Boss, if we are dealing with an ex-elite soldier, that is a whole new ball game, isn't it?'

'Yes,' Sean admitted grimly. 'Let's pray that isn't the case. For now, keep that part to yourselves until we have definite confirmation.'

Twenty-four hours later, when the fax to Colonel Smith was returned, the team was relieved to see that the majority of the dates had been marked with an 'out'. Only three were still causing concern – dates when Peter would have been located within fifty miles of the young women who had gone missing. In addition, there was a newspaper report of a young girl in Cyprus having disappeared, and later found dead. The army base was only twenty miles from the location.

Chapter Seventeen
A new twist

Sean was given the news that Rachel Smith – the Colonel's wife – had agreed to speak to the team via Skype, with her husband sitting in on the call.

Rachel was like many military and servicemen's wives – practical, calm, and self-sufficient. She had to be, bringing up three children while her husband was away on duty, often based in countries far from her own family and friends. Although she desperately missed her husband when he was away, many of his soldiers' wives looked to her for support, so she had to suppress her own feelings.

She told Sean, Catriona and Dougie that she did not mind talking to them but had felt it important that the incident be kept quiet at the time, knowing the impact it would have both on the men and their wives. The Camp Commander had agreed not to press charges, but accept Peter's resignation and get him out as quickly as possible.

With a little gentle prompting, Rachel recounted what had taken place at their home on the Wiltshire army base on September 4th.

'I don't need to check the date,' she explained with a smile. 'The kids had gone back to school.'

She glanced warily towards her husband, sitting off-screen, then cleared her throat and carried on. 'It all happened very suddenly. I was in the back garden bringing in the washing, because a storm had blown up. Peter and his colleague came into the garden from a side entrance; they'd apparently knocked on the front door but got no answer. I knew both men well, so didn't feel any concern.'

Rachel paused, then cleared her throat again nervously. 'I remember my name being called by one of my neighbours, then... suddenly... I was hit by a full rugby tackle and thrown to the ground. I landed in the kids' sandpit, and I somehow managed to rub sand in his eyes before my neighbour and the other soldier pulled him off and dragged him away. I only had minor cuts and bruises from the fall, but my neighbour insisted on calling the doctor.'

She paused again then sat up straighter in her chair. 'I chose not to tell my husband at that time, because I knew he was involved in a particularly difficult operation and did not need any distractions from home. Nor did I feel it necessary to keep going over what happened.'

Catriona cleared her throat and moved in front of the camera. 'Ma'am, I'm Catriona, one of the investigating team. I'm sorry to ask you, but do you remember what you were wearing?'

At that, Robbie Smith exploded. He jumped out of his chair and came close to the camera. 'Are you trying to suggest my wife was inappropriately dressed and warranted this attack?'

Sean interrupted quickly to defuse the situation.

'No, Robbie, Rachel. Sorry if the question wasn't asked delicately enough by my colleague. The victims have all been wearing something similar, so it might be important, that's all. It would help us to complete that piece of the jigsaw.'

Colonel Smith visibly relaxed and sat back down. 'I see. Right.'

Rachel thought for a moment. 'I was wearing my waterproof wind-breaker. It's pretty old. I had thrown it on to run outside and bring the washing in, as it had started to rain.'

'The colour?' Catriona asked tentatively.

'Yellow.'

The couple could see by the way the officers looked at each other that her reply was significant. With no further questions, they thanked Rachel Smith and her husband for their time and assistance.

Before they disconnected the call, Robbie asked if he could speak to Sean alone. When his wife and the two officers left their respective rooms, he drew closer to the camera. 'The truth, Sean. What the hell is going on?'

'The bodies of the women who have been found all had long dark hair and were wearing an item of yellow clothing. A number of them were called Rachel.'

Robbie swore quietly. 'How big is this?

'Seven police forces, including Gardai and now Cyprus, are checking their records.'

'Is there any risk to my wife?' he asked, losing a little of his composure.

'At this stage we don't think so. However, there may be a chance.'

Robbie thought for a moment. 'Remember that place we spoke about years ago, where if it all ended and we needed to go somewhere safe?'

Sean smiled and nodded.

'Well, I will take her there with the kids, if need be. If he comes for her, then I will kill him.'

'I understand.'

'Had I not been deployed and been here when it happened, then he would already be dead.'

'I feel the same, Robbie. I do!'

'One last thing.' The Colonel frowned. 'He isn't highly intelligent. He won't be the leader, so whoever he is acting with will be giving the orders.'

'Thanks for that.'

'Good luck, and if there is any help you need from me or some of my friends, then do not hesitate to call.'

'Thanks, Robbie, I desperately hope it doesn't come to that,' added Sean, and ended the call.

Deep in thought, Sean returned to the ops room where most of the team were gathered. 'It's only a hunch,' he said, scratching his ear. 'Only a hunch, but my left ear is very itchy!'

His colleagues knew all about Sean Maloney's hunches and his itchy left eat. Although they teased him often, it usually meant he was onto something and was several steps ahead of everyone else.

'It's almost twenty-five years to the day since Barry Fitz-patrick was spurned by the girl on the beach. We know it wasn't Peter Adams, as he had joined the army by that stage. What if he remembers that date and that girl? His ex-wife and everyone we have spoken to say he is a vengeful man. He doesn't forgive or forget. What would he do?'

'The sick bastard would come back!' offered another colleague. 'He'd do it again.'

'Any young girl called Rachel is not safe!' Dougie chipped in.

'And what about the original Rachel?' asked Sean. 'What if he found her?'

'He'd kill her, that's for sure. After all these years, he'd kill her.' Catriona sounded certain.

Sean stroked his chin, his brain whirring with questions and possibilities as the team waited. 'Let's assume he knows who she is and where he can find her?'

'Then we need to protect her!' said Catriona.

'But how can he know?' Dougie seemed unconvinced. 'It's just a fluke that we have stitched this all together!'

'Don't you mean good detective work?' Sean smiled.

'Of course, boss, but it is a needle in a haystack.'

'No, not this time, because we may have the original Rachel,' his boss replied.

'Then we need to ensure he doesn't get to her,' Dougie agreed.

'Exactly,' said Sean. 'Or my life won't be worth living!'

Chapter Eighteen
Brainstorming

**Incident Room, Belfast Central Police Office -
Monday, August 3. 8am**

It was the start of a new week. At the morning briefing, the team met to share information and ensure everyone was up to speed with all the current investigations. After having made some good progress, they had still been unable to trace either Barry Fitzpatrick or Peter Adams. Both were wanted for questioning, but the evidence at the moment still looked no more than circumstantial. Nothing could be pinned exactly on either of them, unless they confessed, but any good lawyer would ensure that didn't happen.

'This is niggling me,' said Sean. 'Two girls go missing fifty miles from where Peter Adams is staying in an army camp, when his father is in jail. Does this mean that Peter is an accomplice, or is he doing this in his own right?'

No-one spoke.

'The fact that he attacked a colonel's wife in broad daylight clearly shows Peter has issues with women, but why? Why out in the open, and just before being deployed? What everyone has said is that he is a good guy, loyal; a follower, not a leader. This incident was bloody stupid, and up to that point there have been no mistakes. He would have known this attack would hurt his colleagues, so it doesn't hold up. Billy Brown said that Barry kept in touch with his son, but the prison authorities have no record of his son ever replying to his letters.'

There was silence in the room.

'Let's have some what-ifs?' Sean looked around at his team. 'Come on, the more off the wall the better.'

What-if was a strategy which Sean had learnt at management college, and he liked to use it with his team to help break down barriers and get them thinking outside the box.

'What if... these girls did not all disappear? After all, they're not all called Rachel. And they are not all confirmed a being dead,' suggested Doug. Some of the team nodded. They had been assuming that every missing girl was part of this case, but they might not be.

Sean wrote it on the white board.

Catriona took a deep breath. 'What if the attack on the Colonel's wife was not an attack at all. It's maybe not what it seems?'

There was laughter. Although the rules were not to criticise any contribution, Catriona's suggestion was just too far-fetched for some of the team.

'No, seriously!' stressed Catriona, looking at her colleagues with annoyance.

'Go on,' encouraged Sean.

'I get that if you put a Colonel's wife, a soldier, and an upstanding civilian in a court of law, all swearing the same story, there would be a clear conviction. They all saw the same thing. Agreed?' said Catriona. Most of the team nodded.

'What if something provoked Peter Adams? What if he thought the Colonel's wife was in danger?' she suggested.

'How do you make that out?' Dougie asked.

'What if he thought he was protecting or *saving* her? After all, she is called Rachel, and we have heard a few times the word *saving–*'

'How?' Dougie interrupted, still not convinced.

'What if he thought the neighbour was dodgy and his boss's wife was in danger? Up to that point, Peter would have taken a bullet for that man.'

The laughter stopped.

'That's some what-if Catriona,' said Sean, looking pensive.

'I know, boss, but maybe something in him snapped. This was a man he respected and would die for; he would do anything to save his family. There is a mention of stormy weather in several of the reports. Did something set him off?' Catriona looked around at her colleagues, her gut churning. Had she just made a fool of herself?

The others were starting to nod now; perhaps it wasn't as ludicrous as it seemed.

'Catriona, let's get Colonel Smith back on the line. Good luck presenting that one.' Sean smiled.

Just then a PC came into the room and handed a piece of paper to Dougie.

'Boss,' he told Sean. 'Cheryl Brown is on the line from Spain for you.'

'This will be interesting,' Sean replied, his eyebrows raised. 'Patch her through.'

Dougie pressed the loud speaker and record buttons on his desk phone.

'Mrs Brown,' said Sean pleasantly, 'to what do I owe this pleasure?'

'Detective, you've been fair to me and my family, and I had to tell my daughter the reason why we had to come out to Spain so quickly. She nearly killed her dad.'

Like mother like daughter, thought Sean with a smile.

'Yes, and?'

'Well, she told him straight that if he was holding anything back, anything at all, she'd never let him see those grandkids of ours again. He might be a bastard, but he loves those kids and he would do anything for them... kill anybody who touched them.' She stopped, emotion catching her breath.

Sean's tone softened a little. 'Go on, love. I know this is hard on you.'

'Well, Billy is here on the line, and he has some things he wants to get off his chest.'

Sean and his team waited patiently as the telephone was handed to Billy. After a few minutes, his voice came over the speaker.

'Mr Maloney, I've done something's in my time, but I could never support a perv. You've got to believe me.' Billy sounded worn out. Clearly, the women in his family hadn't given him any peace.

'Barry used to talk about his son – he'd call him Junior, and say he was a chip off the old block,' Billy went on. 'And though the boy was a decorated soldier, Barry knew what buttons to press. One night he ranted about how he had taught the boy a lesson about not trusting women. The boy had been in love and the girl dumped him. He was chasing after her, and Barry soon put a stop to that. He said he'd told the son that he had sorted the... wee... the wee lass. His son had attacked him, but Barry gave him a hiding, too. He said he had done the boy a favour, and that someday he would call that favour in.'

Billy paused to cough. Sean and his team waited tensely, desperate for the man to continue.

'I asked him what the favour was,' Billy went on, 'but he just laughed. I asked him had he called it in yet but he just said, "The time is coming." He scared the crap out of me, quite honestly.'

'When was this?' asked Sean.

'Over a year ago. I asked for a cell move not long after that.'

'Is there anything else?'

'When I met him last month, he told me he had called in the favour. I asked him had his son agreed to do it, and he laughed and said, 'He will. He likes to save people, and maybe this time he can save Rachel.' I don't know what he meant, Mr Maloney. Honest truth,' said Billy.

***

'Do you know how he communicated with his son?'

'By letter. He was always writing letters to him.'

'Billy, one more question. Why did you ever agree to help him?' asked Sean.

Another long pause. 'That might incriminate me, Mr Maloney,' Billy replied eventually. 'Believe me when I say the wrath of my wife and daughter wouldn't compare to that if it was unleashed.'

Sean thought for a moment before answering. 'Well, Billy, if you think the time is right, then you and me should have a wee talk about that. Because, when we bring Barry Fitzpatrick in, he will probably be singing lots of songs.'

'Thanks for that, Mr Maloney, but I think I'll just be staying out here for a while longer.'

Sean nodded. 'Ok. Is Cheryl there?'

'Yes, Sean?' Her voice came over the speakerphone as the receiver was handed back to her. 'I'm here just to make sure he tells you everything.'

'Cheryl, I'll see what I can do for that boy of your sister's.'

'Oh Sean, thanks ever so much. I've not slept a wink of sleep with worry.'

'And Cheryl... If Billy remembers anything else or would like to talk, then you just give me a call.'

'I will. Thanks for your advice.' The call ended.

Sean turned to the team. 'I'm wondering if Catriona might just be right and Peter is more hero than villain. We really need that call with Robbie Smith!' He injected a little urgency into his voice. 'Right, I want the girl in Cyprus checked, and I want the girls that went missing when Barry was in jail triple-checked. We are looking to rule them out.'

***

By 7pm, everyone was tired. It had been another long and frustrating day, but the jigsaw was coming together very slowly.

'Boss, that's Colonel Smith on Skype,' Catriona called from the far side of the operations room.

'Robbie!'

'Sean,' the colonel's voice could be heard across the room. 'I hope you have some good news for me.'

'Well, no, but I need to put a different and difficult scenario to you. Can you hear me out?'

'Not liking this, Sean,' was the cool response.

'I know, but it has to do with the attack on your missus, and could shift the emphasis of this investigation.'

'Yes, I thought it might be. Go on then!'

Sean asked Catriona to explain the scenario. At the other end, Robbie listened carefully, making no response. When she finished, he simply said, 'How far-fetched is that? He was seen by two other people – it was unprovoked.'

'Robbie,' said Sean calmly. 'Before the attack, what was your relationship with him like?'

Robbie let out a big sigh. 'He was part of my hand-picked team. I trusted him; he had my back. He had all our backs. That is what is so bloody shocking. He could have shot me at any time and done me less damage than this, but to go after my missus... Well, you know how you would feel, Sean.'

'I do indeed, and whilst I don't like it one bit, it is critical to rule him in or out of this investigation. We have on our hands the possible multiple murder of young girls over at least a twenty-year period. If there is one iota of chance that he was or was not involved, we need to know now. Can we put this scenario to your wife?'

Robbie went quiet for a minute, then got up and called his wife to come into the room. A few moments later, Rachel's voice came over the speakerphone.

'Sean, hello again. I take it whatever you have just told Robbie wasn't good news?'

'Yes, Rachel, and I'm sorry, this is very delicate.' He nodded to Catriona.

'Hi again, Mrs Smith. It's Catriona.'

'Hello, Catriona, how can I help you?'

'I need to ask you a few questions about the attack again.'

'Okay.'

'Can I ask first of all what the weather was like on that morning?'

They heard Robbie mutter, then Rachel cleared her throat to speak.

'The weather?' she said. 'Yes, it was starting to rain. There was a summer thunderstorm starting. I had been in the kitchen and gone out into the garden to bring in the washing before it got drenched. I had grabbed my rain jacket – the yellow one I mentioned the last time we spoke. The two soldiers came in the side gate. One of them apologised and explained that they had knocked the front door, but I hadn't heard it as I was in the garden.'

Catriona could feel the tension in the room. 'Was there thunder?' she asked.

'Yes, the dog was going mad barking, as he hates thunder and lightning. My neighbour called over the fence. He was calling my name to check I was okay.' She took a deep breath, as though remembering the events.

'That's when Peter... Peter jumped on me. He knocked me over and I fell into the sandpit. He was lying on top of me when the other guy tried to grab him off me. I managed to rub sand into his eyes, which is when he let go. He looked absolutely wild...' Her husband reached over and grasped her hand as she carried on speaking. 'The two men pulled him off and dragged him away.'

'Did he say anything to you at the time?' asked Catriona.

'Yes, he kept saying, "I'll save you. I'll save you." But it didn't make any sense.' Rachel's voice cracked in a sob.

'Sean, let me call you back in a moment!' Robbie Smith cut the call.

Back in the operations room, Sean looked around at his team.

'That, Catriona, is one hell of a what-if! Well done, my girl,' he said.

A few minutes later, the Skype alarm rang; Robbie was back on the line.

'Sean, Catriona. I've talked this over with Rachel and, whilst I cannot quite get my head around it, I put your scenario to her.'

Rachel came back on the line. 'Catriona, I can absolutely see where you are coming from. I never thought of it like that; at the time it just seemed so black and white yet totally out of character. Peter had always been an incredibly polite and respectful man when I had met him before.'

'Is there any chance that he might have thought your neighbour was a threat to you?' Catriona suggested.

'Well, that is the odd thing. Jim can be a bit creepy, if you don't know him, so I can see that, too.'

'Sean,' Robbie interrupted. 'I didn't actually know about the attack until some time later, because I was deployed, as I told you. By that stage, the wheels had been in motion and, to minimise awkwardness for the army, it had been agreed that Peter could leave with immediate effect. I had never considered there maybe another viewpoint.'

'Robbie,' Sean asked, 'the location where Peter was to be posted, had he been there before?'

'Yes, he had. It is one of those classic hell-holes.'

'Could this be a form of post-traumatic stress, do you think? The thunder, the dog barking, your wife's name being called? Does that make any sense?'

'Yes, I suppose it could. But the trigger?' Robbie still sounded unsure.

'We know that he categorically cannot have been at the places where some of the young women went missing. But something happened before he joined the army. His girl-friend, also called Rachel, died one stormy night. She was wearing a yellow dress. She was 16 years old.'

'Dear God, I never knew that,' Robbie replied. 'I can see absolutely that this might have kicked something off. Have you any idea where he might be?'

'At this point, we believe he is back in Ireland, but his objective is not clear at the moment.'

'Sean, if there is anything I can do to help, let me know. Maybe we were all too quick to judge him.'

'Was there anyone he might have been close to? Another colleague? Someone he might have gone to stay with?' asked Sean.

Robbie thought for a moment. 'Let me make some discreet calls and see if I can find anything out.'

'Thanks. One last question. Do you know if he received many letters from home?'

'I'm not sure,' said Robbie. 'But I do remember on one occasion when he was handed an envelope, he appeared to look at the handwriting and then lit a match and burned it without opening it. No-one liked to ask what it was about.'

'Ok, thanks again.'

They closed the call, and Sean turned to the team. 'Any more what-ifs?'

Danny patted a proud Catriona on the back as the others shook their heads.

'Right then.' Sean stood up. 'We still need to find both men. My ear is twitching again. I have a niggling suspicion that Barry is being hunted by his son, but he doesn't realise it yet.' He glanced at his wristwatch. 'Let's call it a night and pick up these pieces tomorrow.'

Chapter Nineteen
Family concerns

Kieran and Megan had been back to visit the house. When they stopped off for a light supper in the bar in the village afterwards, Megan finally plucked up the courage to talk to Kieran about her concerns that their relationship was moving very quickly.

When she'd finished talking, he reassured her that he was happy that they should spend time getting to know each other and not feel pressured or rushed into anything.

'I'm so glad you understand, Kieran,' she said, hugging him as they stood to leave. 'I *am* really happy, please don't think that I'm not. But I just want to be sure that if I move back here, it's for the right reasons.'

'No problem,' he replied, stopping for a gentle kiss. 'I definitely want to buy the house and, while I would love to live there with you, I won't rush you. If you commute for a while from London until you're sure what you want, then I'll just be happy to spend whatever time I can with you.'

It was almost 8.30pm as Kieran started the car for the drive back to Belfast. Within minutes, his phone rang.

'Hi, it's Sean,' his brother's voice boomed over the car speaker. 'How are things?'

'Good.' Kieran smiled briefly at Megan as he replied. 'Megan and I are just heading back from supper in Groomsport. We took the opportunity to pop back and look at the Watch House again while we were there. What's new with you?'

There was a brief silence on the line before Sean replied. 'How did you get on with the house then? Still keen?'

'Absolutely!' Kieran's enthusiasm bubbled over. 'We both really loved it, even more than the first time. I'm waiting for the survey report to come back before making an offer.'

'Good. Erm, could you pop into Mum and Dad's on your way home, and I'll meet you both there? I just want to have a quick chat.' Sean sounded a little nervous.

Kieran took his eyes off the road briefly to glance quizzically at Megan. She nodded. 'Ok, Sean,' he replied. 'Is there a problem?'

'Great. See you there.' Sean cut the call before his brother could ask any more.

***

Replacing the receiver, Sean dashed back to the operations room where his officers were just preparing to leave for the evening.

'Sorry, folks. I have a hunch.'

He smiled as he watched his officers sit wearily back down, some of them already with their coats on.

'I've just spoken to my brother. He and his young lady, Megan – the original Rachel who sparked this investigation – have been to Groomsport this evening. Now, if someone was watching for her and saw them, they might tail them to see where she lives. So, rather than allow them to go back to either of their own places, I have asked them to head straight to my mother's house.'

He looked around at his team. 'Here's a note of my brother's car and his registration. I want the traffic police along the way to watch for any car tailing them. And I need two cars positioned at either end of the road from my mother's house so they can see who drives in. Take a couple of unmarked cars, and if necessary pretend to be smooching couples.' He grinned at the disbelieving looks on some of his officers' faces. 'It's okay, it's work!'

Before he left the office, Sean called his mum to say he was going to pop in and would be there in about ten minutes. Catriona dropped him and Dougie off outside the house, then moved her car out of sight.

***

Although she was delighted to see her son, Sean's mum knew something was wrong when he was visiting so late. Once he'd explained a little about the situation and what he needed them to do, his parents were keen to know if Kieran or Megan were in any danger.

'Not with us all here!' Sean assured them. His phone beeped with a message: Kieran's was just arriving.

A little taken aback by his mother's enthusiastic welcome, Kieran allowed her to lead him and Megan into the cosy living room, where she proceeded to explain that they were playing out a part, and gave him his instructions. After a few minutes, she got up and closed the venetian blinds, then left the room and joined her husband in the kitchen.

When Sean and Dougie came into the sitting room, Kieran couldn't hide his annoyance. 'What the hell is going on?' he asked.

'Sit down, mate. I'm sorry about all the cloak and dagger stuff, but your car has been tailed from when you left Groomsport tonight.'

'What!' Kieran jumped up, looking as though he would punch his brother. 'Why were you tailing us? What's going on?'

Sean put a gentle hand on his brother's arm and gestured for him to sit back down beside Megan.

'Not by us! We are tailing the person tailing you. I didn't want you to take Megan to her mum's house or back to your place, because I suspect that she might be at risk. So this was the easiest and safest place to bring you.'

'At risk!' Megan looked pale. 'Why?'

'Since our chat a couple of weeks ago, we have been investigating the disappearance of several young women who would have fitted the same description as you.'

Megan gasped. 'How many?'

'I can't tell you the number or any more details at this stage, all I can say is that we are concerned and are following up more enquiries.'

Kieran swore.

'And there is a possible link to the Watch House in Groomsport,' Sean went on.

'What, to Hugh Fitzpatrick?' Kieran was puzzled.

'We believe he is part of the tragedy, not a suspect.'

'Oh God, his wife and daughter.' Megan took Kieran's hand, as though looking for some comfort.

'We can't say anything for sure at the moment,' said Sean. 'We think the person concerned might be watching his house. At this stage, we don't know why. But when I heard you were there tonight, I thought there might just be a chance he followed you.'

'You think after twenty years he would recognise Meg?' asked Kieran. 'That's a mighty big coincidence.'

'We don't know, but I'm not taking any risks.' Sean's tone brooked no argument. 'We do know your car was followed up here tonight, and we're checking on that now. There is one more thing. Megan, you said your mum spoke to this man at the caravan site, a few days after the incident on the beach?'

Megan nodded.

'We have some old photos that we would like to show her, to see if she recognises anything. Do you think she would be okay with that?'

Megan nodded and pulled her mobile phone from her handbag. 'Mum's been ill, so she might be asleep, but let me call my dad.'

The three men waited patiently while Megan spoke quietly with her father and explained that she needed to talk to her mum, and would be home in about twenty minutes with Sean and Kieran.

'Does your mum know what happened to you that evening?' Sean asked, as they got up to leave.

'Yes, I told her eventually.' Megan nodded. 'At first I was very scared, and thought she would be mad at me for being on the beach on my own when I shouldn't have been. I know if my dad had caught him, he would probably have killed him.'

Suddenly there was a scream from the kitchen.

Sean and Kieran rushed in to find their father with his arms around his shocked wife. 'There was someone in the garden!' she told her sons.

They opened the door to the garden but it was empty. Sean quickly called the other officers for an update.

'Boss, he pulled up and parked his car and went through the path near the house,' one of the team explained. 'We were following him, but we lost him in the garden when we heard the woman scream.'

'That was my mother!' Sean growled.

'We lost him, boss, sorry!'

Sean swore angrily as he ended the call, then saw his mother's face and apologised.

'Get on and do what you have to do, Sean,' she said firmly, pulling herself together. 'Your dad and I are okay here. He isn't likely to come back.' She smiled reassuringly at her sons. 'If he does, then you'll need a body bag... for him!'

***

Sean spoke to Dougie, and five minutes later a taxi drew up outside the house. Sean took Megan with him, while Dougie was to follow in Kieran's car. Sean gave the taxi driver her address.

'How do you know where my parents live?' she asked, surprised.

'Megan, you're clearly very important to our Kieran. So when I realised this was bigger than just a lucky escape one summer long ago, I've been keeping a closer eye on you.'

'How?'

Sean shrugged. 'The doorman in your office is an ex-colleague; you always like a wee chat with him. He always asks where you are going, and that way we have been able to keep tabs on you. Unfortunately, we lost you earlier tonight as you left when he wasn't on the door.'

'Yes, I was hurrying to get the train to meet Kieran at Groomsport. I don't know whether to be glad or mad.' Megan smiled, despite her nerves. 'Please don't frighten my mum with this, not now.'

'I won't. I promise,' he assured her, looking just like his brother when he smiled.

They sat in silence for a few minutes, then Megan spoke again.

'Sean, the taxi driver tonight when I arrived at Bangor Station. There was something odd about him. He was very chatty, but he asked if I remembered Groomsport when it had been the caravan park. He also asked if I want collected later, but I said my boyfriend was meeting me there and driving me home. When I got out, I noticed that he was wearing gloves, but it's summer.'

'Anything else?' Sean was paying close attention to what she said.

'Hmm. He didn't drive away immediately when I got out. In fact, he was still sitting there when Kieran arrived.'

Sean called the incident room and asked them to follow up with local taxi firms to see if they could find out who had driven Megan earlier that evening from Bangor station to Groomsport.

***

When they arrived at her parents' house, Megan's father opened the door and hugged her warmly before being introduced to Sean.

In the sitting room, her mum was snuggled up on the sofa with a blanket over her feet. Since starting her chemotherapy treatment, she often felt the cold. Megan sat down beside her and leaned over to kiss her cheek.

As she began to explain that Sean was investigating several cases where young women had gone missing, the doorbell rang. Minutes later, her dad showed Kieran and Dougie into the room.

'Mum,' Megan began again. 'Can you think back – it must be about twenty years ago now – to the last summer we stayed at the caravan in Groomsport?'

Her dad nodded as her mum replied, 'Yes, it was the summer before your nan passed away.'

'Do you remember the time I ran away from the man on the beach?'

Her mum nodded, concern etched on her face. Megan squeezed her mum's hand in reassurance and smiled gently. 'I got away. He didn't hurt me.'

'I'd have fecking killed him if I had got my hands on him,' her dad burst out. He rarely swore but his anger was clear.

'I know, Dad. You and the rest of the family, I'm sure.' Megan smiled gently at him then turned back to look at her mum. 'Several days later, a man came looking...' Megan stopped. She didn't know how to express what she wanted to stay.

'Mrs Scott,' Sean took over.

'Jane. Please call me Jane.' The older woman smiled.

'Jane, Megan thought you might remember this man. I know it was a very long time ago, but is there anything you can remember.'

Her mum thought for a few moments. She nodded.

'He was a creepy man. He was looking for a friend of his daughter's, he said. There was a girl in the car...'

'A girl? How old would you say she was?' asked Sean.

'About Megan's age. She had ginger curls. She looked miserable, sad.'

That could have been Sarah, Sean thought. *Might she remember that?*

'Do you remember anything else about the man or the car?' he probed gently.

'Oh God, it was so long ago,' she said, shaking her head a little as though trying to remember.

Megan's dad growled, 'Think, Jane, think!'

'I am bloody thinking,' she snapped back.

Megan smiled and squeezed her mum's hand again. 'It's okay, Mum, take your time.'

Jane took a deep breath then spoke again. 'The car had four doors. It was a dirty beige-type colour, but I don't know what make. I'm sorry, I'm not very good with cars.'

'No problem. That's brilliant,' reassured Sean. 'It really is! And the man?'

'About our age at the time, so probably about forty, I think. He didn't have a beard. Dark hair – dyed, maybe. And his hand... his hand...' She put her hand out. 'That's it... he had his right arm leaning out the window, and his left hand was on the steering wheel. His left hand... it had a scar – a bad burn by the looks of it...'

She traced her finger over her own left hand to indicate where the scar was, still deep in thought. 'I'm sorry.' She looked up at Sean. 'That's all I remember.'

Sean lent over and squeezed her free hand. 'That, Jane, is truly amazing!'

He took some photos out of his pocket to show her. It had been twenty years, but she was sure one of the men in the photo was the strange man who had turned up at the caravan park.

Sean asked if they had a magnifying glass. When Megan's dad produced a small magnifier, Sean showed Jane the photo again. There was clearly a scar on the hand of one of the men.

'So you know who he is?' asked Jack.

'Yes, we do, and we will get him. If Megan hadn't told Kieran the story and then they told me, this man would have got away with some serious crimes.'

Thanking Megan's parents for all their help, Sean and Dougie left the room. Kieran followed them out to the hall-way.

'What happens now?' he asked.

'We know who he is, and we'll find him,' Sean assured him.

'What about Megan and her parents?' Kieran asked.

They were interrupted by the ringing of Sean's phone. 'What?' He snapped his phone shut and looked at his brother. 'It seems there wasn't just one car following you tonight, there were two. Clearly we have stirred a hornet's nest.'

Although there was no indication that they had been followed to Megan's house, Sean suggested Kieran stay at her parents' for the night. 'We're heading back to the station, so just call me if there are any concerns,' he told his brother. 'But we'll leave a patrol car parked nearby as well.'

Once they'd left, Jack checked and double checked all the windows and doors, then smiled at Kieran. 'I wouldn't be too worried,' he told the younger man. 'Megan might be the one protecting us.'

Kieran looked puzzled.

'You haven't told him, have you?' he asked his daughter. She shook her head. 'Aye, after the scare that summer, we sent her to judo classes. What colour of belt do you have, love?'

'Only brown, Dad.' She grinned at Kieran, glad to lighten the atmosphere.

'So you see, lad, there's no messing with her,' laughed Jack. 'And if you do, then her brothers will sort you out!'

***

By the time Sean and Dougie arrived back at the station, the CCTV footage along the Bangor Road and Donegal Road was being analysed. One of the team had spotted that it hadn't just been two cars that had been following them, but also a motorbike. On closer investigation, they were finally able to get the registration plates for the two cars and the motorbike.

'One of the cars was a rental car, which was picked up at Dublin Airport two days ago. We've sent a request to our colleagues in the south to check that out,' explained one of the young officers. 'The other car is registered to a Belfast address, so we are checking that out now.'

'Anything on the motorbike?' asked Sean.

'Yes, sir, it seems it is registered to a house in Groomsport. We've check that, and the property is owned by three people – Sarah and Gordon Fitzpatrick, and Peter Adams.'

Despite the late hour, Dougie made a quick call to Sarah Fitzpatrick in England. When he came off the phone, he explained, 'She says it was their grandmother, Hilda Adam's house, but she had given it to the three of them when she remarried. Apparently, it was rented out until the end of July, but it's now empty as they are considering whether to sell it or not.

'They couldn't make any decision until they found Peter, because he is a part owner. A friend who lives in the village has keys, and has been looking after the place. I've got the details.'

Chapter Twenty
A remarkable woman

Ballyholme Nursing Home - Tuesday, August 4. 10.15am

The nursing home sat back from the sea on a prominent position overlooking the esplanade. The grass bank had wooden chairs and tables positioned to enable the residents to enjoy the view as well as the sea breeze. The yacht club regattas were an enjoyable attraction for the residents to watch and occasionally have a little flutter on. For chillier days, the large cheerful conservatory overlooked the bay, allowing a perfect view of the comings and goings of walkers, joggers, and children playing.

DCI Sean Maloney and DS Catriona Murphy had been shown into the conservatory by a cheerful young woman, who served them with coffee while they waited on the Matron to arrive.

When she did, Sean thought she looked exactly as a nursing home matron should: a big warm smile, but with a glint of steel in her eyes. She extended her hand in welcome to both officers.

'Joyce Lambert. Pleased to meet you. Sorry to keep you waiting, but we were just completing our morning prescription dispensary. How can I help you?' she asked, taking the seat opposite them. 'I believe one of your officers called a couple of days ago looking for a Hilda Adams.'

'Yes, we're looking to speak to Mrs Hilda Hunter, who we believe was called Adams before she was remarried. We believe she is a resident here,' Sean explained.

'Has she been caught speeding again?' Joyce asked with a frown, which broke quickly into a grin when she saw the officers' faces. 'Sorry, a little joke. Hilda is in a wheelchair so I hardly think she is being questioned for breaking and entering!'

Sean found himself laughing. He liked this woman with her no-nonsense attitude.

'Hilda is nearly eighty,' the Matron went on, 'but she does have all her faculties. In fact, she's the life and soul here, putting us younger ones to shame with her energy. A group of our residents went off for a couple of days down to the Mourne Mountains, which is why she wasn't here when your officer called last time.'

'Would she be able to answer some questions for us?' he asked.

'Talk to you?' Joyce Lambert laughed heartily. 'Quite honestly, your problem will be getting her to stop.'

'The thing is,' Sean explained, 'the questions might be a bit upsetting for her, and we are concerned about her age.'

'If it would help, I could sit in with her,' offered Joyce, her expression more serious.

'That would be helpful, but you understand that the conversation will need to be kept confidential at this time.' Sean was sure this woman had kept many secrets over the years.

'DCI, my husband was in the police force for thirty years, so yes I do understand. That won't be a problem. I'll just go and get Hilda, but it may take 10-15 minutes, as she needs to lie down after her medication.' Joyce left the room, and a few minutes later one of the staff brought in some sandwiches and cake.

'Matron thought you might like a bite to eat,' explained the young assistant, who looked a younger version of Joyce.

They had just finished eating when the Matron came back, pushing a smartly-dressed resident in her wheelchair. Sean introduced himself and Catriona, and explained that they wanted to speak to her about her former son-in-law Barry Fitzpatrick, and her grandson, Peter.

The older lady looked both officers over carefully, before replying in a surprisingly strong voice. 'Not before time. I always wondered when Barry's past would catch up with him. Our Peter is a good lad despite how he came into this world. He joined the Army and was in it until a year ago.' She looked down at her hands, clearly upset.

'If you are here asking about Peter, you will know what happened and why he had to leave the Army. He's distraught by it, and not even sure how it happened. I told him he needed to get help. I told him he suffers from that... what do you call it, trauma disease? I mean, the things that boy will have seen in the places they sent him... God help him.' She took a white handkerchief from the sleeve of her jumper and gently dabbed at her eyes.

'Do you have any idea where he is?' Sean asked gently.

She either didn't hear him, or chose to ignore the question. 'Barry, that's a different kettle of fish.' She shuffled in her wheelchair and sat up a little straighter. 'Pure evil that man! Hurts everyone he comes into contact with.'

'How?' asked Sean.

'Well, for starters, he raped my daughter, Rachel, when she was just sixteen. She was a good girl. We didn't know who the father was, because she would never say. I arranged for her to go to Liverpool to stay with my brother-in-law's family, and they couldn't have done enough for her.

'When Peter was born, she had a breakdown. We didn't know at the time that it was to do with the rape. She asked that Peter be put up for adoption, but my husband's nephew and his wife couldn't have children so they offered to adopt Peter. They were offering a good home, so I said yes. We never told Rachel that's where he went until she was well again.'

Hilda sighed and dabbed at her eyes again. 'She didn't want to see young Peter, which I thought was very strange because she had always loved kids. When Rachel got well enough, she got a job on the cruise ships. She lives in Australia now, and has done for about twenty-five years.' Hilda smiled proudly and went on, 'She always wanted to be a nurse, and she is now. She came back for my wedding fifteen years ago, but took a lot of persuading. She only came because neither her sister nor brother-in-law would be there.

'It was only when Peter turned about eighteen that I saw the likeness to Barry. When I called Rachel to ask her, she broke down and told me the whole story. God, I would have killed him, but he just laughed at me and threatened Sarah and Gordon, my other grandchildren. '

'You confronted Barry about the rape?' Sean couldn't hide the surprise in his voice.

The older woman nodded. 'I did. He never threatened Leah, just the two kids.' Hilda's face twisted in disgust. 'Leah's my other daughter. Barry knew it wouldn't bother me if he did something to her, God forgive me. Those two were a match made for each other.' She looked first at Sean then Catriona. 'Have you met her?'

Sean nodded.

'Well, you will know what I mean. She married Barry when he came out of prison for the first time. They say prison is meant to be a punishment, well I tell you, he came out more arrogant and threatening than when he went in. But Leah wouldn't hear a word against him. He was a jobbing builder at one time, working all over the place, England, down south, but if you ask me, he was mainly up to no good.

'I really don't know how they managed to have two such lovely children. Sarah left home when she was sixteen – she told me she was leaving, and where she was going, so I helped her with some money. When Gordon turned sixteen, he did the same and went off to live with Sarah. I'm ashamed to say that my Leah believes the world owes her...' Her voice trailed away.

The Matron, watching quietly, stood and poured a glass of water from a nearby table and handed it to Hilda, who smiled gratefully and took a few sips.

'I saw Peter over the years a few times when we went over to visit my husband's family. He was a lovely child, very happy. Always wanted to be a soldier. When he was eighteen, he turned up at my door. He knew he was adopted and wanted to know the background. At that time, I hadn't seen him for three or four years, and I was shocked. He was the spit of his father.

'Unfortunately, while he was staying with me, Barry arrived unexpectedly. I hadn't seen him for a few weeks. He only usually came by when he wanted money or something. You should have seen the shock on his face when it registered who Peter was. He left but came back the next day with a gun and threatened me to tell him the truth or he would kill Sarah and Peter. And I believed he would.'

Hilda took another sip of her water before continuing. 'He denied raping Rachel. Over and over again, he denied it. Then he said he couldn't remember, as there had been so many lassies and said she had probably been gagging for it. No way, I said. He asked me how I thought Peter would feel if he thought he was the outcome of a rape. So instead, he came up with his own version, of how he had loved Peter's mother but she'd run away leaving him broken-hearted.' She shook her head sadly.

'We understand you were the housekeeper for Hugh Fitz-patrick when both his wife and his daughter, Rachel, died.' Catriona spoke for the first time.

Hilda's smile was sad. 'She was a beautiful woman, Hugh's wife, Louisa. She taught me some old Southern reci-pes. It was an honour to know her. She adored Hugh and that baby. The love and laughter in that house, it was a bless-ing to share. But, of course, Barry couldn't see others happy without sticking his oar in.'

'What happened?' Catriona prompted.

'Barry believed that every woman fancied him. He would come around to their house and hang out. Hugh was good-natured – too good-natured, really – so he didn't see the evil Barry was up to.'

She stopped to think for a moment. Though eager to hear her story, the detectives sat patiently; they didn't want to rush her.

'I don't know what he had over Hugh, although they are cousins, but Barry always liked to have something over you, so he could niggle you. Like a damn fly. I noticed that he started to call round any time Hugh was away. I told him to get out a few times, but he took no notice of me. Just said that as the master, it was his job to keep Louisa safe! I said he wasn't the master of anything, but he turned on me and said he should have been; it was his destiny. He was full of this nonsense that he was somebody.

'The night Louisa died, I left about 6 pm, and she was sitting on the big sofa, cuddling little Rachel.' Hilda smiled wistfully at the memory. 'A beautiful sight the two of them together. "All cuddled in, Nan," she said, because that's always what she called me, "there's going to be a storm tonight. Get home safe and see you in the morning," she said.' Hilda's smile faded and her voice wobbled. 'I never saw her again.'

She sipped her water again, as the others waited in silence for her to continue. 'When I was walking up the road home, I saw a car and thought I saw a man sitting in it. It was too far for me to see clearly. After I turned right out of the Point, I crossed over and took a left up the hill. I looked back and I saw the car moving slowly. It must have driven down the Point, as it never came past me. Hugh was in Dublin at a meeting, so I knew it couldn't be him. I did always wonder.

'I mentioned it to Leah and she said Barry had been at home with her that night, but he wasn't. I've no proof; I don't even know if the car went to the Watch House. All I know is that something must have happened to make Louisa take Rachel out in that storm.' Hilda took another sip. 'Hugh was absolutely devastated. I more or less brought Rachel up until Hugh married Arabella.'

'Arabella?' Catriona probed.

'Arabella Fullerton she is now. Lovely woman. She brought Rachel up as if she was her own. She lives in Galway, I think. Her and Hugh broke up after young Rachel died. It tore everyone apart...'

Hilda stopped talking for a moment and turned to the Matron. 'Joyce, would you mind going to my room and bringing me down my old carpet bag, please?' she asked.

A few minutes later, Joyce came back carrying an old tatty bag. Hilda opened it and pulled out several envelopes.

She handed the first envelope to Sean. 'These are letters Peter sent to me when he was in the Army. You can take them away and read them, but please don't lose them. You'll see that he says his father keeps hounding him for money and to collect on a favour he had done Peter.'

'Do you know what that favour was?' Sean asked.

'Not for certain, no.' She handed over a second envelope. 'These are a couple of unpleasant letters which Barry wrote to Peter. The lad was upset by them, and I don't know why but I kept them, just in case they might be needed one day.'

Sean noticed the letters were dated and postmarked, which could prove useful in tying up Barry's whereabouts in connection with the investigation.

Hilda opened the third envelope, removed a tattered notebook and held it out to Sean.

'It's a diary that used to be in Hugh's study at the house, but Barry must have stolen it. When I was moving to live in Spain, after I remarried, I found it hidden inside an old bag he had left in my garden hut. Hugh was away in America at the time, and I always meant to return it to him.

'But I've never been able to face Hugh after... after what I learnt about Rachel's death. I was going to post the diary back to him, but it went into a bag and I forgot all about it.' When her voice broke in a sob, Joyce took the older woman's hand and asked if she wanted to continue.

Hilda looked at Joyce gratefully. 'I have to. I have to say it, otherwise they will believe it's Peter's fault.'

'Mrs Hunter. Hilda. We really understand this is difficult for you,' Sean said kindly, 'but can you tell us what
happened the night Rachel died?'

Hilda kept hold of the Matron's hand as she replied. 'That
was the worst night of my life. Peter had been courting Rachel
– a summer romance. They were very happy together, but
there was no funny business going on. Peter always treated
her with respect. He bought her a lovely yellow dress for her
birthday – her sunshine dress, she called it – and a little sea
horse necklace. They were a lovely young couple.

'He was besotted by her, but he wanted to join the Army.
Rachel wanted to follow in her mother and father's footsteps
and go to university, so she decided to finish the relationship. But I tell you, she was heartbroken over it. She really
liked him, but she had dreams and she thought it better that
they cool things off. Peter was devastated. They agreed to
meet up for a final goodbye before he left to join the Army.'

She gripped the Matron's hand a little tighter as she went
on, 'They went for a walk, and said goodbye at the harbour
where they had first met – all very sweet. They promised
they would write to each other, but with no commitment.
Peter left her walking towards her house, and he came home
and sat and cried with me.

'A storm was starting up. It must have been about ten
o'clock when Arabella called. She was frantic. She hadn't
known anything about Peter and Rachel being close, but she
asked if I had seen Rachel or knew where she might be. I told
her that my grandson had been with me since seven o'clock,
and had seen Rachel down at the harbor just before that.'

Tears rolled slowly down Hilda's wrinkled cheeks. 'They
found her body the next day. It near killed him,' she sobbed.
The matron wiped her own eyes, then put a comforting arm

around the older woman. 'I swear to God that Peter had nothing to do with it.' Hilda put her head in her hands.

'And Barry?' Catriona prompted.

'The night after the funeral, Barry had too much to drink. Things were said and he was cursing and swearing, and Hugh decked him. One punch and it floored him. Then Arabella slapped Leah a good one. If it had been under any other circumstances, I would have cheered. The pair of them were too drunk to drive, so they ended up at my house. All the insults and slights came pouring out of the two of them.

'Peter was distraught. Barry told him to get over Rachel, that she was a slag and... And that... he had done Peter a favour!'

Joyce couldn't contain a loud gasp. Sean and Catriona said nothing, but Sean hunched forward a little, eager for Hilda to keep talking.

'Yes, he said, "I've done you a favour, lad, there'll be no more making a fool of yourself over some girl." Peter asked him what he meant. Barry said, "She winds you in when she wants you, and throws you away when she doesn't. She won't be doing that any more." But Peter was furious and he thumped Barry. Every ounce of strength went into that punch, but the fight turned nasty.

'Then Barry started to laugh. He told Peter, "She tried to fight me that night, but one wee slap and whoosh, splash... Bye bye." The fight just went out of our Peter. Then Leah started on at him that his mother was a slut and had tried to trap Barry.'

'Why did Peter not go to the police?' Sean asked.

'Barry said it was his word against Peter's. He said he would tell the police that he had seen Peter push her. No-one could prove anything. The last thing he said to Peter was...

"I'll call in that favour sometime." I threw Barry and Leah out, and I told Peter the truth about his mum. It was the toughest thing I ever had to say to the lad. He left the next day.'

'Did he believe you?' Catriona asked.

'Yes, he did. He said he would kill his father one day, though.'

Sean cleared his throat gently. 'Hilda, have you have any idea where Peter might be now?'

The old woman looked exhausted, as though all her fighting spirit had gone. She looked briefly out of the window then back at Sean. 'I believe the time has come now.' Before they could ask her any more questions, she slumped over in her chair.

Joyce Lambert immediately sprang into action, pressing an emergency button on her wrist which brought the nursing team rushing into the room.

Sean and Catriona were asked to wait outside while an ambulance was called. A few minutes later, the matron left her nursing team with Hilda and asked the officers to join her in the office.

'I am totally shocked at what she has told you,' she said, visibly shaken at the turn of events.

'Yes, it's quite a story. Does she strike you as a lady who would lie?' Sean asked.

'No, she's honest as the day is long,' replied Joyce, shaking her head. 'What a truly evil person this man must be. You asked where her grandson, Peter, might be. He has been here a couple of times in the last few weeks.'

'Really, when?'

'Last Sunday before the residents went away for the trip. He comes on a motorbike usually. A polite lad, very caring.'

'How did Hilda get in touch with him?' asked Catriona, looking puzzled.

'She has a mobile phone.' Joyce shook her head and gave a little smile. 'She's forever texting. I have his number in her file, as one of her next of kin, in case of an emergency.' She looked through some folders on her desk and wrote a number on a piece of paper before handing it to Catriona.

'Do you know, by any chance, where he might be staying?'

'I think he may be staying in Groomsport – in her old house. I'm not sure for definite, though. Obviously, I'll have to contact her relatives to let them know she is being taken to hospital. It's normal procedure, you understand.'

Sean thought for a moment before replying. 'Can you give us about half an hour then call them, just so that we can arrange to get some officers at the hospital?' She nodded. 'I hope Hilda is okay. If you could give Catriona a note of all Hilda's next of kin contacts and numbers, I'll go and make a few calls. And thank you for all your assistance today. We really appreciate it.'

***

Outside, Sean made a call to the office to instruct that a plain clothes team be sent immediately to the hospital. He advised the dispatcher that one of the suspects – Peter Adams – might be driving a motorbike. He was not to be approached, but allowed to go to his grandmother's bedside. He was not to be made suspicious or he might run.

As he finished his call, Catriona came out to join him. She told Sean that the Home's files showed all of Hilda's grandchildren on the Next of Kin list, along with her daughter, Rachel. But not Leah.

'I've asked the Matron to call Peter last, just in case he checks with the others,' she explained.

Sean nodded. 'Good idea. Okay, if you drop me off at Dundonald Hospital and then head back to the office with Hilda's bag, you can start getting it processed and logged. If there is anything significant, call me.'

They got into the car and Catriona began the drive to the hospital.

'Are you planning on arresting Peter if he turns up at the hospital?' she asked.

'Not at this point,' Sean replied, 'but if there is any suggestion that he will do a runner or harm anyone, then yes.' He took in her look of disappointment. 'I know you would prefer to be coming to the hospital, but whatever information is in the bag could be the pieces to the jigsaw we need. At this moment, all we have is still hearsay and circumstantial evidence.'

Catriona smiled. 'Sure, boss. I understand.'

***

Two miles away, Peter was in the shower when his mobile rang – the caller left a message on his voicemail. He had been staying at the house, but only using the upstairs so that anyone looking in the windows wouldn't see him.

When he checked the message, it was the Matron from the nursing home telling him that his nan has been taken into Dundonald Hospital and could he please call back.

The old lady had been the one constant in his life since he had discovered that she was his real grandmother. He owed her.

He called the nursing home and was reassured that they had taken her to the hospital as a precaution after she had collapsed that morning. He then called the hospital. They confirmed that an elderly lady had been brought in from Ballyholme, but could not confirm her name or any other details at that stage.

He would go there. He needed to be with her. Peter was about to get on his bike when he hesitated. Nan was always so robust and healthy. What if it was a hoax? He called Sarah.

She was relieved to hear from him, but angry that he not been in touch. When she confirmed that she'd had a call from the Home and was making plans to travel to Belfast, he assured her he would go straight to the hospital and update her from there. In the meantime, she would contact her brother to see if he was able to travel over with her.

In Australia, Rachel – Peter's mother – was wakened by the telephone to be told that her mother had collapsed and been taken to hospital as a precaution. She thanked the Matron, then got up and made herself a cup of tea. She thought for a while and then made her decision. She would return 'home'. She wanted to be with her mum whatever the consequences.

Chapter Twenty-One
Peter's story

Peter got on his motorbike and headed to Dundonald, taking a roundabout route through the back streets, paranoid that he might be followed. He arrived at the hospital convinced that there was no problem, and made his way to A&E.

The receptionist confirmed that his grandmother was awaiting tests, and he was directed to a small room, where he found his nan hooked up to several machines. A nurse was checking her blood pressure.

'Hello,' said the nurse, as she finished her checks and headed towards the door. 'The doctor will be in shortly to talk to you.'

'Will she be okay?'

'Yes I will,' croaked his grandmother, opening her eyes. He sat down on the chair beside her and took her hand.

'Peter, it's all going to be okay.'

He thought she meant she would be well.

'Peter, I've told the police... everything...'

'Nan,' he said reassuringly, stroking her hand.

'Peter, they need to deal with him, not you. Please. I can't rest for worrying about you,' she pleaded.

At that moment the door opened and Sean entered, Dougie close behind him.

Peter jumped up from his seat. 'I've not done anything wrong!' he shouted.

'We know,' Sean soothed. 'Sit down, Peter. Your gran has told us everything, and we've had statements from other people, too. We're looking for Barry Fitzpatrick. Would you know where he might be?'

Peter sank back into the hard hospital chair and ran a hand through his hair. 'I nearly got him the other night, but you guys lost him at the back of the garden up in Belfast. When I realised you were there, I scarpered pretty quickly. I saw him going into the Watch House in Groomsport a few times. He's been driving a taxi. I don't know where he is now.'

'Peter, we need you to stay with your nan and not go chasing after him. Do you understand?' Sean's tone was more forceful.

'Please, Peter,' Hilda pleaded, grasping his hand. 'It'll destroy your life.'

'He destroyed my life the night he murdered Rachel,' retorted Peter.

'He's destroyed many lives, but he won't any more,' Sean assured him. 'We have enough evidence to lock him up and throw away the key.'

'Okay.' Peter smiled down at his worried grandmother. 'I'll stay here.'

'We will need to take a detailed statement from you,' Sean went on, 'but that can wait for the moment.'

The door opened and a harassed-looking young doctor entered. 'We need to run some tests on this lovely young lady.' He smiled at Hilda. 'Would it be possible for you all to wait outside?'

'How long will it take?' asked Sean.

'Hard to say, but we want to do a thorough check over, so it might be a couple of hours. We also have to give her some medication, which will probably make her sleepy.'

Sean looked at Dougie, then turned back to Peter. 'Why don't we go and have a coffee, Peter? Your nan is in good hands.'

Hilda nodded her approval, then relaxed back on her pillows as the three men stood and left the room.

***

Over a cup of coffee in a quiet corner of the spacious hospital café, Peter haltingly opened up to Sean and Dougie.

'I always knew I had been adopted, but my parents couldn't have been kinder. They couldn't have kids of their own and the waiting list for adopting a baby had been very long, so when my mother got pregnant at sixteen and went to Liverpool, they adopted me when she decided she couldn't keep me. They were wonderful, but as I grew into my teens I knew that I wanted to meet my birth mother,' he explained. 'It was easy to trace her, because Nan – who I then discovered was my real grandmother – had kept in touch over the years. My adoptive parents were related to my grandfather, her first husband.

'When I was 18, I was at a loose end. I wasn't really academic and had dropped out of school. I needed to get a job but had no idea what to do, so I decided to come to Northern Ireland and see my nan. It was Easter 1986. Her house had a view over the village green from upstairs out into the Irish Sea, there were lovely walks along the coast, and I loved going out fishing. Nan would fry up any of the fish I caught, and I never ever tasted anything so delicious.'

Peter sipped at his hot coffee while the officers waited patiently for him to go on.

'I hadn't seen her in a few years, though we often spoke on the phone and she sent me a birthday card and some money every year. She looked really shocked when she opened the door, even though she had known I was coming. By that time, I had shot up and was over six foot tall, with broad shoulders, and the Celtic colouring of ginger hair and blue eyes.

'It was a couple of weeks later that I found out the reason for her shock. My father...' Peter's voice faltered briefly, '... the sperm donor, turned up at the house. I didn't know at that time who he was. She tried to fob him off and wouldn't let him in, and when I heard her voice getting angry and a bit of a commotion, I went to the door to sort it out.

'I was looking at an older version of me.' Peter gulped, as though reliving the moment. 'He looked taken aback, too; clearly, he hadn't known I existed. There was an almighty row and he left. Nan started to cry and said that my mum – Rachel – had always refused to reveal who my father was, and it wasn't until I had showed up at the door that she realised. That was why she had looked so shocked.

'Nan showed me some old photographs of my mum. There were a few of my mum's sister, Leah, and *him*, but none of my mum and *him* together. Nan said that there would be a problem when Leah found out – and there was. She dropped in a few days later and there was a screaming match. She called my mother a lot of names. A hypocritical slut being one of them!'

He took a few more sips of his coffee then continued. 'Nan phoned my mum, who lives in Australia. Whatever my mum said, my nan cried even more but she wouldn't tell me. She just said that my mum didn't want to make contact with me, and she was very sorry. I offered to leave but Nan said that she wanted me to stay and I had more right to be there than either my father or Leah. I met my cousins, Sarah and Gordon – I look quite like them, too – as they came round to Nan's house quite a lot. They were nice to me.

'Nan worked as a housekeeper in the Watch House at the edge of the Point, so one day I went there with her as she needed help to take curtains down for washing. I learned later that the owner was my father's cousin, but I never actually met him; he was always away in Dublin or someplace else.

'The house was beautiful. While I was helping Nan, I looked out of the window and saw the most beautiful creature I have ever seen, lying on the grass. She was wearing shorts and a t-shirt and had long, dark brown hair. She turned round, saw me, and let out a scream. Nan ran outside to reassure her, and she came in and introduced herself as Rachel. She was studying for her 'O' level exams which were coming up. I was tongue-tied. I had never been good at chatting to girls.'

***

Peter's eyes took on a faraway look as he recalled his time with Rachel, and Sean and Dougie were left in no doubt how much he'd loved the girl. 'I saw her a few days later walking back from the village shop. I had been walking along the coast path from Bangor, where I had got a part-time job working in a record shop. It was a beautiful June day and I was just turning into the Point when I saw her up ahead. I didn't have time to turn around when she saw me.' He smiled. 'She was very excited. She had just sat her first exam that day and it had gone well. She asked me how my job was going and I asked her how she knew I had a job. She laughed and said my nan had told her. She said she would pop into the record shop that weekend with her friends. My heart skipped a beat. I wished her luck for the rest of her exams and walked on, but I couldn't wait for Saturday.

'She did come into the store that day with two of her friends – Linda and Jenny. They were nice girls, too. I was leaving the shop at 5.30, and since it was a nice night I decided to walk back along the coast road. She was standing at the bottom of Main Street. When she saw me, she laughed and said, "I guessed you would come this way." We walked back along the coast road together, through Ballyholme and along Ballymacormick Point. She chatted so easily, and asked me loads of questions. I told her I was adopted and she told me about her mum being killed.

'When we reached the turnstile that led out onto the Point, she stopped. "Have you ever kissed a girl?" she asked me. I was embarrassed but said no. "Can I be your first then?" she asked, looking up at me. I bent down and kissed her. She pulled my head down and we stood there for a couple of minutes kissing. Her lips were soft and her mouth warm. I could feel things happening to me. "How about we meet here every night at 6.30 on your way home from work?" she suggested.

'I was delighted. I couldn't wait until work finished every night, and I practically ran the whole way home. She was always there waiting for me. She would watch for me from her bedroom window then leave the house in time to meet me. We would sit there talking and kissing, hidden from view. She said I helped her to manage her stress during her exams, and she helped me to gain confidence in myself. I loved her.' He gulped. 'For her 16th birthday I bought her a silver seahorse necklace and a yellow t-shirt dress she had admired. I couldn't afford much, but she was delighted.'

Peter's smile of reminiscence faded and his eyebrows lowered into a frown as he went on. 'Nan would go into Bangor every Wednesday night for the dance that was held at Pickie Park on the seafront. One Wednesday I was getting ready to go out to meet Rachel when Barry arrived at Nan's house, carrying a six-pack of beer. He told me we needed a man-to-man talk. I said I was going out, but he didn't listen. He just sat down, opened his beer, and put his feet up on the table. I didn't know what to do.

'He asked me, "Got a girlfriend?" I shook my head. I didn't want him to know about Rachel; I didn't want anyone to know, or it would be spoiled. "You're not some poofter, are you?" was his reply. I was embarrassed, but shook my head again. "What's wrong with you, then? At your age I had the girls fighting over me." I said nothing, then he leaned forward. "I mean, your mother and her sister. Well, I have to admit your mother was the much better looking one, but your aunt... well, she was easy. An easy lay. Tricked me into marrying her by telling me there was a kid on the way, when there wasn't. Still, I have two kids now... Three, including you."

'I looked at him, wanting to know more about my mother. "What about my mother?" I asked him. "I would have married Rachel if I'd known a kid was on board, but she ran away before I knew!" "Why did she run?" I asked. "In those days, it was a big shame on a girl if she got pregnant before she got married. She wouldn't have been able to face that cow of a mother of hers."

'I tried not to show that I was annoyed. "Do you mean my nan?" I asked. "Aye, that old witch!" "But my nan knew about me," I blurted out, not thinking. "She came and visited me every year. She arranged my adoption." He exploded in anger and jumped up. "She what! That fecking old cow. I'll bloody kill her!"

'I wasn't having that. "You leave her alone," I said. I was as tall as him, but he probably weighed a couple of stone heavier than me. Just then there was a knock on the door. My heart sank. It was Rachel. I was late meeting her.

'I made for the door, but he tripped me and I fell heavily. I got up quickly but my lip was bleeding. He opened the door. "Why if it isn't the beautiful young Rachel Fitzpatrick!" he said sarcastically. "Does Daddy know you're here?" Rachel looked at me standing there embarrassed, my lip bleeding. "Your dad wouldn't be too happy at you slumming it with my son!" he told her. "Can't have any interbreeding going on."

'There was no hiding the shock on Rachel's face. "Your son?" she asked, then she looked at me. "He's your dad? He's my dad's cousin." I could only nod. "Oh, so we have incest in the family?" he taunted, taking another mouthful of beer. He was leering at her. It was disgusting. "It's not incest," she told him. "Not how your dad will view it, young lady." He was laughing, enjoying some part of this that I didn't know or understand.

'Rachel turned to go. I called after her to wait, and made to go with her. "Just like your mother, you are. Running away." He laughed at her again. But she stopped and turned to glare at him. "My mother?" She was indignant, her eyes were blazing. "Aye," he said, enjoying himself. "How did you know my mother?" she demanded. "Let's just say, your dad was away a lot of nights and it got mighty lonely over in that big house." He gave that leering smile again.

'Rachel was furious. "You're sick!" she screamed at him. "I can't imagine anyone wanting you." He just grinned back and licked his lips. "Yes, you've got her spirit alright!" he said. Rachel turned to leave and as she was almost out the door, he shouted after her, "Who's the daddy?"'

Peter stopped talking.

'Another coffee? Or a glass of water, Peter?' Sean offered, realizing that the young man was struggling with his memories.

'Water, please,' he replied. Dougie got up and went over to the counter. He returned minutes later with a glass of iced water.

'Thanks,' the younger man said gratefully, and took a few sips.

'Go on, please,' Sean said gently. 'What happened next?'

'Rachel ran and ran. When I caught up with her, she was crying. I tried to put my arms around her, but she pushed me away. "No!" she shouted. "What if... what if he is my father?" "He's not. He can't be!" I tried to reassure her. "But you don't know!" She was really distraught. "You don't know!" Rachel ran off home. I didn't follow her. I was frightened.

'The next night she wasn't at the rocks, nor the next or the next. I learned that she had gone away with some of her school friends. I moped around. Nan kept asking me what was wrong, but I couldn't tell her. As the summer holidays were coming to an end, Rachel came back, but I didn't see her. She never left the house on her own, and I didn't have the courage to go to her house.

'It was a Thursday night, near the end of September. The nights were drawing in. I had come in from work and was sitting watching the TV, but not really paying attention to it. Nan came in, turned the TV off, and sat down. "Right, my lad, tell me what is going on with you," she said. I wouldn't look at her. "Okay, I'll ask you again. What is it?" she pressed me. "Is it that young Rachel?" I couldn't meet her eyes. "Her stepmother is worried about her. She's stopped going out. All she does is sit in her room and study. Now don't tell me you two weren't friendly." I nodded. "Did you break her heart, lad?" she asked. I shrugged.

'There was a pause then Nan looked worried, as if realising what the trouble might be. "She's not pregnant, is she?" I jumped up. "No, Nan. No, we never... We never did anything like that!" "Thank God for that," she said with a sigh of relief. "Well, whatever it is can't be that bad." I sat back down and started to tell her about what had happened the last night that I had seen Rachel. Nan was furious. "Dear God, I will fecking kill that man!" she said. And she probably would have. "Listen to me, and listen good," she said. "There is no way on earth that he could be Rachel's father. None whatsoever, and I know!" She was adamant.

'I was puzzled. "How can you be so sure?" I asked. She smiled at me. "Rachel was a honeymoon baby. They got married in the USA in June, and spent their time travelling over that summer. They came back in mid-September and Louisa was just pregnant. She had the worst morning sickness I had ever seen, so I knew from very early on because I was looking after her." Relief washed over me. "And secondly," she went on, "that father of yours was doing some time at Her Majesty's Pleasure, so he was not about. He was gone until Rachel must have been about eighteen months old. When he came back, he wasn't long before he was playing with that stupid daughter of mine, Leah. She thought she had got herself a good catch! She couldn't be told."

'I could see an opportunity to ask more about my own circumstances. "What about my mum?" I asked. "Peter," she said sadly, "I don't know how to tell you about her. She was a lovely girl. Wanted to be a nurse. She is a nurse now." "Please, Nan, please tell me why she abandoned me. I mean my adoptive parents were just the best, but I have always wondered." "She didn't abandon you," Nan said, "not in the way you think. I didn't know the whole story until recently – she wouldn't tell me – but your mum was coming home from the youth club at the church hall one Friday night. She was a good Christian girl, never gave me a moment's worry." She stopped and wiped her eyes. "Your father... she was walking back... he started to walk with her, chatting to her. He asked her out. She said no. She was sixteen and he was about twenty-four, I think. The following week he was waiting for her. The lane beside the church. He raped her." Nan started to cry.'

Peter took a few gulps of his iced water. 'Nan said, "I never knew. She came home, had a bath and went to bed. A few weeks later, she realised she was pregnant. She didn't believe in abortion. She didn't tell me who he was, or what had happened. I sent her to my sister-in-law's house in Liverpool, away from prying eyes. When you were born, she had severe post-natal depression. The adoption was for the best. Initially, you were put into care, but then your adoptive mum and dad offered to take you. She begged me... begged me to tell no-one she was pregnant. And I didn't. I just thought she was ashamed. She didn't tell me about the rape until the night you turned up here a couple of months ago. I phoned her when I realised who your father was. That's why... that's why she has never been able to meet you." I cried then. That man had destroyed so many lives. I hated him. I was determined to kill him, but first I would have to let Rachel know the truth.

'The next day I took the day off work and waited for her getting off the bus. I handed her a note then went to sit at the rain shelter near the harbour to wait for her. It had started to rain and the wind was howling. A storm was brewing off the sea, but there wasn't anywhere else we could meet. She turned up after about half an hour, and I told her what my nan had said. I told her everything. About how she had been a honeymoon baby, and about my own mum. She cried. I put my arms around her to comfort her, then I kissed her. She responded at first, but then then she pulled away and ran back towards the harbour.

'I ran after her. I begged her to give me another chance, but she said she couldn't. She said every time she would look at me, she would think of that evil man. She was sorry and asked me to forgive her. But I understood. I took one last look at her and then walked away. I left her standing there on the pier and walked back to Nan's. I didn't see anyone. I couldn't. I was crying my heart out.

'When I got back to my nan's house, I was soaked. She made me have a hot bath, and she put my clothes in the washing machine and made me hot chocolate. I told her what Rachel had said. She was angry that I had left Rachel down at the pier in the bad weather, and went to put her coat on when the phone rang. It was Rachel's step-mum. She said Rachel was missing and she was worried.'

Peter's hands shook as he lifted the glass to his lips. 'They found Rachel's body the next morning. I looked into my nan's eyes and swore on the Holy Bible that Rachel had been alive when I left her. She believed me, and it's the truth.' He looked directly into Sean's eyes. 'I would never have hurt her. I loved her.

'I was going to go to the funeral, but when I reached the church I saw my father there, dressed in black, mourning the death of the beautiful girl he had taunted. He was standing behind Rachel's father. I stood at the edge of the cemetery as her coffin was lowered into the ground. I just wanted to get in beside her.' Peter's voice broke and his hand shook slightly as he held onto the glass. 'I didn't go back to the house afterwards; it didn't seem right. Instead, I walked from Bangor to Groomsport, as we had done many times. I sat in our little nook and remembered the girl I had loved. I swore that I would never love another woman.

'When I went back to Nan's that night, there was an almighty row going on in the sitting room, between my dad and Leah and my nan! I caught the tail end of what was being shouted. "He pushed her. I saw him. He pushed her. I tried to save her. I did. I tried to save her." It was his voice. Then I heard Nan. "So you were there that night?" He realised that he had said too much, and didn't answer. Nan asked him again, "Tell me now, were you there when that child died?" He didn't answer her. "Why were you there?" Nan demanded. "Were you spying on that family again?" He still said nothing.

'Then Nan shouted, "You better get out, the pair of you. Don't come anywhere near me or Peter ever again." "I'll stop you seeing my kids!" Leah threatened, but Nan gave a harsh laugh. "That's a joke," she said. She sounded furious. "They wouldn't recognise you as any kind of fit mother." "Oh yes, I am not the holier-than-thou daughter, am I? The one that got herself pregnant at sixteen!" Leah's voice was sneering. "Ask your husband about that," Nan replied. "Ask him what really happened! Go on."

'I stayed in the kitchen listening. There was a brief silence, and then I heard Leah demand, "What does she mean?" Then there was the sound of a slap. "Shut up!" His voice again. "Go on," Nan taunted, "tell her. Tell her how you raped her sister on her way home from the church, down the church lane. Yes, what a big man you are. She was sixteen, for God's sake!" Then Leah started screaming. "You raped her? You raped her?" There was a thud, as if someone had been pushed over, and Leah's screams sounded more like a whimper. "I never raped her," he shouted. "She was gagging for it, always flirting around me. But that night she got what she really wanted." Leah wasn't giving up. She shouted back, "No way. That wasn't our Rachel. She wouldn't have looked twice at you and that's what goaded you, I bet. You thought you were the big man and every woman fancied you. You make me sick, you bastard." There was the sound of another hard slap, then a few minutes of silence before he replied. "Bitch!" he screamed. "Well, no woman has ever made a fool of me again. And I made sure that wee slut hasn't made a fool of my son."

'I couldn't hold myself back any longer, and burst into the room at that point. "You did what?" I demanded. "Oh, here's lover boy!" he laughed, and started to taunt me that he had seen Rachel. He claimed she had pushed past him, and he had warned her to leave his son alone or there would be consequences. He said she had laughed at him and said he didn't deserve to be anyone's father. "She slapped me, the little bitch, so I slapped her back and she fell, hitting her head. She was dead, and there was nothing to be done, so I lifted her body up and threw her off the pier."

'I couldn't contain my fury. I punched him with every ounce of strength I had. He went down hard, and I started kicking him, everywhere I could. His head, his stomach, anywhere. He wasn't getting up anytime soon. It took all my nan and Leah's strength to get me to stop.'

Peter's body was rigid, as though he was reliving the fight. 'Nan spat on his face and told him to get out. She said if he came near her family again, she would go to the police and tell them everything. He struggled to his feet, then he said, "Aye well. It gets easier every time. You go to the police, and I'll just say that I had reason to believe she was my daughter and I tried to stop them, as it was incest. There was a row, and I saw him push her off the rocks. Go on, stir the hornet's nest!"

'Nan seemed shocked at his callousness. There was no remorse, he didn't care how many lives he ruined. "It's not true, no-one will believe you," she told him. "Maybe," he said, hobbling to the door, "but it will make life difficult for him. And the Army won't touch him then, either." When he left, Nan told Leah to get out, too. "You've made your bed," she said. "You better go and lie in it, too." When they left, Nan crumpled. She kept moaning, "Oh God, that poor child, and you... You poor child."

'The next day I left and enlisted in the Army. I kept in touch with my nan, but I never came back. Until now. I haven't been in the same room as him since that night, but he wouldn't leave me alone. He kept writing to me when I was in the Army. First of all, he said that he hadn't hurt Rachel, it had been the drink talking. He kept saying I owed him a favour, and he would call it in. The letters just kept coming. I stopped reading them. Then, about a year ago, I stupidly read a letter. He said he had "saved" lots of Rachels over the years, as recompense for his sins.

'I was stressed and worried. I was due to be deployed again to Afghanistan, but his words kept haunting me. I was staying at Sarah's house for a few days in Godalming. We've kept in touch since she moved there. Anyway, there was a storm, and I've always hated storms since that night Rachel died. There was a crash of thunder and I went indoors. On the TV was a police officer asking if anyone had any information about a missing girl. She was sixteen. They put a photo up on the screen, and she had long brown hair and was wearing a yellow t-shirt. I lost it. I just lost it. I left their house. I was terrified that he had done it again. I went back to the barracks. I probably shouldn't have been driving my bike, but I had to get away.'

Peter stopped talking, then looked searchingly at Sean and Dougie. 'I expect you know what happened to Colonel Smith's wife?' he asked. They nodded.

'It was a few days later, and I was still wound up by it all.' He looked down at his hands, embarrassed at the events of that day.

'But, Peter, there's a different theory about that incident,' Sean said, and offered Catriona's suggested scenario. Peter shook his head. 'I could never be trusted again,' he said, his voice almost a whisper.

'Where did you go when you were discharged from the Army?' Sean asked.

'I went to stay up in Scotland on a farm belonging to an old ex-colleague who asked no questions. I was there until about two months ago.'

Dougie noted down the details so that they could confirm Peter's story later.

'So why did you come back to Belfast?'

'I wanted to see Nan again. When I left the Army, all my post was forwarded to Nan's house in Groomsport, so when I arrived there was a letter from *him* in amongst all the other stuff. It said that he had found the first Rachel back in Groomsport, the one that got away, and now it was her time.

He finished the letter by asking if I'd be able to save her this time. I had no idea what it was all about, but I couldn't let it happen to another family. I had every intention of killing him, so I've been hiding out at Nan's old house.

'One morning I was looking down at the Watch House, and I saw a man. At first I thought it was Hugh Fitzpatrick, but then another man came out and I realised it was Barry.'

'When was this?' asked Sean.

'Probably the end of June, early July. About a week or so later, I saw a woman and a man at the house. To be honest, I got a shock. The girl looked like Rachel might have, had she lived, with her long dark hair. I've been watching the house since and the couple have visited again.

'When they left the last time, I noticed a car had been sitting on the Point and then it followed them. I realised it was Barry driving, so I got on my motorbike to follow him, and that was the evening I saw the police chasing through the garden.

'I've been watching the house since then but I haven't seen that man back there. Well, not in a car anyway. He could get round the back, if he walked from Ballyholme. I've noticed lights going on in different rooms, even though I am pretty sure Hugh Fitzpatrick has been away, so I was going to do some night surveillance and have a closer look. But now that Nan's ill, she is my priority.' He looked at his watch. 'Do you think I might be able to see her now?'

Sean checked his own watch. It was 5pm. 'Why don't you go and ask? I'll need you to make a formal statement, but that can be done later.'

Dougie went with Peter to check on Hilda's condition, while Sean headed outside to make some calls. It was time to speak to Hugh Fitzpatrick, but first he wanted to check that Megan was safe.

Before he could contact Kieran, his mobile rang with a call from Catriona.

'Hi, boss, the incident room has traced the other vehicle that was following Kieran and Megan's car,' she said excitedly. 'The first car had stolen licence plates. It was registered as off the road, so our guys checked out the owner. The car was locked away in a garage under cover and hadn't been used in 2-3 years.'

'And the other one?' asked Sean.

'The second one was a hire car, hired three days ago from Dublin Airport by two Americans – Colin Fairburn and Thomas Kells.'

'Should the names ring a bell?' Sean was puzzled.

'Thomas is Rachel Fitzpatrick's step-brother. His mother is Arabella Fullerton, as she is now.'

'Hmm, why would he be in town now?'

Catriona told Sean the two men were staying in a hotel not far from Groomsport.

'Well, I think Dougie and I need to pay them a visit. Anything on the bag contents?'

'Not yet, boss,' Catriona replied. 'The letters and the journal are being analysed, as we speak, and Forensics have recovered fingerprints on the letters so they are checking them out now. Hopefully, we should have some results soon.'

Chapter Twenty-Two
American tourists?

Seaview Hotel, Bangor - 6.20pm

As Dougie pulled into the hotel car park, Sean wondered aloud why the two Americans might be in town.

'Hard to say, boss. Perhaps his mother called him after we went to see her in ...' Dougie suggested. 'Maybe he wants to find out what happened all those years ago and—'

Sean's phone bleeped with a text. It was from Catriona. *Just a heads-up, boss. Colin Fairburn is an ex US marine.*

Sean read the message out to Dougie with a wry smile. 'That might change things a little,' he said.

A brief word with the young receptionist in the hotel entrance told them that the two guests were in the bar. She discreetly pointed them out.

'Mr Thomas Kells and Mr Colin Fairburn, I believe?' Sean approached their table in the corner of the snug room.

'Yes, who's asking?' They said, both standing up.

Sean showed them his ID. 'Please sit down, and if you have any weapons, please hand them over now.'

'We're not carrying anything,' said Thomas indignantly.

Sean nodded and sat down at their table. 'My name is Detective Chief Inspector Sean Maloney, of the Police Service of Northern Ireland. I'd like to know why after all these years you felt it was the time to visit your old home, Mr Kells?'

'Does every visitor get such a warm welcome, officer?' Thomas asked sarcastically.

'That depends on their reason for being here, sir,' Sean replied pleasantly.

'We're on holiday,' said Thomas.

'Good. We welcome tourists. But can I ask why you might have been following a car on Tuesday night, up into an area where tourists don't normally go?'

Thomas looked at Colin, who shook his head. Neither men answered.

'Don't be saying now that you got lost,' Sean went on with a smile, 'because your car was tracked from Groomsport – your old home village – up to Belfast and beyond, at a time of night when most tourists are in the bar or in bed.' Neither man spoke.

***

'Now to help jog your memories, you could have been looking for Hugh Fitzpatrick, your stepfather... or Barry Fitzpatrick, his cousin... or Peter Adams, your late stepsister's boyfriend... or—'

'He wasn't her boyfriend,' snapped Thomas, clenching his fist and tightening his jaw. 'He's a cold-blooded murderer.'

'Who exactly?' asked Sean.

'Peter Adams,' replied Thomas.

'Now what makes you say that?' asked Sean, looking surprised.

'He murdered my sister... my stepsister, Rachel.' The man's voice cracked with emotion.

'Where and when might that have been?'

'The night she died, I saw Rachel leaving the house,' he began. 'I asked her where she was going but she said she wouldn't be long. I was frightened, because there was a big storm coming, but I saw her running towards the harbour. I got the binoculars from upstairs and saw her waiting in the rain shelter waiting for someone. Then Peter turned up. I knew she was friends with him, although my mum and my stepfather didn't.

'They walked down to the pier, and I saw Peter kiss her then she pushed Peter away. A car drove into the car park, and it looked like Hugh's, my stepfather, so I turned the binoculars to look closer. A man got out, but I couldn't see his face, he had a big anorak pulled up over his head. When I moved the binoculars back towards the pier, Rachel and Peter were nowhere to be seen.'

Thomas paused.

'Go on, please, sir,' Sean said quietly.

'I waited for her to come in, because I knew Mum would go mad if she knew Rachel was out. She was meant to be in her room studying. When it got to nine o'clock I told Mum that Rachel wasn't in her room, and she started to phone round some of her friends. Eventually she phoned the police, then called Hugh in Dublin.

'We sat up all night waiting... just waiting,' Thomas stopped to wipe a stray tear running down his cheek. 'Next morning they found her body.' He coughed gently to clear his throat. 'I told Mum that it was Peter Adams, but she said that Mrs Adams, our cleaner, had said he had been at home with her all evening.

'Hugh's cousin, Barry Fitzpatrick, must have heard our conversation and that afternoon he grabbed me by the arm and told me to stop spreading lies about Peter. He said if I didn't stop, he would get into the house one night when Mum and I were alone, and cut our throats. He said if I didn't believe him, I was to think about what had happened to my dog. He smiled when he said it and then laughed.' Thomas shuddered at the memory. 'After that, I never mentioned Peter again.'

'What happened to your dog?' asked Sean.

'I've no idea. He never came back,' replied Thomas. 'I was thirteen, and I was terrified that was what would happen to me.'

'You didn't mention this to your mum?'

'No. Barry had been unpleasant to her, too. She tried to get Hugh to stop him calling round, but he never did anything about it and in the end Mum and Hugh split up and she left with me. I... I had a nervous breakdown.' He paused again, trying to regain his composure. 'I tried to kill myself, and was admitted to hospital for a while. When Mum mentioned that the police had been to visit her recently, I felt...' he looked across the table at his friend, 'we both felt it was time to close this chapter off.'

'Can you be absolutely sure it was Peter?' Dougie asked.

'No doubt!'

'And did you see him throw Rachel into the sea, or hit her?'

'No, but... she wouldn't have killed herself!' he shouted.

'You say you saw a car pulling into the car park?' Sean said.

'Yes, I don't know what type it was exactly, but it looked similar to my father's... Hugh's.'

'Could you identify the driver?' Sean asked hopefully.

Thomas shook his head. 'I don't think so.'

'So instead of it being Peter who killed Rachel, could it have been someone else... for example, the person in the car?'

'Well, I don't know.' Thomas was flustered. 'For years I've believed it was Peter Adams. And why would Barry threaten me if it wasn't him?'

'Were you at Mrs Adam's house the other night?' Sean continued questioning.

'Yes, but we were told she didn't live there any more and it was sold a long time ago.'

'Have you spoken to or seen Hugh Fitzpatrick since you have been back?'

Thomas shook his head again. 'We saw him leave the house. We were sitting on the bench on the green when he walked past. He didn't know me.' The young man's voice cracked again, his shoulder slumped. 'Why would he, after all these years?'

'Do you intend to see or speak to Hugh Fitzpatrick during this visit?' Dougie asked.

'I've nothing to say to him. I know he lost his daughter, but he also lost his son. Only, he clearly didn't consider me to be that, did he?'

'What are your plans for the rest of your holiday?' asked Sean. There was no reply. 'Did you honestly think that Peter Adams would break down and confess to you?' He looked at the two visitors, shaking his head scornfully. 'Peter Adams is a decorated trained combat soldier who has carried out tours of duty in hell-holes around the world. Does that tell you something about the man you think you can take on?'

The two younger men looked surprised. It was clear they had no real knowledge of the man they had planned to track down and confront.

'I suspect that a highly skilled soldier, SAS-trained, would outgun you both... US Marine or not, with all due respect.' Sean's exasperation was obvious. He didn't need former militia taking on their own mission.

'So, gentlemen,' he said, standing up. 'Let me strongly suggest that you take yourselves off to Bushmills or the Mournes, and see some of this beautiful country, or go and visit your mother. If for any reason at all, I find you within five miles of Peter Adams and his family, then you will be visiting one of our highly respected establishments. One where you won't hold the key to the door. Do I make myself clear?' He waited til both men nodded their acknowledgement before he and Dougie left.

***

When Dougie and Sean were five minutes away from the police headquarters, they received a call to confirm that Colonel Robbie Smith and his wife, Rachel, had arrived at the city airport.

'Have them taken straight to the hospital, please, and I will meet them there,' Sean instructed.

When the couple arrived, Sean and Dougie led them to a side room, close to where Hilda Adams was being monitored.

'Sorry, Sean,' Robbie Smith apologised, 'but Rachel absolutely insisted on coming. She believes Peter will listen to her.'

'You could be right,' Sean admitted, shaking hands with his friend's wife. 'Make yourselves comfortable and I will get him.'

When Sean gently opened the door to Hilda's room, she was asleep but Peter was sitting by her bedside.

'Peter, would you mind coming with me for a few minutes. There's a couple of people I would like you to meet,' he said. The younger man followed him.

When Peter was led into the side room, he immediately snapped to attention when he saw his former colonel. But when Rachel Smith put out her arms to hug him, Peter recoiled in shock. He started to stammer an apology, but Rachel shook her head.

She held his hand as she and her husband tried to explain to Peter what they believed had happened on the day of the BBQ.

'I'm sorry this has taken so long,' Colonel Smith told him, 'but I'd like to put you in touch with one of the Army doctors who specialises in post-traumatic stress. I think he will be able to help you moving forward. Will you let us help you?'

As Peter nodded, there was a tap on the door and a nurse entered.

'I'm sorry,' she said. 'But Hilda is awake and she is a little concerned that her grandson has left.'

Peter stood to leave, then invited the Colonel and Mrs Smith to come and meet his gran. Sean waited until all the introductions had been made, then made his excuses to leave.

When he returned to the office, the experts were still working their way through the letters and the diary which Hilda had given them.

And the investigation team had been carefully reviewing the timeline they had created based on the letters from Barry to Peter, matching the dates, postmarks and locations with their knowledge of the crimes that had been committed across the country.

Everything seemed to point to Barry Fitzgerald. But where was he?

Chapter Twenty-Three
Where is Megan?

Malone Road, Belfast - Tuesday, August 4. 7pm

K ieran was finishing for the day. The oak kitchen that he had designed with the owner was almost complete. The deadline was tight to have it finished before the end of the summer holidays, but it was almost done. Kieran liked to keep his hand in by doing some of the hands-on work himself; he loved the challenge of putting the different parts together; the feel of the wood.

He was going to bring Megan to see the kitchen when it was finished, as he was sure something similar would look fabulous in the new house and he was keen to see if she agreed. Kieran smiled to himself. He couldn't believe his luck at meeting Megan on a plane just a couple of months before.

He knew she was the one for him, he just needed to give her time to realise it, too. The ringtone of his mobile snapped him out of his daydreams.

'Hi, bro, where are you?' Sean sounded cheerful, but his tone was far from casual.

'I'm still at work finishing the kitchen off over near Newtownards. Why?'

'Where's your girl this evening?'

'I got confirmation today that my offer for the house in Groomsport has been accepted, so she offered to go down and get some measurements. You know what women are like!' He laughed, remembering Megan's excitement at helping to choose colour samples and furniture for his new home. 'I am going to meet her there in an hour when I finish here.'

Sean swore quietly under his breath. 'Do you mind giving her a quick ring and check if she's still there? Nothing to worry about, but we would like to talk to her about a couple of details.'

'Sure. I'll call her now and get back to you.' Kieran hung up, then dialled Megan's number. It was ringing but she wasn't picking up. He texted her. No response. He called Sean back.

'She's not picking up.' Kieran could feel a fluttering in the pit of his stomach. 'Is there a reason to be concerned?'

Sean tried to sound reassuring. 'Probably not, but let me check and I'll call you back.' He ended the call and grabbed his jacket. 'Call Hugh Fitzpatrick, see if Megan Scott is with him,' Sean barked at his team. 'And call the boys in Groomsport. Tell them to get over to the house as quickly as possible, to check everything is okay.'

Two minutes later, Dougie shouted to him. 'Boss, Hugh Fitzpatrick is on the line.'

'Professor Fitzpatrick,' Sean began, 'I'm sorry to bother you, but is Megan Scott with you?'

'Yes, yes, she is right here. Do you want to speak to her?' Hugh was clearly taken aback at the call.

'Please,' said Sean, hugely relieved. He waited while Hugh Fitzpatrick called Megan and she came on the line. 'Hi Megan, Sean here. We were just concerned about your whereabouts.'

'Sean, what's going on?' she asked.

'I'll explain when I get there. Can you put Hugh back on, please?'

Megan handed the receiver back to Hugh with a shrug of her shoulders, then went to her bag. Her mobile showed five missed calls from Kieran. She called him.

'Thank God!' he said, not attempting to hide his relief. 'Are you okay?'

'Yes, I'm fine,' she said, puzzled. 'Do you know what is going on?'

'No, but stay there. I'll be there in less than thirty minutes!'

Replacing the receiver, Hugh looked anxiously at Meg, then walked over to the window. The lighthouse on the Copeland Islands was flashing; the fog siren was being sounded; the night was drawing in. Hugh could see a small motorboat, but couldn't make out if it was coming towards the house or leaving it.

'Do you know what is going on, Professor?' Megan asked, her gaze following his out of the window. She shivered when she saw the fog coming in. She wouldn't want to be out on a boat on a night like this.

'Let me just check something first,' Hugh Fitzpatrick replied. He went and checked that both front and back doors were locked, then went into his study and took a small handgun from his desk drawer and tucked it carefully in the back of his belt, hidden under his jumper.

Returning to the living room, he looked out the window again towards the Copeland Islands. He saw the small boat heading away from the house, and sighed with relief.

'Let's sit down and I'll tell you what I know,' he said. 'In 1805, a ship was sailing from Belfast to Demerara, in South

America. On board was the usual cargo of candles, linen, soaps. But also about one hundred human slaves, worth about £2.5 million pounds.

'Slaves from Africa?' asked Meg, astonished.

'No, my dear. About one hundred and fifty years before the African slave trade, there was a very lucrative business in Irish slaves which went on for centuries. Men, women, and children – families. Anyone getting into trouble or failing to pay their rent could find themselves being sent as a slave.'

Megan gasped. 'I had no idea! How awful for them being crammed into a ship to be taken to God-knows-where.'

'The ship they were on was one of the last to leave these shores before the Slave Trade Act abolished slavery,' the professor went on. 'For some reason, they had to stop at Groomsport for some repairs before the vessel made its treacherous journey to the Caribbean. The human cargo had to be taken off the ship; at least, the women and children were. There was a revolt and a number of them escaped. Most were quickly recaptured, except for a woman and two men. The woman's name was Rachel.'

'How do you know all this?' asked Megan.

'It's part of the research I do,' he said. 'It's how I met my first wife, too.'

Megan nodded, keen for him to continue.

'The other reason I know so much information is that the junior customs officer, based here, kept a diary. We had to fix the old chimney after a fire took hold, not long after I bought the house, and his diary was found in a tin box buried in the old chimney. Some of the book was unreadable, but what I could make out was that the junior officer found Rachel. He managed to hide her for several days.'

'Were they caught? I mean, Rachel and the customs officer?'

'Yes, I'm afraid they were. The customs officer was called Barry Fitzpatrick. The pair had managed to take a small boat and row over to the Copeland Islands, but the senior customs officer, who had come under suspicion, told on them. He had probably been threatened that he and his family would be put on the boat – a punishment that would mean certain death for some of his family.'

'That's dreadful.'

'Yes. It was a crime to harbour a fugitive, or to help a slave to escape. The couple were brought back to Groomsport – to this house, in fact. Barry was put in the ship to replace one of the men that had escaped, and the ship sailed the next day. The senior customs officer later found Barry's diary and made the final entry himself. He then buried the journal behind a brick in the chimney of the house. According to his entry, the last words that Barry ever spoke as he was led away, were: "I should have saved her!" The senior customs officer added a note that he prayed for their souls.'

Megan sat quietly for a few minutes, clearly digesting the tragic story before she replied. 'Your daughter was called Rachel, wasn't she?'

'Yes. Yes, she was. I was following up on the story in the Caribbean to see if I could find out what happened to the couple. When I was there, I met my wife, Rachel's mother. She would be described as a "mulatto" – a derogatory term now for someone who comes from a white parent and a black parent. In her case, an African woman and a white Irish father. They were forced to interbreed, even though it was illegal.'

'Did you ever find out what happened to Rachel and Barry?'

'It seems Rachel died on the voyage. Because he was educated, Barry was used by the captain to keep records of the ship, but he was still a slave. When they finally reached the Caribbean, he was handed over to the plantation land owner. He died five years later. Many of those taken from this land didn't survive well in the heat and conditions.'

'So what has this to do with now?' asked Megan, her brow wrinkled in confusion.

'I have a cousin with the same name – Barry Fitzpatrick. He is not a direct relation of the customs officer, though he likes to pretend he is the reincarnation.'

Megan didn't know how to reply. She was unsettled at the story, and beginning to feel a little concerned.

'He was with me when we found the diary,' Professor Fitzpatrick went on. 'Barry was fascinated with this house and the diary. He always resented the fact I had this house. He even tried one day to see if he could row from here to the Copeland Islands, to prove that if it was him, he could have saved the slave girl, Rachel.'

'Why was he resentful?' asked Megan, uncomfortable about discussing such close family matters.

'Our grandfather owned a large farm estate and left most of his wealth to my father, his second born. Although the older child, Barry's mother – as the daughter – wouldn't inherit anything. My father was never a farmer, so he sold the farm and made a lot of money, as it is where lots of new houses were built. My aunt resented this, believing she should have been allowed to farm the land. Unfortunately, she suffered severe post-natal depression after Barry was born and again with Barry's younger sister.' Hugh took a deep breath and shook his head. 'Barry's sister died whilst still an infant, and his mother ended up killing both her husband and herself. Barry came to live with us, but sadly all the trauma and resentment got handed down to him. To be fair, it wasn't usually an issue unless he had been drinking, or if someone had upset him. I'm afraid he believes the world owes him.' Hugh Fitzpatrick shook his head sadly. 'We haven't spoken since my daughter died.'

'Your cousin...' Megan began haltingly. 'Does... does he have a scar on his left hand – a burn scar here?' She pointed to her left hand, just above the wrist.

'Yes, he does. He burnt it at some camp fire, I believe. It was around the time of my wife's death, as I remember it being bandaged at her funeral.' He looked away, as though gripped by a sad memory, then swiftly turned his attention back on Megan. 'How did you know he had a scar?' he asked. 'Do you know him?'

Before she could answer, the house phone rang. They both jumped.

Hugh picked up the receiver. 'Yes, yes,' he said. 'I'll open the door.'

A few minutes later, he returned to the living room with Sean Maloney and his two colleagues, Dougie and Catriona.

'Professor, Megan,' Sean began. 'Glad to see you are both alright.'

'You know each other then?' Hugh looked confused.

'Yes, this young lady could well be my future sister-in-law,' Sean explained, and winked at Megan. She gave a gentle laugh, a warm blush creeping over her cheeks.

Sean's smile faded, and his tone became more formal. 'Professor... a question, please. Is there a place your cousin would run and hide, or someone that he would stay with?'

'Actually, Detective, I have a number of questions myself tonight,' he replied. 'But to answer your question, yes, he would take himself off in a small boat and go over to the Copeland Islands. He would either camp or stay on one of the derelict houses. He often used my old car and would leave it parked in the old outhouse at the bottom of the garden, then take the little boat out from the harbour. The car is still there, as far as I know. I never got round to getting rid of it after I left here, following my daughter's death. I haven't been in that garage for years.'

Sean nodded at Catriona and Dougie, and the pair quietly left the room.

They had no sooner gone than the door burst open and Kieran rushed in. With anxious eyes only for Megan, he went quickly to her side and pulled her into his arms.

No-one spoke for a few moments, then Hugh Fitzpatrick gave a gentle cough. 'My dear,' he said, smiling kindly at Megan. 'You asked if my cousin had a scar. How would you know that?'

Megan's hand flew to her mouth and she looked straight at Sean, who nodded. With Kieran's arms still wrapped protectively around her, she took a deep breath and began to explain.

'Back in 1989, when I was eleven, a man tried to grab me on the beach beside the caravan park. He had first asked me my name, and I told him it was Rachel. It was my pretend name, one I used when I was playing with one of my friends. I didn't want to tell him my real name. The man had a scar on his hand.'

'Dear God!' Hugh looked stunned, and sat quickly down in his armchair near the window.

Sean took over the story. 'A couple of weeks after the incident with Megan, a young girl died down near Millisle – she was called Rachel. She fell off some rocks. Her mother was having a relationship with your cousin at the time.'

Hugh put his head in his hands, then asked wearily, 'My daughter... did he... did he kill her?'

'We think so, but we have no actual evidence; it's all hearsay at the moment. We know he tried to blame it on his son, Peter.'

Hugh Fitzpatrick looked up, puzzled. 'He doesn't have a son called Peter.'

'Yes he does. Mrs Adams, your old cleaner, had two daughters – Rachel and Leah.'

'That's right.' The professor nodded. 'Barry married Leah.'

'Yes, but before that, according to Rachel he raped her one night when she was walking home from the church.'

'Rachel Adams was raped?'

'Yes, she left for Liverpool soon after, and gave birth to a son, Peter. Hilda never knew the whole truth until Peter turned up at her door. He was living with Hilda the summer your daughter died.'

'I can't get my head around this, I really can't,' said Hugh, shaking his head.

'I'm sorry to say there's more.' Sean explained that they were investigating other disappearances or accidental deaths of young women. Further investigations had revealed that Barry Fitzpatrick was also wanted for questioning in Cambodia regarding several offences there.

'We are pretty certain he is back in the area,' Sean explained. 'And we have reason to believe that he might be after Megan here, because he thinks she is Rachel – the one who got away.'

Hugh Fitzpatrick spoke first. 'Do you think he... he really had anything to do with Rachel, or even my wife Louisa's deaths?'

Before Sean could answer a question that he was reluctant to address, Dougie came back into the room and whispered in his boss's ear. He excused himself and both officers left the room.

'I can't take this in,' said Hugh. He turned to Megan. 'You poor girl. This must have been dreadful for you!'

***

Outside, the officer who had been watching for any cars or people approaching the house, reported that he had noticed a small boat. 'It was drifting, sir,' he said, 'but when the police car arrived, the boat made a turn, heading back out towards the Irish Sea. I couldn't see where it was heading, because it turned its lights off.'

'Damn!' Sean cursed. 'We didn't think to check boats. We were looking for cars.'

Dougie and Catriona had discovered that the garage door appeared to have been opened recently. Inside, under a tarpaulin, was the beige saloon car that they had been searching for; hidden right under their noses.

Sean went back into the house where his brother and Megan were waiting.

'Take this girl back to her parents and stay there tonight, just to be sure. You got that?' he said. Before Kieran could argue, Sean stepped forward and poked him forcefully in the chest. 'That is an order. Now go!'

Kieran stepped back and took Megan's hand. 'We will be at her parents', no worries.'

Taken aback at the way Sean had spoken to his brother, Megan hesitated slightly then gave Sean a hug. When he whispered something to her, she nodded, then she and Kieran headed out to his car.

Sean ordered his officers to close the garage off, so that if Barry did return he wouldn't be alerted to the activity. In the meantime, they would apply for a formal search warrant, to ensure everything was above board.

'We'll be back in the morning, Professor, with the relevant paperwork,' he said. 'Thanks for all your assistance.'

Chapter Twenty-Four
Find Barry

Groomsport - Tuesday, August 4. 9.20pm

It was too misty now to launch a boat search, or to approach the Copeland Islands without being seen or being well prepared. They needed to have someone who knew the rocks out there.

Sean instructed his officers to arrange for boat patrols at dawn the next day. They would need the lifeboat men who patrolled the waters as their best resource. The Copeland Islands was made up of three individual islands; each one would have to be landed and searched. It would take time.

He made a call to the captain of the Donaghadee lifeboat to ask for detailed maps and his team's assistance; they were the people who best knew the waters in and around the area.

When he finished his call, Sean saw Catriona and Doug apparently arguing as they stood outside the Watch House. He quickly approached them.

'What's going on with you two? We can't have the team divided at this time!' He glared at them.

'I'm not convinced that Hugh Fitzpatrick is as innocent as it all seems, to be honest, boss,' offered Catriona.

'Well, I think he is as much a victim as anyone. I can't

believe he would murder his wife or daughter,' added Dougie.

Sean thought for a moment. 'What's your reasoning, Catriona?'

'Don't get me wrong, sir, it is horrific what happened to his wife and daughter, and I don't think he was responsible directly for either of their deaths but... but we haven't found an alibi for him the night of his daughter's death. And he was with another woman the night of his wife's accident. The key suspect's car is nicely hidden in his garage. We haven't checked his whereabouts for the dates of the other alleged victims...' Her voice trailed off. 'I'm just saying.'

'Another of your "what ifs"?' asked Sean, shaking his head. He turned away deep in thought and made a few more calls before walking back to them.

'Okay, Dougie, you focus on getting this search ready for six o'clock tomorrow morning. Use the helicopter. If Barry's on the islands, he has nowhere to run but into a boat. Work with the lifeboat team to have our own boats positioned ready for interception, so that he doesn't make it to the mainland. Catriona. A word.' Dougie went off to make the preparations.

'Right, Catriona,' said Sean. 'If you think Hugh is involved, what would be his next move?'

'He needs to make contact with his cousin, to warn him. If his cousin is caught, he could well spill the beans on Hugh's involvement.'

Sean summoned over a young PC. 'Check any incoming or outgoing calls from Hugh Fitzpatrick's phones. Tell the watch team to contact me if he leaves the house or if there are any other comings and goings. Report anything suspicious at all!'

He turned back to Catriona. 'Next?'

'He may make a run for it,' she suggested. 'If he thinks his time is up.'

Sean summoned another officer. 'Put the ports and airports on alert for either Hugh or Barry Fitzpatrick,' he ordered.

'Dublin and Shannon as well, sir,' prompted Catriona. Sean looked at her with surprise.

'Sir?'

'I think I'll be keeping a closer eye on you, my girl, going forward!'

Catriona reddened, not sure if it was a compliment. 'I don't think he would take the risk of going after Megan, though, boss. I mean, that would be suicidal now he knows her connection with you.'

'Hmm,' Sean nodded. 'I've already warned Kieran to be alert, but nevertheless I've sent reinforcements.'

Catriona looked at her boss closely and then gave a little laugh. 'You didn't send her to her parents, did you?'

Sean smiled. 'Nope. Couldn't afford to take any chances. My family would kill me if something happened to that girl. I'll let you into a wee secret, Catriona. When we were lads, if I gave him an "order" he would always do the exact opposite. So they've headed to somewhere that is a bit like Fort Knox. Anyone turning up at her parents' tonight will have a surprise. Her parents are safely with mine up in Bushmills, too, just in case.'

'Kieran is following that order?' asked Catriona.

'Yes, I just checked and then double checked.'

Catriona looked confused.

'He says he is there, and so do the watchdogs that I have checking them in. No-one will get through the watchdogs tonight, or ever.'

Catriona looked even more confused.

'Colonel Robbie Smith owes me an old favour, so tonight he and some of his former colleagues are protecting my wee brother and Megan.'

'I wouldn't like to take them on in a surprise,' laughed Dougie, catching the last part of the conversation as he rejoined them.

'No,' agreed Sean, 'that was what I thought, too.'

'Peter Adams?' Catriona was trying to tick everyone off in her head.

'He's sitting right beside his old boss, as we speak.'

'That's good!'

'Yes, he would die or kill for that man. I just hope tonight he doesn't have to prove it. He seems like a decent man actually, despite his father and what he has been through.' Sean turned to Dougie. 'Okay, so back to this. Find out the time and destination of the first flight out of the harbour airport tomorrow morning. If Catriona's suspicions are correct, Hugh will head for that and then we'll have lost him. Two of the team have set up surveillance on the Watch House from a cottage along the main road. I want you both to go there and take the lead on that watch.'

'Yes, boss.'

'If he makes a run for it, then let him. Don't jump on him too soon. And be prepared that he has another passport. Report anything back to me.'

'Right, boss.'

Both officers got into the car and drove off, as though heading out of the village, then doubled back and parked their vehicle out of sight as they made their way to the cottage where their colleagues had set up watch.

Inside the cottage, Catriona was approached by an enthusiastic young constable. 'Ma'am, a few minutes ago I noticed a flashlight or torch down near the house.'

'Could it have been a dog walker?' Catriona suggested.

'Ma'am, it could be of course, but I was a Boy Scout...'

There was laughter from the other two officers.

'Go on!' Catriona frowned at the others, warning them to be quiet.

'Well, the most commonly known Morse Code is SOS – save our souls!'

'Yes,' Catriona agreed, 'usually sent when a boat is sinking. And?'

'Yes, or in any type of danger. That's what I think is being sent.'

'You've lost me!' Catriona frowned, trying not to snap at the young officer.

'Well, what if the person in the house is trying to warn someone offshore that there is a problem?'

Behind Catriona, the other two officers had stopped laughing. All four quickly made their way into the front room of the house, careful to ensure that no light could be seen from the window. Catriona took the binoculars. In the mist it was difficult to see anything.

She watched for a couple of moments, her heart beating loudly in her chest. Just as she was about to turn away, she spotted it. The light was definitely flashing in a sequence.

. . . - - - . . . And again.

She lowered the binoculars and turned to the young PC with a dazzling smile. 'Let's thank God that you were a Boy Scout. Well spotted.'

Ignoring the sheepish looks of the other two officers, who were clearly embarrassed that they had missed something so important, Catriona took out her mobile phone and called Sean with the information.

'That certainly changes things,' he acknowledged. 'Barry will know we are coming now. Okay, as soon as Hugh makes a move, trail him!'

Catriona asked the surveillance team if they had noticed any taxis coming and going while they'd been watching. She was told there had been two taxis which had been noted near the Watch House – one was the firm which Barry Fitzpatrick had driven for; the other, a taxi company based at the railway station which had dropped off Megan Scott earlier that evening.

Catriona's mind was in turmoil as she tried to process everything. It seemed likely that Barry had been in close contact with Hugh all along. What if Barry had been hiding right under their noses in the Watch House itself? With his car hidden in the old garage, that was a possibility. They had never thought to check that. What if he had been in the house that night when Megan had turned up, or had been on his way there, having been tipped off by Hugh? How far was Hugh Fitzpatrick involved?

She made her way through to the kitchen and poured herself a glass of cold water, sipping it slowly to try and calm her thoughts. Sean's ear might be twitching, but her gut was churning. She hadn't eaten much for the last few days, though, so that probably didn't help.

Her phone rang. It was a call from a colleague in Belfast who had checked the booking lists for the following morning's flights. No Hugh Fitzpatrick or Barry Fitzpatrick. Catriona asked her to keep checking for any late bookings in any name, and to call her back with anything new. Catriona's gut was telling her more and more that the professor was involved.

She called on the surveillance team to come through to the dimly-lit kitchen and bring their map of the area. 'Right.' She pointed to Ballymacormick Point, the tip where the Watch House sat on reached Ballyholme Bay. 'We need a watch put down here. I suspect that if Hugh Fitzpatrick leaves, he won't come out the front but will go this way. He'll know we are watching so may well have a taxi pick him up from around here.'

The eager young PC who had spotted the Morse Code signal, volunteered to take the position on the coastal path. He knew the area well and explained that there was a point where, if you knew the path, you could go one of two ways. He knew how to reach it by cutting across the farmer's field.

'The first flight leaves the harbour airport at 6.15am,' Catriona explained, 'so to catch that flight he'd need to be at the airport by 5.15am, which means leaving here around 4.45 am.'

'It would take about 45 minutes maximum to walk from the house to the pick-up point,' the young officer said, keen to show his local knowledge.

'Okay.' Catriona glanced quickly at her watch. 'It's just gone 11pm. I reckon we can expect some movement between 3 and 4.30am. Grab something to eat and whatever you need then head up there. And, Officer,' she paused, recognising the lad's youthful enthusiasm, 'don't try to be a hero. Keep in contact with updates on *anything* you spot, and don't make any moves without authorisation. Okay?'

'Yes, Ma'am,' he replied, thrilled at being given such an important task.

Catriona sighed as she watched him leave. The boy was keen to show initiative but she just hoped he wouldn't do anything daft. Before she could reconsider, her mobile rang.

Her colleague in Belfast reported that a late booking had been made on the 6.15am flight leaving for London City Airport.

When she called Sean with the update, the name on the flight booking surprised him. He agreed that neither taxi company should be contacted in case they tipped Barry or Hugh off.

'Let me know as soon as Hugh makes his move,' Sean instructed. 'Once he leaves the house, I want you to head to the airport. Don't approach him until he is inside the terminal building, and simply ask him to accompany you to assist with their enquiries. If he resists... only if he resists,' Sean warned, 'make an arrest on the grounds of being an accomplice in multiple murders.'

'Okay, boss, I understand.'

'I'm arranging for a search warrant for the Watch House, but I don't expect we will get that before the morning so it might be easier to get Hugh's voluntary agreement for the search first.'

***

'Once Hugh leaves the house, will I get one of the team to have a quick look around?'

'Yes,' said Sean, 'but tell them not to go inside. Get a couple of officers to wait discreetly front and back, just to stop any comings or goings once he has left.'

Catriona ended the call and sat down on a comfortable armchair with a large bag of cheese and onion crisps and bottle of mineral water. When she had finished, she told the surveillance team to wake her if there was any movement, then curled herself into the chair for a much-needed nap.

Chapter Twenty-Five
Will he run?

**Observation house, Groomsport -
Wednesday, August 5. 4.30am**

A gentle hand on her shoulder wakened Catriona. One of the young local officers reported that movement had been spotted from the house. As expected, the person was taking the path along the coast towards Ballyholme.

Catriona went to the bathroom and splashed cold water on her face to help her waken quickly. She could feel butterflies churning in her stomach again; she knew the importance of the next few hours.

The sun had not yet risen, but the moonlight provided a level of brightness. When the eager young officer out on the path texted some 10 minutes later, he reported that Hugh Fitzpatrick was taking the inland route. A taxi had been spotted waiting for him where the path reached the road.

Catriona sent a quick message to Sean and Dougie to say they were on the move. Within minutes, she was in an unmarked car being driven to the city airport, 30 minutes away.

Belfast City (George Best) Airport - 5.45am

They watched as Hugh was checked in. He was carrying only a small back pack, and moved through the security checks without any delay.

Just as he cleared security, he spotted Catriona and her colleague waiting for him. His initial surprise couldn't hide his disappointment, but he seemed resigned to the inevitable and simply nodded and half smiled at Catriona.

She approached him and asked if he would voluntarily accompany them to the station in Belfast, although she did advise him of his rights. He agreed, without asking why.

Once they reached the police station, he was signed in by the duty officer, and allowed to call his solicitor before being shown into an interview room.

Hugh was given breakfast with a strong black coffee, and asked to wait in the holding room until both his solicitor and DCI Maloney arrived.

Donaghadee - 5.30am

Sean and several of his team approached the Copeland Islands with the support of the lifeboat and some fishing boats. Overnight, the police helicopter had used infrared camera to detect a presence on the island, and at first light the officers were ready to land.

As they approached the island, they spotted a small boat hidden in one of the inlets. Sean asked the lifeboat team to position one of their vessels to block the smaller boat in, to prevent any chance of escape.

When Barry saw the police officers approaching, he had nowhere to run. Reasoning that they had little or nothing to pin on him, he was prepared to bluff it out but looked shocked when informed that he was being arrested in connection with the disappearance or suspicious deaths of six women.

Composing himself again, he simply shrugged and said nothing throughout the drive back to Belfast. At the police station, he was booked in and provided with breakfast whilst waiting for the duty solicitor.

Belfast Central Police Station - 9am

Before any interviews began, Sean wanted to take some time with his team to review the information they had. The postmarks from the letters which Hilda had provided, showed that Barry had been in the various locations at the time when a number of the disappearances had occurred. He had often used hotel stationery to write to Peter, so checks were also being made with the various venues to confirm any records of his stays.

Sean ran a hand wearily through his hair and sighed. Although they had enough justification for arresting Barry and questioning him, the links were still tenuous and circumstantial. Any good solicitor would be able to provide enough doubt to make them worthless, so without further evidence or a confession, they were still on icy ground.

He decided they would question Hugh Fitzpatrick first, particularly as he was there voluntarily and they didn't want his goodwill to run out.

***

Hugh's solicitor arrived just before 9am and spent thirty minutes in earnest conversation with his client before DCI Sean Maloney and his colleague, DS Catriona Murphy, began the formal interview.

Sean began by advising the professor that while he had not been arrested, he was helping with their enquiries regarding a number of disappearances of a number of women, and the potential deaths of several others. Hugh Fitzpatrick confirmed that he understood.

In previous conversations, his alibi for the night of his wife's death was that he had been attending a historical society meeting at Trinity College, Dublin. With the help of their colleagues down south in Dublin, the investigating team had checked the records of the historical society and found that he had not been there on the night in question. Contact had also been made with one of the society members, Professor James Donnelly, who remembered he had been extremely miffed that his colleague and competitor had not turned up that evening to hear his maiden speech.

'I suppose he was off with that woman he had been with before he got married, because she wasn't there either,' Professor Donnelly told the investigating officers. Unfortunately, he had been unable to identify the woman concerned.

Hugh Fitzpatrick's alibi for the night of his daughter's death had again involved the historical society in Dublin. Although the team had confirmed his attendance as one of the speakers that night, had been intrigued to learn that Fitzpatrick had been issued with a speeding ticket that night, on the road coming north, but just south of the border. Yet he had told Sean and his officers that he didn't drive.

While the time of the speeding ticket provided him with an alibi for his whereabouts that evening, Sean realized that Fitzpatrick must have been on his way back from Dublin before he was called to tell of his daughter's disappearance. *Did he already know there was a problem?*

'Perhaps we could begin by looking at your whereabouts on the evening of the death of your daughter, Rachel, please, Professor Fitzpatrick?' Sean asked.

His solicitor – a well-dressed, elderly man, with thinning hair and wearing gold-rimmed bifocal glasses – was about to object, when his client shook his head. 'No, it's okay,' Hugh Fitzpatrick told him. 'This needs to be resolved.'

Sean asked Hugh Fitzpatrick to explain why he'd told them he didn't drive.

'I was ashamed to admit that I no longer drove. In fact, my licence lapsed because one night, after Rachel died, I was driving home... drunk... and I hit and killed a dog.' The professor looked down at his hands as he carried on. 'I realised that it could easily have been a child. That was when I admitted to myself that I had a drink problem, so I checked into a rehab clinic and joined sobriety. I stayed sober until...' His voice faltered.

'Until, sir?' probed Catriona.

'Until two months ago – mid-June – when my cousin, Barry, got back in touch with me. He had just got out of prison and had nowhere else to turn; he was broke. He reminded me of our old bonds and that I still owed him a few favours.'

'What were those favours, and did he call them in?' asked Sean.

'Yes, he needed a place to stay, so he came to the Watch House. He had stayed there before. The summer after my daughter died, I went to the US for two years, and he "rented" the place from me. Actually, it was more like squatting. He left at some point when he was sent to prison.

'I told him last month that I was selling the house, as I planned to move back to the States, and he got very angry. He felt that half of the house should have been his.'

'Why would he think that?' Sean continued questioning.

'Our grandfather left the farm and the farmhouse to my father, who would continue to farm it, according to the will. Barry's mother, as the daughter, couldn't inherit in those days, and only received a small amount of money in the will, but not the farm. My father was no real farmer, and was subsequently offered a very substantial amount of money for the land, as it was prime real estate. He left me a sizeable amount, which I used to buy the old Watch House.

'I offered to give Barry some money when the house was sold, but he wanted all of it. He said he had evidence of my affair, and he was sure that my friend would not want it disclosed.'

'Your affair?' Catriona asked.

'When I was at Trinity as a lecturer, I had a relationship with a post graduate student. In those days, any whiff of a scandal could damage your career.'

'But surely as part of academia, this was less of an issue?' Catriona suggested.

'Not for me, but it was for her. She was starting out in politics. I was in Dublin with her the night Louisa died,' he looked down at his hands, embarrassed, 'but it was a chance meeting. No more than that. I called home the next morning to speak to my wife, and Mrs Adams our housekeeper was there. She was crying, and that is when I learned about my wife's death and that the baby – Rachel – was in hospital.

'Had I gone home as planned, my wife wouldn't have been out driving.' His face crumpled. 'I've never been able to forgive myself for that.'

'And were you with this same woman when your daughter died?' Catriona suggested.

He nodded. 'I had kept in touch with her, although I did love Arabella, my second wife. That night my friend and I met at a reception in Dublin, got talking, and we went back to her apartment. Arabella rang me to say that she knew I was with this woman, so I left to drive back and face the music. I was stopped for speeding. The young PC was kind enough to suggest I stop for a sleep, rather than arrest me for being over the limit. That is why I never made it home until the morning.'

'Who told Arabella about your friend?' asked Sean.

'I don't know. You would have to ask her.'

'And this woman,' Catriona went on, 'she would confirm you were with her, on both occasions?'

He hesitated. 'I'm not sure if she would, but I was certainly seen by the doorman both arriving and leaving.'

'The lady's name, sir?'

He smiled gently. 'Marianne Daly.' He looked at their surprised faces. 'Yes, the Minister for Culture and the Arts. I don't know if Louisa ever knew or suspected, but had I gone home as planned that night, my wife would not have gone out. I wish I could assure you, it was absolutely all above board. I've never been able to forgive myself for not being there.'

'How did your cousin, Barry Fitzpatrick, know about this relationship?' asked Catriona.

'Apparently he saw us one night going back to her home in Dublin. He must have been following me.'

'Given that it was a long time ago, you will understand that we will want to check?' Sean said.

'Yes, I understand, but please be discreet. She has worked extremely hard to get to the position she has reached.'

'Was this why the lady in question was as supportive of your TV programmes and the funding you might have received from her department?' Catriona asked innocently.

'Certainly not!' Fitzpatrick blasted angrily. 'It was absolutely all above board. The project had been approved by her predecessor. But, of course, if there was a whiff of scandal, the newspapers would no doubt make something of it.'

'Has the affair been going on all these years?'

'No. We have seen each other at social and cultural events, but nothing ever happened again. She is very happily married... to her job! Barry, unfortunately, tried to blackmail me with this on more than one occasion. He also liked to hint to Arabella that it might still be going on, just to wind her up.'

Fitzpatrick sighed wearily. 'I had told Arabella everything when we met. She and I actually met in rehab, and it is part of the process to admit the truth about your past. Barry didn't like the fact that he couldn't get to Arabella, or have something to hold over me.'

'So am I right in thinking you have been in rehab twice?' Sean asked.

'Yes, the first time was after my wife died, and I relapsed after the death of my daughter.'

'Was there anything else Barry held over you?'

'When I was a student, I had been dating a really nice girl and we talked about getting engaged. She left the university one day and didn't come back. Her parents came looking for her.

'About three weeks later, she came back but she refused to see me. When I eventually managed to speak to her, she begged me to leave her alone. Her face had signs that she had been bruised and battered, and when I pressed her about what had happened, she said she had been jumped from behind by a man who attacked her and told her to stay away from me. I'm fairly confident it was my cousin.'

'Do you have the name of the girl?'

Catriona made a note of the name he gave them.

'Another time, we were on holiday together in Spain and

met two girls. The girls started to demand money from us, so Barry attacked them. We left the next morning before the police arrived. He laughed about it, and said I could always rely on him.

'In a way, not speaking out against my cousin has meant he has got away with many things over the years. He regularly extorts money from me, and has done so for many years. I was relieved when he went to prison.'

The professor sat a little straighter in his chair and looked directly at the senior detective. 'I know you think I was running away this morning, and to an extent I was, but not from you. From him. I left a bag with a number of items in my wardrobe. My solicitor here will confirm that I called his office last night and left a voicemail telling them where they could find the items, and that they were to be handed into you, Detective Maloney. I believed that by the time you received them, I would be far away.'

'Where exactly are these items?' Sean asked.

'There is a blue holdall in the wardrobe of the spare bedroom, under a pile of folded sheets and towels. I would like to assure you that I will do everything I can to help in any way to convict my cousin. He has ruined many lives. Unfortunately, I was too weak a man to have dealt with this before. I was thinking only of myself and my own reputation.'

'What do you think we could convict your cousin of, Professor? For the record?'

'In the holdall is a journal kept by my cousin. It is similar to one kept in the 1800s by a young customs officer who tried to save a slave girl, named Rachel. The original journal was found when work was undertaken to fix the chimney in the Watch House some twenty-five years ago, then later it went missing. It seems Barry thought he was repeating history by "saving" any girl on her own called Rachel.'

'I see.' Sean nodded. 'Anything else?'

'There is also a handgun in the bag. I don't know what it was used for, but it does look quite old.'

'And how did you come by these articles? How can you be sure they belong to him?'

'Since your visit to me, I have been mulling over what happened to my wife and daughter. Things that I remember at the time just didn't seem quite right and I challenged Barry last night, just before Megan Scott arrived. I knew she was due to visit, so I wanted to get him out of the house.

'When I explained that the young woman was coming to take measurements, he said he had already seen her when she first came with her boyfriend to view the house. He asked me her name and was confused when I said it was Megan. I happened to say that she and her boyfriend had been regular visitors to the caravan sites in the area some twenty years ago, and I noticed a look in his eyes which frightened me.

'He laughed and said I was right up to my neck in it, but not to worry, he would bail me out as usual. When I asked him out of what, he said it was all in the journal. Before he could say anything else, the phone rang. It was Megan to tell me she was on her way. I was frightened, so pretended it was yourselves phoning to say that you wanted another meeting and would be there in ten minutes.'

Sean frowned. 'We would never have given you a warning before visiting.'

'I know, but it was all I could think of. Barry panicked and wanted to go and get the holdall. I told him I had put it in a safe place, but would bring it to him once you had left. He took the boat and was heading to the Copeland

Islands. Our signal as boys when everything was okay was the Morse Code SOS – the opposite from what it means! I used the flashlight last night to send him that signal so that he thought all was okay, but I guessed you would be watching me.'

'And you were right.' Catriona was glad she had listened to the eager young officer.

'I have read some of the journal,' he went on, 'but quite honestly I didn't want to read the whole thing. The bits I did read where horrific. I just don't know how my cousin ended up with such a warped mind.'

At that point, Sean decided to stop the interview and return Hugh Fitzpatrick to his cell, while his solicitor agreed to accompany Catriona and another officer to the Watch House to retrieve the holdall.

Sean took Catriona aside for a few minutes before she left. 'I don't want you driving, because you must be shattered. Try and grab some shut-eye in the car on the way down to Groomsport. I want you to ensure that his solicitor is with you when you find the bag, so that there can be no accusation later of tampering with evidence.'

'Sure, boss.'

She managed a short nap on the thirty-minute drive, and wakened with a start when they arrived at the house. A couple of uniformed officers were stationed outside, and they checked their colleagues' identity documents before allowing them to enter the property.

The holdall, with a travel lock on it, was exactly where Hugh Fitzpatrick had told them it would be, in the wardrobe. Catriona made sure the solicitor was with them when the bag was removed from the house and put into the car, then they headed back to Belfast.

Belfast Central Police Station - 2pm

Still under caution, the professor revealed the combination lock for the bag and Sean put on thin gloves to ensure his fingerprints would not contaminate any of the evidence. With the solicitor still in attendance, Sean slowly opened the bag.

Inside were several envelopes. The first – a letter for the lawyer – was handed over unopened. The second contained a journal-type notebook. A third was addressed to DCI Sean Maloney.

At the bottom of the bag was a transparent plastic sandwich bag, which contained a handgun. The holdall and its contents were signed over as evidence, and countersigned by both Hugh Fitzpatrick and his solicitor.

Forensics officers would have to examine the contents of the bag and take fingerprints before Sean and his team could proceed to read the journal. He was conscious that any failure to follow procedure at this stage could scupper the entire case further down the line.

'Professor Fitzpatrick,' he said, 'I have to warn you that you are still under caution, and anything you may say can be used as evidence.'

'Yes, I understand.'

'Can you please explain the contents of the holdall?'

'Yes, Detective. There is a handgun, and I have taken every precaution not to get my own fingerprints on it. It belongs to my cousin, Barry. I found the gun and his diary hidden in a secret alcove in the Watch House in Groomsport. I've read a few of the pages of the journal, but again tried not to get my own fingerprints on it. I know the journal will give you the times, dates, and type of offences which my cousin has perpetrated. As for the gun, I've no idea what crimes it may have committed. As I said, I left a voicemail message with my solicitors to collect the bag and take it to you. The letter to my solicitor is confidential and between him and me.'

The solicitor nodded, but advised Sean that the voicemail was available for his officers to listen to.

Switching off the tape, Sean indicated that Hugh Fitzpatrick should be returned to a waiting room this time, not a cell.

As he was led from the room by a police officer, the professor asked Sean if he could give him some advice regarding Barry Fitzpatrick and how best to approach him. Sean, never too proud to accept advice, duly nodded. The two men spoke quietly, out of earshot of the others, then Sean thanked him and Hugh left.

Although the team were itching to get their hands on the journal, they would have to wait a little longer until their forensics colleagues did their job.

Chapter Twenty-Six
Barry's story

Belfast Central Police Office - Wednesday, August 5. 8am

When he was brought into the police headquarters, outwardly Barry was full of bravado and bluster but he couldn't understand how they had caught up with him.

The previous night he had left the Watch House in a hurry, angry at Hugh's refusal to give him his bag. His cousin said he'd had a call from the police to say they were on their way, but once Barry was in the boat and heading out from the shore he had looked back and spotted the young woman going into the house.

Hugh had said her name was Megan, but Barry would always think of her as Rachel. *Why was she there?*

He turned the boat around, planning to take her and Hugh by surprise, and was just about to anchor the boat when he saw a car arrive – this time it *was* the police. Barry had swiftly turned the boat around again, and headed to the islands as originally planned.

He made himself comfortable on the cell mattress. He knew the police were playing a waiting game, but he was confident they didn't have anything on him.

Hugh would be out of the country by now. Barry laughed to himself, remembering the signal last night telling him that everything was okay. The signal was a throwback to when they were children. It meant the opposite of what anyone looking thought it meant; they weren't in danger, they were safe. It often angered Hugh's father when he thought the boys were in trouble at sea.

Barry would soon own the house, he was sure of it. For now, he would have a little kip.

Wednesday, 3.15pm

Sean, Dougie and Catriona took time to discuss their strategy before interviewing Barry Fitzpatrick. After all their work and investigation, they knew the importance of getting their questioning right.

'From what Hugh Fitzpatrick has said, Barry is extremely jealous of him,' Sean began. 'So I'm going to blame the professor for the crimes, and hope that will annoy Barry. Hopefully, his arrogance won't allow someone else to take credit, even if it means digging his own grave.'

'Let's hope so,' agreed Dougie doubtfully.

'We know he has a real problem with women,' Sean went on.

'That's putting it mildly, boss,' Dougie commented wryly.

'Hm, true. I think you, Catriona, should come across as quite rude, almost insolent, when you're talking to Dougie. Give the impression that you think you're superior to him. Hopefully, that might wind Barry up as well.'

Catriona grinned across at her colleague. 'No problem, boss. I can do rude and insolent. In fact, being superior to Dougie is just too easy.' They both laughed.

'Right then.' Sean stood and gathered up his files. He took a deep breath. 'Here goes.'

When Barry was escorted into the room, along with the duty solicitor, Sean began by pointing out that, following normal procedure, the interview would be recorded. He advised Barry that he was being interviewed as an accomplice to crimes committed by Professor Hugh Fitzpatrick.

Barry sat very still with his arms folded, but Sean noticed a slight facial reaction to the word 'accomplice'.

'Have you ever watched Hugh Fitzpatrick's history programmes?' Sean asked, almost conversationally. Barry shook his head.

'Well, he's clearly an extremely clever man. So when he explained that he was writing a book about how he attracted these young girls to him, based on a history story, we became very interested. In fact, we couldn't quite believe that all these girls had gone missing over years and no-one had realized a connection.'

Barry said nothing, but his facial muscles and body language indicated he was ready to burst. Sean watched him closely, watching for his agitation to increase at his cousin being given the credit for *his* work.

'We did tell him, though, that the story was a bit far-fetched,' Dougie chipped in. 'No one person would be capable of all that, or that clever. He took our comments on board, and said he would adjust the book and welcomed our input.'

'He's a liar!' snapped Barry.

'A liar?' Sean asked innocently.

'He wouldn't have the imagination or guts to do any of it.'

'But it's just a story,' said Sean. 'Don't worry about it. We're not taking him seriously! We have him here in the station answering questions as well.'

'So why exactly is my client here then?' asked the solicitor, looking up from taking notes.

Before they could answer, Barry leaned forward and thumped the table. 'It is bloody true. It is!' His solicitor, clearly used to all kinds of reactions from his clients, put his hand on his arm to calm him down.

Sean leaned back in his seat and put his hands behind his head. 'Which bit exactly?'

'All of it!' Barry snapped.

'You mean he *has* done all those things – the kidnapping, the assaults, the murders? Really?' Dougie sounded astonished.

'No, not him. Me! Me! I did them!' He leaned back in his chair, sneering at the officers facing him. 'Me.'

Sean gave a hollow laugh. 'He said you would say that!' he goaded.

Barry leaned forward again, his shoulders tense, his expression angry. 'Hugh doesn't have the balls. The one time he got himself into a bit of trouble with a woman, he called me. I had to bail him out.'

'To be fair, he did say you sometimes acted as his support act. I take it you're the Bonnie to his Clyde,' Dougie said quietly, ensuring his words had impact.

'No way am I a support act to anyone!' Barry fumed.

'Which woman did he get in trouble with?' asked Sean, changing the direction of the questioning.

'How many do you want? The stories I could tell you would make any book he wrote look like a children's one.'

Dougie smiled. 'I loved his history programmes. It's amazing how he can tell a good story. I got him to sign a book for my missus, she'll be well chuffed.'

His comments were met with silence. The veins on Barry's neck were pulsating, his face turning slowly red. He was clenching his fists, the knuckles turning white.

Sean drummed his fingers on the table. Before he could continue his questioning, there was a knock on the door and Catriona entered.

'Excuse me, sir.' Her dark hair, usually scraped up into a tight plait, lay loose across her shoulders. She handed Sean a note and waited while he read it.

'Thanks, Rachel,' he said, smiling at her.

'Hey, doll, any chance of some coffees in here?' Dougie threw her a leering look.

'Get them yourself, you lazy fecker.' She glared at her colleague. 'You forget I'm your superior officer.' She turned and walked out, ignoring Dougie's grin.

Sean leaned over top his colleague, speaking loud enough for Barry and his solicitor to hear. 'Hey, watch yourself, mate. She'll kick your ass.'

Picking up on the comment, Barry started to laugh. 'What a wimp! You gonna take that crap from a female? I'd never have a woman telling me what to do.'

'You're a lucky man then,' Sean returned his attention to Barry. 'I've been married twenty years and my wife is definitely the boss!'

'She needs a good slap then. That'll show her.'

'I'd be frightened she hit me back,' joked Sean.

'Nah. There's a way to do it that shuts them up and has them begging you for more.' Barry was preening now he had everyone's attention.

'No way!' Sean shook his head.

'Aye, I had to teach Hugh that a couple of times. But he never learned.'

'In what way?'

'We were in Spain one summer, and took these two girls along the beach. They started to demand money. A couple of sluts, they were. I slapped the one I was with, and that shut her up. I told Hugh to slap his, but he couldn't. So I slapped her for him. The bitches threatened us, so I took out my knife and carved a wee memento for them.'

'What kind of memento?' Dougie sounded impressed.

'The sign of the cross, just here.' Barry pointed to his left cheek. 'When they look in the mirror, they'll always remember not to mess with Barry.'

'Really?' Dougie scoffed. 'That's easy to say, but you've no way of proving that, have you?'

Barry stiffened. His solicitor bent towards him, whispering that he should perhaps stay quiet or to reply 'no comment', but his advice was ignored.

'I was always saving him. I saved him from drowning. I even saved him from that stupid wife of his. She was going to leave him and take his kid to the States.'

'What kid?' Sean prompted.

'His wee girl, Rachel. A beautiful wee thing.' Barry's voice softened.

'But his wife died in a road accident!' Dougie looked puzzled.

'She found out he was doing the dirty on her, so she took the wee girl and was headed to the airport. She shouldn't have been driving. It was a wet night and she wasn't a good driver.'

'You were there?' asked Sean, pretending to be surprised.

'It's not what you think! We were in love. I thought if I could make her see the truth of what a bastard he was, she'd leave him. She laughed at me. Laughed at me,' he said quietly.

'Leave him for *you*?' sneered Dougie.

'I knew she loved me. It would only be a matter of time, and we could be together.'

'What did *you* have to offer her? What were you doing at that time – odd-job man, living off the goodness of your cousin?' Dougie suggested.

'No!' Barry's anger rose again.

'Did you tell her you loved her and she laughed at you? Is that what happened?' needled Dougie.

'I told her where she could find him with his lover. She was angry, so angry. She got in the car to go and confront him. She put Rachel in the back, she was sleeping. Louisa was driving too fast; she didn't know the road and must have forgotten she wasn't in America when she was going round the bend on the wrong side.' Barry shook his head, as though trying to erase the picture from his mind. 'I was following a bit behind her, and I saw her car swerve sharply then hit a wall. She was dead by the time I got to her, but the car had started to burn. I got Rachel... I got Rachel out. I burnt my hand.' Unconsciously he rubbed the scar near his wrist. 'I left the little one sitting in the field away from the car. I drove off. There was nothing I could do.'

There was silence.

'That bastard was off shagging that bloody MP, and his wife... his beautiful wife... was dead.' Barry let out a cry of anguish, then took a deep breath. 'I made sure he felt every ounce of guilt.'

'But you never told him you had saved Rachel, did you?' asked Sean.

'No. No, that was my calling, to save Rachel... like the history book.'

'What history book?'

'Ach, it's long gone. Hugh and me found it hidden in the old chimney breast. It told the story of a young lad, called Barry Fitzpatrick just like me, and he tried to save the life of a young slave girl called Rachel. I always felt it was my calling, to save Rachel, just like my ancestor.'

'But young Rachel died, too, didn't she?' Sean countered.

Barry's face turned stony. 'I would watch them,' he said at last.

'Who?'

'Rachel and Peter. She was so like her mum, full of life. But Peter was my son.'

'So why should that matter?'

'She was messing him about. I warned her to stop, but she laughed. I told her I would tell her father and she told me just to go ahead!' He stopped for a moment, as though replaying memories in his head. 'I saw them that night on the pier. One minute she was kissing him, and the next she was pushing him away. It wasn't right.'

'What happened?'

'Peter left, so I went to speak to her. She told me to fuck off and called me a perv. She had seen me watching them. She went to push past me and I grabbed her arm. She hit me so I slapped her. I told her I had loved her mother and she had loved me. She laughed at me, saying there was no way her beautiful mother would love an ugly, nasty cretin like me.'

There was a pause.

'I told her I had saved her that night from the car. But instead of thanking me, she screamed at me, "You killed my mother." I told her it was an accident, but she didn't believe me. She tried to run. I grabbed her and she tripped and fell, hitting her head on the harbour wall. I fell, too. I was dazed. I got up but she was dead. There wasn't anything I could do. I couldn't save her. I threw her body into the sea.'

'You threw her body into the sea?' Dougie repeated.

'Yes. She was dead. No-one would have believed it was an accident,' Barry replied.

'She was dead before she went into the sea?' Sean asked.

'Yes, she was dead,' Barry confirmed.

There was a pause, then Sean spoke quietly. 'She fell over, hit her head, and you lifted her body and threw it into the sea.'

'Yes, there was nothing that could be done!' Barry shouted, running his hands through his hair. 'Nothing!'

Sean let out a deep sigh. 'She wasn't dead. Rachel wasn't dead. She was unconscious. When you threw her into the sea, she drowned. Your actions effectively murdered her.'

'No. No.' He turned with an anguished look at his solicitor. 'It was an accident.' He repeated, 'It was an accident.'

His solicitor requested a break.

Belfast Central Police Office - 7.30pm

When they reconvened, Barry looked drawn and grey; the enormity of what he had done was starting to sink in. He had confessed to killing Rachel Fitzpatrick. It was manslaughter, not murder, not deliberate, but he was on edge now.

Sean started to speak. 'The year after Rachel Fitzpatrick's death, a young girl – also called Rachel – died in similar circumstances off the rocks in Millisle. You knew her, didn't you?'

Silence.

'You knew her mother, Angela Porter. She has confirmed that you were having a relationship. You were still married to your wife, Leah, at the time.'

Silence.

'Angela Porter suspected you had an interest in her daughter, too. A beautiful young girl, with long dark hair – not unlike Rachel Fitzpatrick.'

Silence.

'Bit of a coincidence, some might say,' said Sean. The officers waited in silence. They needed Barry to acknowledge he knew the girl.

'She misunderstood,' he said at last.

'What?'

'I only meant it as a joke. It was only the one time.'

'Tell us.'

'I had been with her mother and had gone to the bathroom for a wee. I hadn't locked the door. She walked in.' He shook his head with a sigh. 'I asked her if she'd like some of this.'

'For the tape, suspect points to his penis,' said Dougie.

'I was joking. Her mother heard me and slapped me. I wouldn't have touched her; she was just a kid.'

'Did you see her after that?' asked Sean.

'It was the bank holiday weekend. I was driving to my own place when I saw her staggering home. She had clearly been drinking. I knew her mother would go mad if she caught her.'

'So what happened?' Dougie asked calmly.

'There was one hell of a clap of thunder and a flash of lightning. I couldn't leave her like that, so I stopped and offered her a lift. She said no. She swore at me. I had bought her a present, so I flung it out the car window at her and said it was to say sorry. And I drove off.'

'And that was the last you saw of her?'

'I know I should have just kept driving, but I have a daughter, too, so I stopped and waited for her in the car park. I mean, it was nearly four miles for her to walk home, and she was staggering.' He took a brief pause before continuing. 'She saw me. She started running, and she tripped and fell.

She tore the dress she was wearing, and she was bleeding. I went to help her. I used the part of the ripped dress to wipe her knees and her hands. She just sat there on the ground.

'I suggested she put on the new dress I had bought her, and then I would take her home. I walked away to get back in my car and when I turned round, she had put the dress on. I got in the car, but she turned in the opposite direction. I started the car but as I got closer to her, she ran faster. I drove off and left her. I already felt that she was going to accuse me of molesting her when I had only been trying to save her.

'About half a mile from my own home that night, I had a puncture. I tried to change the wheel but I couldn't get the bloody nuts off, so I left the car parked there and walked home. By the time I got in, I was soaked. My wife gave me hell for it.'

'In which direction did she run?' Dougie probed.

'Towards the beach. The rocks.'

'Your son Peter's mother is called Rachel, isn't she?' Sean suddenly moved the conversation in another direction.

'Yes,' replied Barry, a little confused at the change of questioning. 'But I didn't know about him until he turned up at his nan's door when he was eighteen, for God's sake.'

'You seem to have a thing about ladies called Rachel, don't you?'

'Coincidence.'

'Your son's grandmother has given us a statement that you raped her.'

'Lying cow!'

'You deny it?'

'I've never had to force myself on any woman.'

'So why would she say it, after all this time?'

'She was gagging for it!'

'Really?' Dougie looked skeptical.

'I mean, her and Hugh were at it like rabbits. I admit I liked to watch them, but I didn't rape her.'

'So what happened?'

'She was waiting for Hugh after church one night, at the lane beside the church. It was dark. She didn't realise it was me at first, cos Hugh and I looked alike in those days and I was wearing his jacket. We went down the lane and had sex – willingly. She finished with Hugh just after that.' Barry laughed. 'I mean, once a girl had me, there was no comparison.'

The officers waited for him to continue.

'When I realised that both Peter and Rachel could be mine, I had to put a stop to it. You know what I mean?' Barry said.

***

Catriona, who had been watching the interview through one-way glass, requested to speak to Hugh Fitzpatrick and his solicitor. She was accompanied by DC Niall Levin.

'Professor Fitzpatrick, I'd like to ask you a couple of questions, but would remind you that you are still under caution,' she advised.

'Yes.'

'Did you know Rachel Adams, the daughter of your housekeeper?'

'Yes.'

'When she was 16?'

'Yes, we went to the same church. We often went to church events together. She was a really lovely young woman, but we were just friends. I was ten years older than her and due to be going to America to work.'

'Did you ever have a sexual relationship with her?'

'Absolutely not!' He looked outraged at being asked.

'Where you surprised to learn that she had a child?'

'Very. I only became aware of this recently and it was quite a surprise. As I said, I was in the US for a couple of years, then I met my wife and we came back to Groomsport to live.'

'How well did Rachel Adams know your cousin, Barry?'

'Actually, I didn't know that they knew each other. Barry wasn't the church-going type, so I don't know how they actually met.'

'So you were surprised to find out that he was the father of her son, Peter?' Catriona asked.

'Shocked would be a better word.'

'Why?'

'She wasn't that kind of girl. I mean, she was very sweet. Strong Christian views – believed you should wait until marriage, so yes, I was shocked.'

'Professor Fitzpatrick, if you heard that she had accused Barry of raping her, would that also shock you?'

'Barry? Rape?'

'Yes, rape. Knowing Rachel as you did at that time, does she strike you as the type of girl who would be "gagging for it"?'

'Really, Officer.' Hugh Fitzpatrick flinched in disgust.

'Please, Professor, just answer the question,' said Catriona firmly.

'No, Officer, she never struck me as that type of girl.'

'Would you consider her a liar?'

'No,' he said, shaking his head. 'Nor that either. I mean, I only ever saw her in connection with church events.'

'Thank you, Professor Fitzpatrick. That will be all for now.'

As Catriona and her colleague stood to leave, Hugh's solicitor challenged why his client required to remain at the police station if there was no evidence against him.

'We can charge him with obstructing the course of justice, and therefore hold him, if you prefer?' Catriona snapped.

'No,' said Hugh sharply. 'I am willing to stay here voluntarily until this is resolved.'

The officers left the room.

***

Along the corridor, in the interview room, Sean was still questioning Barry.

'Over the years, there have been a number of young women who have gone missing or suffered unusual accidents. Many of them called Rachel,' Sean stated.

'Coincidence,' replied Barry, looking confident that they had nothing to link him to anything.

'If we were to ask you to confirm your whereabouts for those dates and times to rule you out, could you do so?'

Silence.

'Your cousin has provided us with dates and whereabouts for himself. It is hard to believe that one man could be able to do all this. How he never brought attention to himself is a mystery,' said Sean, shaking his head. 'He'll be making the history this time, isn't that right, Dougie?' He looked at his deputy.

'That he will, boss,' confirmed Dougie, nodding.

'What's unusual is that the person usually wants the publicity, the notoriety. He said that's why he has owned up now, and the publicity for his book will be amazing. You said yourself he had a relationship with a member of the government.' Sean smiled at Barry. 'The book will fly off the shelf. He'll make a fortune!'

'He is a liar!' Barry snapped back, the vein in his temple pulsating. 'A liar.'

'I understand you want to protect him. It was always you who saved him when he got into trouble, but honestly, Barry, you can't save him now.'

Silence again. After a few minutes Barry leaned across the table, pointing his finger at Sean.

'I kept a journal,' he said smugly.

'A journal? Like a diary?' asked Sean innocently.

'Yes.'

'Of what exactly?' Sean shrugged his shoulders, appearing disinterested.

'Times, dates, places... the details.'

'Of what?

'The girls I saved.'

'Saved from what?' Sean's tone was dismissive.

'Slavery.'

Silence.

'Slavery?' Sean sat back and folded his arms, shaking his head in disbelief.

'I helped them escape their troubles. They thanked me. They would give me gifts. Tokens of appreciation.'

'Really?'

'I took a leaf out of my ancestor's life and kept a journal of details.'

'Your ancestor?'

'Yes, he tried to save the girl Rachel from the slave trade. It was my job to continue his work.'

Barry's solicitor touched his arm gently, trying to suggest he should stop talking.

'So where is this journal now?'

'Ha!' said Barry, his natural arrogance returning. 'Without it, you have nothing. I'll take it to my grave.'

'So this journal is all your own work?'

'Yes, it damn well is!' hissed Barry.

'And not your cousin Hugh's?' asked Sean.

'My cousin hasn't got the bottle. It was my job to save them. Me, Barry Fitzpatrick. I did it!' spat Barry. 'I should be given a bloody medal.'

'These tokens that the women gave you, where are they now?' asked Sean.

'Saved me a bloody fortune.'

'Let me guess,' Sean laughed. 'You gave them to your missus for presents, didn't you?'

'Stupid cow! And not just her. What they would do for you when you gave them some piece of glitz. They thought you loved them.' Barry was almost preening himself. 'My ex, she was just like the woman in the Bible. Second choice. She trapped me into marrying her just like in the Bible. It is only Rachel who is the prize, and my job was to save Rachel.' He sat back in his chair and folded his arms. 'I think I need a break now,' he said smugly.

Barry was escorted back to his cell grinning. Sean and Dougie managed to hide their smiles until he was out of the room. Little by little, Barry was using his own words to hang himself.

Chapter Twenty-Seven
Closing the circle

Belfast Central Police Office
Wednesday, August 5. 8.15pm

Back in the incident room, the team were studiously ploughing their way through the copies of pages of the journal. They were cross-referencing names, dates, and places with the list of women they had already identified. So far they had ticked seven off the list.

The forensic team were examining the gun, and the handwriting analyst was checking the writing. It would take hours of painstaking work to put the final pieces together. Along with Barry's letters, his latest confession should be enough to convict him. Now all they had to do was find some of the jewellery to close the circle.

Sean had just sat down at his desk to make some notes when there was a sharp knock on his door, and Chief Constable Davis entered.

'A few minutes, Sean?' he asked.

'Of course, sir.' Sean stood and gestured for his boss to sit down.

'I've listened in to some of the interview with Barry Fitzpatrick,' he told his senior detective. 'Good work so far.' He cleared his throat before continuing. 'I have just spoken to the Minister, and she confirms that she and Hugh Fitz-patrick had been in a relationship whilst she had been a student, before he went to America and met his wife. She has confirmed his alibi that he spent the night at her flat in Dublin and left around 7am, and distinctly remembers the details because of the tragic death of his wife and also because she had the worst hangover ever.

'She said the irony of it is that the professor had ended the relationship, and nothing had happened between her and him. They drank too much whisky and he fell asleep on the sofa. It seems Hugh was never unfaithful to his wife; or, at least, not with her. She admits that she has seen him on a number of occasions over the years at cultural events, and is adamant that the funding for his TV programme was approved by her predecessor and had nothing to do with her.' The Chief Constable paused before adding with a smile, 'She is willing to make a statement to that effect, if required.'

Sean breathed a sigh of relief. 'That's good news, sir.'

'You definitely have your man now,' said the Chief Constable.

'Yes, but there is still something niggling at me.' Sean frowned. 'I can't quite put my finger on it, though.'

'Keep it simple, Sean. There is more than enough here to charge Barry Fitzpatrick with the kidnappings and deaths outlined in that journal. Has the handwriting analysis come back yet?'

'No, sir. It could take another day at least.'

'Fair enough. We need to ensure that's watertight,' the Chief replied. 'What about the gun?'

'Still waiting on forensics, sir.'

The Chief nodded. 'How's his brief doing?'

'Duty solicitor, sir. Completely out of his depth, and Barry isn't taking any of his advice to shut up, either.' Sean grinned.

'Good, but just make sure he can't play that card at any appeal,' stated the Chief. 'What time are you planning to reconvene?'

'We've a couple more things to check, so I think we'll let him and his solicitor have a good night's sleep, and then tomorrow, hopefully close the trap.'

'OK. I'd like to watch.' The Chief stood and paused briefly before opening the door to leave. 'Nice seeing you in action, Sean. Slowly, slowly, reel him in.'

'Yes, sir.'

As soon as the Chief Constable had left, Catriona and Dougie came in.

'Boss, Rachel Parker, Peter's mother, has landed in Aldergrove. She should be with us in about thirty minutes.'

'Okay. Catriona, you take her statement when she gets here.' Sean looked at them both. 'Is there any reason we should keep Hugh Fitzpatrick here tonight?'

Catriona spoke first. 'I'm still not convinced that he's completely innocent, sir. He did try to do a runner last night.'

Dougie added, 'I agree, boss, but we don't really have anything concrete to pin on him.'

'Okay.' Sean stroked his chin, deep in thought. 'Let's get Rachel Adams' statement first. If she names Barry, we'll charge him; if she names Hugh, then it's a different ball game. Hugh Fitzpatrick doesn't know we have Rachel Adams arriving, does he?' Dougie shook his head.

'Good. If Rachel cannot confirm it is Barry, then get a DNA sample from the professor so we can check. Can we also get a sample of Peter's blood?' asked Sean.

Dougie shook his head doubtfully. 'We'd have to ask Hugh Fitzpatrick for permission for the DNA sample, boss.'

'Okay, hold off on that for the moment then,' advised Sean.

Belfast International Airport
Wednesday, 9.25pm

Rachel Parker, nee Adams, still looked fresh, despite more than a thirty-hour trip from Sydney, Australia. When she emerged from International Arrivals at Aldergrove, Catriona approached and introduced herself, before leading her out to a waiting car.

During the trip to Belfast Police HQ, Catriona explained that they had a man in custody, and hoped she would be willing to make a statement about the rape which had occurred in Groomsport when she was 16 years old.

Rachel nodded. 'I hope it won't take long, though, Detective. I'm keen to get to the hospital to see my mother.'

Sean had told Catriona he wanted Rachel's statement to be taken before she met any of her family.

Declining refreshments, Rachel was shown to an interview room by Catriona and one of her junior colleagues, DC Elaine Duffy.

'Mrs Parker, I do realise after all this time and trauma, that this might be very difficult for you,' Catriona began. 'But I do need to ask you some questions. Is that okay?' Rachel nodded.

'Are you absolutely sure that it was Barry Fitzpatrick who raped you on your way home from church that night?'

'Yes, I am!'

'Is there any chance that it could have been Hugh Fitzpatrick, his cousin?'

'No.' Rachel Adams was adamant. 'I am absolutely sure it was Barry.'

'Why are you so sure? Did you clearly see his face? After all, it was dark.'

'Hugh wasn't like that. He was kind and considerate, but Barry was just an oaf! You're right, it was dark, but I could smell the alcohol on him. Hugh never drank. I could also smell cigarettes; Hugh never smoked. Barry did both. It had to be him.'

'Did you clearly see Barry's face?'

'Yes, erm, yes... I did.'

'You don't sound so sure. I'm sorry. I do understand this was a long time ago,' Catriona asked gently.

'I've lived that night every night for thirty years, Officer.' Rachel looked down at her hands, clasped tightly in her lap.

'So why the hesitation?'

'He... he jumped me from behind. He pinned me down on the ground... I never did see his face fully, because my face was in the grass.' Her voice broke and her eyes welled with tears.

Catriona apologised and reached across to gently touch the older woman's hands. 'I'm so very sorry to have to put you through this again.'

Rachel Parker nodded, pulling herself together. 'I understand. I needed to say it. I've had counselling for years, and they said I needed to confront it. Will I have to testify in court?'

'It's unlikely. He has already confessed to several other crimes,' said Catriona.

'Oh, thank God. Thank God.' Rachel slumped back in the chair, clearly relieved.

'There is one thing, though, which would help,' said Catriona. 'Could I take a cheek swab for a DNA test, to be completely sure?'

Rachel looked surprised, but immediately gave her consent. Catriona took a swab from inside her mouth, then thanked her and arranged for a driver to take Rachel to the hospital.

As she watched the elegant woman hurry off to the waiting car that would take her to the hospital to see her elderly mother, Catriona's gut was twitching. Was it hunger?

Belfast Central Police Office
Wednesday, 10.20pm

Catriona headed for Sean's office, where he and members of the core team were just starting a recap of the day's events.

'We need another visit to Leah Fitzpatrick,' Sean told them. 'Which of you would prefer that pleasure?'

Dougie and Catriona both laughed.

'We'll also need a search warrant,' Sean explained. 'We're looking at her jewellery specifically, and any other items that are listed against the missing girls. Did Arabella Fullerton make a list of pieces she had lost? We might want to use that as the reason for the search, and not mention Leah's ex-husband just yet.'

'Yes, she did,' Dougie confirmed. 'We'll get the custody officer to write it up. We can serve the warrant first thing in the morning, or do you want us to go tonight?'

'I think the morning is fine. I'd like us to have a summary of the key information coming out of the documents which Hugh Fitzpatrick had in his holdall,' Sean replied. 'The question I haven't yet found the answer to is how involved is Hugh Fitzpatrick? Any thoughts?'

'He must have known, boss. How could he not?' said Dougie.

'He seems so wrapped up in his own stuff, though,' offered Andy Gibbs, one of the detective constables. 'He doesn't strike me as the type of man who would kill a woman. In fact, he seems a bit of a wimp.'

'His solicitor will ask for his release, and at this point we have not one iota on him,' Sean told them. 'He's still here voluntarily. Maybe that was bad judgement, but that is it.' Sean looked around the room. 'Catriona?'

'I'd say that if he had known of Barry's involvement with the deaths of his wife or daughter, he would have killed his cousin himself. So, no, I don't think he is involved with the killings, or at least not all of them.'

'Clarify that, please?' asked Sean, puzzled.

'I think he...' She paused, still trying to rationalize her thoughts. 'I think Hugh is the father of Peter Adams.'

Sean raised his eyebrows. 'So effectively, you're suggesting he was the one that raped Rachel Adams?'

'If it was rape,' Catriona replied.

'Ouch! That's going to be a difficult one.' Sean winced. 'What are your thoughts behind that?'

'I don't know exactly, it just all feels a bit too black and white really. She went home, had a bath and did her washing, then didn't say anything for several weeks until she realised she was pregnant. Those were different times from now. In those days, it was the worst thing that could have happened to a young girl, to get pregnant.' Catriona shrugged, knowing she was on delicate ground here.

There was silence.

'Don't get me wrong, boss,' she added. 'I absolutely feel for the woman whatever happened. Is it possible to hold Hugh until a paternity test comes back?'

'Do we have Peter Adams' consent to the paternity test?' Sean looked around the room.

'We would need to ask him specifically for it,' said Dougie. 'We haven't yet. He is meeting his mother for the first time today. It would be a difficult conversation to have with both of them.'

'But if a crime has been committed?' argued Catriona.

'We have Barry admitting to sex with Rachel Adams, so we would be on thin ice to force consent. Let's focus on the rest of the evidence; we're keeping the forensic team busy enough. Release Hugh under caution and request that he surrenders his passports voluntarily – both his British and Irish one,' Sean directed. 'He can't return to the house in Groomsport, though, as we will certainly want to search the car, at the very least.'

Wednesday, 11pm

Before Hugh Fitzpatrick was given permission to leave, Dougie and Sean had one more discussion with him – with his lawyer – to clarify when he had first become aware of his cousin's activities.

'I admit I was very naïve,' the professor sighed. 'I knew he had been in trouble with drugs and had spent time in prison, but we lost touch for many years when I was in America. In fact, I only came back to live properly in Groomsport about three years ago, when the TV programme was being made. I intended to return to the US, but a health issue prevented me.

'Sadly, the news on my condition is not good...' his voice cracked slightly, 'and I've been looking at alternative therapies to ease what time I have left. That's why I want to sell the house and return to the US. If I'm being honest, I don't feel I belong in Ulster any more.'

'When did you see Barry again?' Dougie asked.

'I was at the house mid-July, and he turned up one evening. I didn't tell him about my illness, but said I was selling the house. He was furious at first, then calmed down and said he had nowhere to go, so I agreed he could stay for a couple of nights because I would be away on business.

'He asked me for money and, because he was clearly down on his luck, I gave him a couple of hundred pounds. But when I got back from my business trip a few days later, he asked for more. We had another row and eventually I told him that if he just left, I would transfer a large sum of money to him once the house was sold. The one condition was that he would never contact me again.

'Then last week he turned up wanting to know why the police had been calling. Clearly, he has been watching the house, but I've no idea where from. He had been drinking, and began shouting and threatening me that he had evidence which would shame me so that I'd never be able to show my face again.'

Hugh Fitzpatrick rubbed a hand over his weary face; the long wait in the police station and the sporadic questioning were catching up with him. 'When he eventually left the house, I went and checked the room where he had been sleeping, and that's when I found the journal and the gun. When I read the contents of the journal, I was shocked. And frightened, I admit. I realized I would have to give the information to yourselves, but I was also desperate to get away from Groomsport, to avoid any further confrontation. The strain of the last few weeks has undoubtedly taken its toll on my health.'

Dougie advised Hugh Fitzpatrick and his solicitor that he was being released under caution, and would need to surrender both his British and Irish passports. He also explained that the professor could not return to the Groomsport house as it was due to be forensically examined.

'I understand, Officer,' Hugh replied, nodding towards his solicitor. 'I have friends here in Belfast I can stay with.' He wrote down a name and address on Dougie's notepad, and returned it to him.

'I would like to have a presence on site when the house is being searched, Detective,' the solicitor added. 'I take it my client is not required to be there?'

'No problem,' Sean replied. 'The search is scheduled to start at 8am tomorrow. And no, your client is not needed. For the moment, he is free to go.'

Chapter Twenty-Eight
Final pieces of the jigsaw

Belfast Central Police Office - Thursday, August 6. 8am

Before resuming questioning Barry Fitzgerald, Sean met the Chief Constable to discuss the findings of the journal and several other strands of the investigation.

The diary entries from Barry's journal confirmed that eight of the missing women had been his victims. Five other women on the team's original list of missing people had now been accounted for. Three had been confirmed as still alive, but had chosen not to return to their families for fear of abuse or retribution; the police had agreed not to disclose their whereabouts. One other woman had returned to her family nine months after the original report had been filed, but had not notified the police. Her case could be closed.

In the case of the fifth woman, her then partner had broken down and confessed to her murder as a drunken accident; he had lived with the guilt for years. He had been arrested.

The missing woman in Cyprus, who had initially been thought to be linked to the case, had been found safe and well. She had run off with a much younger man, and was happily living with him and their three children in another part of the island. There was an issue with her using false papers, which the Cypriot police were discussing with her, but it was unlikely she would be prosecuted.

'There are other entries in the diary which have not been identified, sir,' Sean told the Chief, 'so the investigation looks likely to continue for a few more months. But for now I believe we have enough evidence to charge Barry Fitzpatrick. He doesn't know yet that his cousin handed in the evidence and didn't keep his side of the bargain.'

'Anything on the gun?' the Chief Constable asked.

'Forensics have confirmed that only Barry's fingerprints were on the weapon, but the weapon has been linked to a man wanted by both sides of the paramilitary organisations. If Barry was to be set free and news of the gun possession became known, it is unlikely he would find a safe hiding place.

'The gun has been linked to the armed robbery shooting in Newry when a leading politician on one side of the divide was severely injured. It was also linked to an internal feud where a member of the opposing paramilitary organisation was murdered. We believe this connection with the gun could be what Barry held over Billy Brown, an ex-con we interviewed at the start of our investigation.'

'I shouldn't be smiling,' the Chief Constable said, making no attempt to hide a grin. 'But this means he is a dead man walking, by all sides. There is no prison in Northern Ireland, or the Republic for that matter, where this man would be safe.'

'Yes, sir, I agree. He might prefer to be convicted of sex offences, given that he would at least be given a secure cell by himself. If he can provide us with some additional information regarding the gun, he might even be welcomed in Broadmoor Prison, for his own safety.

'Obviously, the gun is my bargaining chip,' Sean went on. 'Whether Barry himself was directly involved in any of the shootings I've mentioned, he will soon realise the significance of the gun and the interest that people will take in it, and might not put on such a brave face. If he was holding the gun for someone, they won't want Barry opening his mouth, either.' He gave a wry smile. 'He is damned if he stays quiet, and damned if he doesn't.'

Groomsport - Thursday, 8.30am

Led by Dougie, a forensic team began the search of the Watch House in Groomsport, starting with the garage and Hugh Fitzpatrick's car, which had been housed there for 18 years.

Although the vehicle would be removed for more detailed analysis, a search of the boot found what initially looked like a scrap of torn yellow material, bearing several oil and other stains. The material was hidden under the spare wheel in the boot of the car. The wheel itself was punctured.

Millisle - Thursday, 8.30am

A separate team of officers – led by Catriona - arrived at Leah Fitzpatrick's house. They were met by a stream of foul-mouthed obscenities from Leah, who was clearly not a morning person.

Catriona smiled brightly and handed over the search warrant, enjoying the scowl on the older woman's face turn to shock when she explained that they were looking for Arabella Fullerton's missing jewellery.

'If the fecking cow had been civil, I would have returned them!' swore Leah. 'And it wasn't me who took them, but Barry. I swear on my mother's grave.'

'You could, but your mother isn't dead,' Catriona laughed.

'What do you mean? She's been dead these last 12 years...' Leah looked totally confused.

'Nope, she's very much alive. Anyway, we're here to look for items of jewellery taken from Mrs Fullerton, and also from several other women.'

'Eh?' Leah clutched the piece of paper to her chest. 'What other women?'

'We have reason to believe that your ex-husband may have given you jewellery over the years which had been stolen. Do you have any jewellery that he might have given you as gifts?' asked Catriona.

The cigarette dropped from Leah's mouth. She staggered back into the living room and sat down on the tatty sofa with a thump. 'The feckless bastard. I knew he was up to no good. I knew it, but he always swore that the presents were a token of his love.'

'And where would this jewellery be now?' asked Catriona kindly.

'Some of it I pawned over the years, when I needed a bit of money. The rest is in the jewellery box on the dressing table in my bedroom.'

An officer went upstairs and quickly returned with a dark wooden box.

'This one?' asked Catriona.

'Yes.' Leah nodded.

Catriona opened the box and sifted through several items before spotting the ring which Arabella Fullerton had described. She put the entire box into an evidence bag and sealed it.

'Right, Leah. If you'd like to get some clothes on, we'd like you to accompany us to the station and give us a statement as to how you came about this jewellery.' Catriona read her the statement on her rights.

Belfast Central Police Office - Thursday, 10.35am

It took 90 minutes to get to Belfast, as the traffic was busy heading into the city. Catriona had phoned ahead, and a duty solicitor was waiting to represent Leah, so that they could proceed as quickly as possible with questioning her about the items in the jewellery box.

Once settled in the interview room with the tape recorder running, Catriona opened the jewellery box and lifted out two velvet-covered trays. Slowly, she removed every item of jewellery and laid them on the table in front of Leah, while a young junior officer catalogued each one.

While it was clear to everyone that some of the items were cheap tat, there were also several expensive-looking pieces which stood out. Underneath the second tray were a number of receipts for a well-known Belfast pawnbroker, who was still in business in the city centre.

Another officer took the receipts and photocopied them, before heading off to the pawnbrokers to check if any of the items were still being held.

As Leah's statement about the contents of the jewellery box was being signed, the officer called to confirm that a small bag of jewellery was still being held in the pawnbroker's back cupboard. Most of the contents were relatively worthless, but one piece was significant.

It was a distinctive custom-made charm; unique. It matched the description of a charm worn by a young woman reported missing the year after Rachel Porter had died in Millisle.

Several hours later, a contrite Leah Fitzpatrick was released on bail, pending further enquiries. She had been warned that she may face charges of receiving stolen property.

Midday

Back in the investigating team's office, Catriona telephoned Sarah Drummond. She was at the hospital visiting her grandmother. Sarah stepped outside to take the call.

'Did your father ever give you any jewellery?' Catriona asked.

The other woman hesitated briefly before replying. 'Nothing much, a couple of items which I keep at home in England. I can arrange for them to be sent over, if you want. Why do you ask?'

'At this stage, we think they may have been stolen,' Catriona explained, not wanting to give any more details.

'That doesn't surprise me,' scoffed Rachel. 'Sadly, nothing either of my parents does surprises me any more.'

'One other thing, if you don't mind. We spoke to Leah, your mother, this morning and she seemed to be under the impression that your grandmother died. Why would that be?'

Sarah laughed. 'I can answer that easily enough. We wanted it that way. When Nan remarried, Tony had a bit of money and we all knew that Leah would pester her continuously for handouts if she knew. She had already borrowed a lot of money from my nan and never paid it back.

'My brother, Peter, and I had clubbed together to buy Nan's house for her when the council were selling it, but she gave it back to us when she got married. If my mother had known we owned the house, she would have expected to be put up in it for life. So we decided to rent the house out and we told the tenants that if anyone came looking for Nan, to say she had died. Nan's friends and neighbours couldn't stand Leah either, so they went along with it.

'No doubt at some point my mother must have gone to the house and been given that message. Detective, my nan deserved some happiness after all that Leah and Barry had put her through. We didn't want her caught up in anything to do with my father and the sort of people he mixed with. When she and Tony got married, they moved to Spain and lived there for ten years. They came back when Tony became ill, and bought a little place in Ballyholme, where most of his family lived. Nan hadn't wanted to live in Groomsport again. When Tony died, Nan moved into Ballyholme Nursing Home. They look after her very well.'

'Thanks, that explains things. How is Hilda now?' Catriona asked.

'She's doing okay, thanks, and delighted to have us all here. There's talk of her being discharged back to the nursing home in a couple of days, and she is keen to get back there. I'll stay until she leaves hospital.'

She continued. 'Peter is staying in the house in Groomsport while some issues with the Army are being resolved. It seems one of his former commanding officers is helping with that.'

'And your aunt?' Catriona pictured the elegant woman who she had collected from the airport in Belfast.

'She is staying in a hotel in Belfast. It's handy for her to be near the hospital and visit Nan; she said she couldn't bring herself to visit Groomsport.'

12.45pm

'Boss.' Catriona knocked sharply on the door to Sean's office and entered before he could answer. 'Hugh Fitzpatrick's solicitor is on the line. Apparently the professor called the lawyer's office this morning early, and told the receptionist he would come in for a meeting around 11am, but never showed up. He has tried calling, but there is no answer on his mobile phone.'

'We have his passports, right?'

'Yes, but it wouldn't be hard for him to drive, or be driven, across the border. There's no security check.'

'Put out an alert for him,' Sean barked. 'Contact our Southern partners to advise them.'

Did an innocent man run? Sean mused, as he watched Catriona leave. *And where would he run to?*

Belfast Central Police Station - 4pm

When Colum Fullerton called DCI Sean Maloney, he was in a foul mood. He had been in the High Court in Dublin all week and had spoken to his wife, Arabella, at home in Galway yesterday, but had been unable to get hold of her this morning.

'When I got home this afternoon, there was no note but I discovered four suitcases missing, along with some of my and Arabella's clothes, her jewellery, and some other valuables. When I checked the safe, both our passports are missing, and I've checked our bank accounts. They have been drained of more than 30,000 euros.'

Sean asked for a check to be done with his Southern colleagues, and two hours later received confirmation that a Mr and Mrs Fullerton had flown from Dublin to New York early that morning. Further checks revealed that the couple had transferred directly to a flight to a Caribbean island, without clearing immigration.

No sooner had the information come through than Sean had Colum Fullerton back on the phone. On cancelling his wife from his credit card, he had discovered that she had booked two business class tickets to the Caribbean – and he was liable. Fullerton was furious and demanding some kind of police action.

When Sean finally got Fullerton off the phone, he allowed himself a wry smile at their cheek. How long had Arabella and Hugh been planning to run off together? With some hair dye and a shave, Hugh could probably pass for Colum Fullerton, and by avoiding going through customs and immigration in the US, his fingerprints would not have been checked.

Sean called Hugh's solicitor and broke the news to him that his client had done a runner. They agreed to meet on Tuesday morning. This would give Sean and his team time to review the evidence collected from Hugh, and the search of his house.

Chapter Twenty-Nine
A place in the sun

Caribbean island of Grenada - Saturday, August 10. 11am

The little house was beautiful. They had stayed there years before when Hugh had been carrying out research for his book on the white slave trade routes, and had happy memories of being there with the children, Rachel and Thomas.

Arabella breathed a contented sigh as she relaxed on a sun lounger, a cold drink at her side. Thomas and Colin would arrive in a couple of weeks for a holiday. Her son had never warmed to Colum Fullerton. Although he had understood his mother's reasons for marrying the man, Thomas had encouraged her to follow her heart and spend what time was left with Hugh.

It had been a stressful few weeks, but she was happy. The visit from the police had opened up old wounds, but it had also reminded her of how content her life had once been with Hugh. Before Rachel's death, they had been extremely happy. A deeply caring and sensitive man, she had loved him deeply.

Raking up the past also brought to the surface the emotional compromise Arabella had made in marrying Colum Fullerton. While not exactly miserable, she was mature enough to admit that their marriage was barely more than adequate; soulless really, with no passion and no real laughter. In return for a comfortable lifestyle, Colum expected a housekeeper and an attractive escort to functions; someone who would neither embarrass nor upstage him.

When she had asked Colum to leave the room when she was being interviewed by the two police officers, he had been aggrieved and taken himself off to Dublin the following morning without any conversation.

A couple of days later, Arabella – still troubled by the memories which had been reawakened – had written her former husband a short note, and waited. When he telephoned a few days later, they agreed to meet in a café in Enniskillen, away from any prying eyes. Arabella stretched out in the sun, smiling as she remembered now how nervous she had felt, like a schoolgirl on her first date.

They had talked for hours, with Hugh telling her what little he knew about the police investigation. He was convinced it was a simple review of a closed case, and had been surprised and defensive when Arabella said she suspected the probe related to his cousin Barry.

'When Mrs Adams told me that she felt she had to leave as our housekeeper, I went to her house and asked her to reconsider, but she was adamant,' Arabella told him. 'I asked her outright if her grandson Peter had had anything to do with Rachel's death, and she looked me in the eye and swore on her other grandchildren's lives. She begged me to believe her. But when I asked if Barry had been involved, Mrs Adams told me she could not lie to me but nor could she tell me the truth. I could sense she was in a difficult position so I did not press her any further. And I had no proof to take it any further.'

Hugh had been shocked but admitted he didn't want to reopen old wounds with Barry again. It was then that he had told her about his illness.

Arabella shifted slightly on her lounger and wiped a tear as she remembered their conversation. It was then that she had made up her mind to take care of him for the time he had left.

It had been easy enough to buy two new mobile phones and SIM cards, allowing them to talk without any suspicion arising or their calls being traced. Over the following few weeks, they spoke every day and met in different locations where neither of them were known.

Hugh kept her up-to-date with the police visits, and she told him of Thomas's surprise trip, and his conversation with DCI Maloney. Hugh had also shared two confessions with her – the first concerning Rachel Adams, Peter's mother; the second, that Barry was hiding in his house in Groomsport.

Arabella had been shocked, but time was short. She smiled wryly as she recalled his surprise when she revealed her plan, but she had been adamant that she would not lose Hugh a second time. She begged him to search the house for any evidence that Barry was up to no good, and that was when he found the journal and the gun. He had read the journal; its contents had shocked them both to the core.

They had agreed a plan A and a plan B. Plan A was for Arabella to meet Hugh in London, from where they would cross the Channel and lose themselves in France. The idea for Hugh's identity change had, ironically, been Thomas's. He had casually mentioned to his mother how alike the two men were in terms of height and build, the only difference being hair colour and Hugh's beard.

Arabella knew Plan A had gone wrong when she did not receive a text to confirm Hugh's departure from Belfast, nor one about his arrival in London. She had been frantic. Her calls to the house had gone unanswered, but she could do nothing but wait and continue to act the part of Colum's faithful wife.

As soon as Hugh had been released from the police station, he had called Arabella and it was plan B which swung into motion. The Dublin Airport express bus left Belfast at 4.30am on the Thursday morning and would arrive in Dublin Airport by 8am. After checking in, Hugh had called his solicitor via their switchboard, so that his call could not be traced, and agreed to meet later that morning.

The flight to New York had left just after 10am, and they had been fraught with nerves every step of the way, from check-in at Dublin through to landing at JFK, and the transfer to their follow-on flight. Only when their plane finally touched down at Grenada in the Caribbean, could they begin to relax. One last short flight had brought them to this picturesque little island, which did not have extradition with the UK or Ireland; even if it did, the process would be too late for Hugh.

Arabella knew Colum would be furious at her leaving him, and even more so when he realised that his credit card had been used to pay for the one-way business class flights to the Caribbean. But she had no regrets. Better to have the time left with Hugh, even if it was short, than remain stuck in an emotionless marriage.

Her quiet musing was interrupted by a smiling Hugh wandering out into the garden. He looked happy and rested, already benefitting from their relaxing surroundings. He had left written instructions for his solicitor to complete the sale of the house to the young chap, Kieran Maloney. Hugh and Arabella would enjoy the peace and tranquillity of their Caribbean home for as long as they could. She smiled at him. They deserved some good fortune.

Epilogue

12 months later

DCI Maloney was working his way through a pile of paperwork when he received a call from Peter Adams asking if he could meet him for a coffee in the cafe in Groomsport.

When he arrived, Peter looked well. Fit and healthy, he was no longer the gaunt, tense young man of some 12 months ago.

As they waited for their order, they discussed the life sentences Barry Fitzpatrick had been given, and how he had been moved to a prison in England which dealt specifically with sex offenders.

'I can only thank God he pleaded guilty, so that none of your family needed to testify, and the families of the victims were spared a lot of the gruesome details,' Sean admitted. 'So how have you been?'

'Good, thanks,' Peter replied. 'The Army have been very supportive and I have been receiving counselling for post-traumatic stress disorder. I believe it's helping me.'

'Good.' Sean smiled, delighted to hear that the young man was finally receiving the help he needed.

'I'm due to take up a role with an organisation which Colonel Smith put me in touch with, so I'll be moving to the

UK, and the house in Groomsport is up for sale. You know that my nan died two months ago?' He looked at Sean for confirmation.

'I had heard. Sorry to hear that, Peter. She was quite a character.'

Peter smiled, but couldn't hide the tears welling in his eyes. 'She passed away quietly in her sleep at the nursing home. I'm just glad she lived long enough to see that Barry got what was coming to him after all those years.'

The waitress arrived and placed two cups of coffee down on the table before leaving.

'I'm keeping in touch with Rachel... my mother... though it's still early days for us both.' Peter stopped to sip his coffee. 'I'm just very thankful for the love and support of my family.'

'Great. Glad to hear it,' Sean replied. 'So why did you want to see me?'

'This came in the post a few days ago.' Peter handed Sean a letter. 'I didn't know what to do with it.'

Sean scanned the letter quickly. It was from Professor Hugh Fitzpatrick, with instructions to be forwarded to Peter three months after Hugh's death. In the letter, Hugh explained that he was deeply ashamed to admit that in all likelihood he was Peter's father.

He revealed how he had got drunk with Barry one evening then gone to meet Rachel, as arranged. He admitted he had taken advantage of her, and nothing he could say would alleviate the hurt or shame that he had caused her, and the difficulties for both of them. Hugh ended the letter by saying he was deeply sorry for his actions.

Sean looked across at Peter. 'How do you feel about it?'

The young man shrugged.

Sean's mind was racing. Catriona had always suspected Hugh's involvement to some degree, but they had been unable to pin anything specific on him and, given Barry's confessions, there had been no further investigations.

In the end, Barry had not been charged with Rachel's rape. Given the magnitude of offences against him, she had requested that for her family's sake she did not want the offence included and everything dragged up again. After discussion with the Crown Prosecution Service, the charge had not been pursued.

'What do you want to do with the letter?' Sean asked Peter.

'Burn it!' the young man replied with a deep sigh. 'To be honest, my mother and I will never have a real relationship. She has believed strongly all these years that it was Barry who raped her, but what difference would it make to her now to have it all dragged up again? My greatest fear was always that nature would overcome nurture. Whilst my start in life was under the worst possible circumstances, I was lucky to have the love of my adoptive family, as well as my nan, and Sarah and Gordon.'

He smiled shyly at Sean. 'Actually, I feel as though Robbie and Rachel – Colonel Smith and his wife – are intent on adopting me as well.' The men both laughed, then Peter added more seriously, 'Dragging all of this up again would just reopen all the hurt.'

'That is incredibly thoughtful of you,' said Sean.

'I wanted to talk to you because... well, because I wanted to tell someone. You and Robbie provided immense support to our family, for which we are very thankful. I was also worried that if this letter came out, it might give Barry some grounds for appeal. I would not want him to put anyone through that again.'

Sean shook his head. 'It could bring up some questions, that's all. The evidence against Barry for the other crimes was so overwhelming. Clearly, Hugh committed that offence and Barry held it over him for life.'

'Can we walk?' asked Peter, gesturing to the waitress for their bill and waving aside Sean's offer to pay.

They headed out of the café and walked slowly towards the harbour. Peter took a cigarette lighter out of his pocket, flipped the flame, then held it to the edge of the notepaper. In less than a minute, the letter was destroyed.

'Hugh's house here was sold, as you probably know.' Peter looked to Sean for confirmation.

'I do indeed. My younger brother bought it,' Sean explained with a broad smile. 'He and his girlfriend moved in a few months ago, after some renovation work. They are due to marry later this year.'

'That's good.' Peter paused briefly before continuing. 'On his death, Hugh left a sizeable fortune to be shared amongst me, Sarah, Gordon, and Arabella's son, Thomas. I spoke with Sarah and told her that I did not want to keep the money, so I have donated my share to the soldiers' charity for rehabilitation. At least it will do some good for people who deserve it.'

Peter stopped walking and turned towards the detective. 'This is where it ends,' he said. 'I hope Rachel can now rest in peace.' He shook Sean's hand firmly, turned and walked away.

THE END

About The Author

Born in Northern Ireland, Groomsport was our summer camp where my imagination developed.

Thirty years on I have lived in so many places around the world. I eventually took time out to write or rather to prove to myself if I could do it, to stop procrastinating. What happened next has been a life changing experience that has enabled me to continue my travels and add to my collection of wonderful friends and family.

I currently spend my time house sitting, travelling and writing.

Contact
BarbaraAnnlawther@gmail.com
www.barbaraann.co.uk